Storm Born

THE WITCHES OF WHEELER PARK: BOOK 1

CHRISTINE POPE

STORM BORN

Copyright © 2020 by Christine Pope

ISBN: 978-1-946435-33-0

Published by Dark Valentine Press

Cover art by Lou Harper/Cover Affairs

Book formatting by Indie Author Services

"The wound is the place where the light enters you."—Rumi

PROLOGUE

JAKE WILCOX PULLED OUT HIS PHONE TO CHECK the time again. Five minutes after two. In the grand scheme of things, being five minutes late wasn't that big a deal, but he wanted this meeting over with so he could roll up his sleeves and get to work. True, Connor Wilcox, the leader —*primus*—of the Wilcox witch clan in Flagstaff had already signed off on the project, but Jake wanted Connor to see what had been accomplished since the *primus* had given the go-ahead some six months earlier.

From the outside, the place looked like an ordinary two-story house, built in the Craftsman style of the turn of the last century. The neighborhood around Wheeler Park was filled with those types of homes, some of which had been converted to office space, just as this house had been. However, Jake very much doubted that the graphic design companies and nurse-practitioners and contractors who'd taken up space in similar venues nearby had any idea what was actually hidden inside the white house with the green trim and the modest "Trident Enterprises" nameplate next to the door.

If asked, he would have told any of those neighbors that Trident Enterprises was an information technology company that specialized in various low-cost computing solutions for small businesses. However, although he'd exchanged greetings with a few of the people who occupied homes in the area, no one had ever asked him for that information. No, they just seemed happy that the formerly rundown property had been painted and spruced up in general, thus improving the overall look of the neighborhood.

On the house's second story, not all that much had been changed—there were still three bedrooms and a bathroom, although everything had been updated and redone. Jake figured it couldn't hurt to keep the bedrooms furnished for the time being, since he didn't know whether there might be occasions where he or one of the other Wilcox witches or warlocks working for Trident Enterprises might not need to crash there. If any outsiders had peeked into those rooms, they would have seen beds and night-stands and dressers, carefully framed prints on the walls. Jake's cousin Laurel had made the design decisions, clearly all too happy to be set loose on the local furniture stores with Trident's generous budget funding her purchases.

Downstairs, however...the contents of the downstairs rooms probably would have shocked their neighbors, while the spaces themselves would have been well-nigh unrecognizable to the home's original owners.

The living room was split into three worksta-tions, each outfitted with a Mac Pro computer and a pair of large cinema displays. The dining room had four more workstations equipped with the best PCs money could buy. A dedicated high-speed line had been run to the property, and a host of anti-surveillance equipment installed—all under the supervision of Jake's younger brother Jeremy, who was a genius with computers and electronics. Actually, computers were his magical "gift," a talent that no one in the Wilcox clan had ever heard of before. No one among the McAllisters or the de la Paz clan had ever encountered it, either, making Jeremy unique even among their already rarefied population.

In a way, it was Jeremy's talent with computers and code that had first prompted the germ of the idea that became Trident Enterprises.

"Hello!" came Connor's voice from the living room. Jake immediately left the dining room, where he'd been hooking up the new color laser printer that had just been delivered a few hours earlier, and went out to meet the *primus*. The front door had been locked, since there was so much valuable equipment stored in the house, but locked doors weren't much of a barrier for witch-kind.

"Hi, Connor," Jake said. "Glad you could make it."

"Oh, I didn't want to miss this," Connor replied, looking around with approval in his greenish-gray eyes. "Sorry I'm a little late—I was working at the vineyard this morning."

Connor was a silent partner in Angel Hill Cellars, a vineyard down in Page Springs run by Anthony Rocha, the husband of Connor's wife Angela's best friend. As far as he could tell, Jake guessed that Connor let Anthony do most of the heavy lifting, since he was the one with an enology degree, but even so, Angel Hill seemed to occupy a good deal of the *primus's* time. Even though it was early June, and Connor and Angela would normally have relocated their family to their home in Flagstaff by that point, they were still down in the large Victorian house in Jerome that Angela had inherited when she became *prima* of the McAllister clan.

Still, Jake wouldn't comment on the tardiness of the Wilcox/McAllister household's return to Flagstaff. The biannual move was Connor and Angela's business, and not the sort of thing that a peripheral third cousin should be commenting on. Or at least, Jake viewed the situation that way, even though he knew Connor tended to be pretty easygoing about those sorts of things, and was far less bound up in formalities and tradition than his older brother Damon, who'd been the previous *primus*. Not that Jake had had many dealings with Damon; he'd been in high school when Damon passed away, and there had never been any real reason for the two of them to interact beyond an exchange of greetings at the Wilcox holiday potluck, that sort of thing.

"No worries," Jake said in response to his cousin's apology. "I was just getting the last of the equipment set up."

Connor raised an eyebrow. He was tall and dark-haired like most of the Wilcox men, with high cheekbones and a long nose that betrayed the Navajo heritage of his line, even though the

Native American witch who'd been his ancestor was now seven generations back or so. "I thought Jeremy was handling that stuff."

"Oh, he did most of it," Jake said, not at all offended by his cousin's assumption that he might not be up to a lot of technical tasks. "But while I'm not exactly a computer genius like he is, I can handle hooking up a printer. He had to go over to Lowe's—he needed some fasteners to finish installing the radio equipment in the next room."

The *primus* absorbed this explanation without comment. He silently surveyed the room, taking in the sleek wood and glass desks that held the Mac Pros, the large whiteboard that covered most of one wall. The modern furniture was a direct contrast to the house that contained it, and yet it somehow seemed to work together harmoniously enough, probably because Jake and his cousin Laurel had done their best to choose office furniture that spoke of this century while still allowing a nod to the hundred-year-old house.

"How many people do you have on board right now?" Connor asked at last.

"Just me and Jeremy and Laurel," Jake said. "Since she just wrapped up getting her degree in computer science at NAU, we figured she'd be a good person to help us compile data. And because her talent is healing, she could be a handy person to have around...just in case."

This comment elicited another raised eyebrow. "I'm surprised Eleanor was willing to let Laurel go that easily."

While Jake was doing his best to seem professional and on top of everything—even though this was his first try at being a manager and he realized he honestly didn't know what the hell he was doing—he couldn't help grinning at Connor's remark...mostly because it had taken a lot of persuading to convince the clan's healer that Laurel's talents couldn't be put to better use elsewhere. "Who said it was easy?"

"Well, I kind of have to side with Eleanor on this one," Connor said, his expression now completely serious. "Healers are always desperately needed."

"True," Jake allowed, "but Laurel promised Eleanor that if anything happened that required all hands on deck, then of course, she would help out. But really, Eleanor isn't swamped. We all have our own doctors—she's even admitted that she advises people to see a specialist for a lot of things."

The *primus* didn't argue with that statement, probably because he knew it was the simple truth. In fact, he and his wife had gone to a civilian—nonmagical—doctor for Angela's pregnancies. Eleanor was a very good healer, but even she couldn't handle all eventualities.

"So, you're going to 'flip the switch'—so to speak—tomorrow?" Connor asked next, apparently deciding that he wasn't going to argue the point as to whether babysitting Trident Enterprises' data flow was really what Laurel should be doing with her gifts.

"That's the plan," Jake replied. Although he tried to sound casual, he couldn't help but feel a stir of anticipation—well mixed with anxiety—somewhere deep inside. After all, the idea of this project had consumed him for far longer than the six months that they'd been actively working on making Trident a reality.

No, if he wanted to admit it to himself, the thought had taken on a life of its own almost three years ago now. Three years since he'd lost Sarah, and had desperately started searching for something to consume his empty days, some sort of project that would maybe help him forget—if only for an hour here and there—the gaping hole she'd left in his life.

On the surface, the idea was simple enough. It had floated into his mind one day as he listened to his mother talking to another Wilcox cousin on the phone, discussing how the cousin's oldest child had just turned eleven, and how her magical talents had begun to manifest. The conversation had been cheerful enough—the little girl's ability was working with plants, helping them grow—and almost matter-of-fact. After all, that was just how it happened in a witch clan. Around the age of ten or eleven, or possibly a little younger if a child was precocious, like Connor and Angela's oldest daughter Emily, those magical gifts began to manifest, and others in the clan encouraged them and helped them along, assisting the child with learning all the facets of their gift and how best to use it without hurting themselves or anyone around them.

Only...what would happen if a witch or warlock was born outside a clan? At first, when Jake had broached the idea to his mother, she'd frowned and said that magical talent was heredi-tary, and so there weren't any rogue witches or warlocks suddenly appearing amongst the civilian population, since all of witch-kind was bound by the clans that people were born into. Which all seemed pretty neat and tidy, but didn't really cover any witch or warlock hook-ups with civilians. It would be nice to pretend that such things didn't happen—and they were probably pretty rare, just because the tendency among witches and warlocks was to find your match fairly early on, and to get married and start a family right away. After all, he'd known with Sarah from the time they were both barely twenty-one that they were meant to be together. They'd decided to wait, though, just because she wanted to get her master's degree in education and thought it was better to focus on school rather than get married immediately and set up a household.

They shouldn't have waited. They should have gotten married as soon as they both earned their undergraduate degrees. But Jake had agreed, figuring another two years wouldn't matter so much in the grand scheme of things. They were already together, and waiting for a little piece of paper wasn't such a big deal.

Except it was a big deal, because she'd been a year away from getting her master's when she went on the camping trip that changed everything.

At any rate, Jake speculated that there must be children out in the world who had no idea one of their parents was a witch or warlock. Most likely warlock, just because the sad truth was that women were generally the ones who got left with any unplanned children, and even if a witch had an affair with a civilian and had a child by him, she'd know what to do once that child got old enough to start showing signs of magical ability.

What would it be like, though, to have no idea who your father was, to start to manifest those powers and not know what in the world to do about them? Jake guessed it would have to be frightening as hell, especially with no one to guide you along and explain that it was all perfectly normal...for someone born to witch-kind, anyway.

And that was when he resolved to figure out a way how to track down those lost witches and warlocks, to do his best to discover who their parents actually were so they could be reunited with the clans where they belonged. He'd brought up the idea to Jeremy, figuring if his computer-genius brother couldn't figure out the logistics of such a project, then it was basically impossible and would be dead in the water before he even got started. But Jeremy had seized on the notion immediately, and said it actually wouldn't be that hard, that he'd write algorithms to analyze news from all over the world, to scan through Facebook and Twitter feeds, through police and emergency scanners and any other sources of information available, and so track down the bits and pieces that sounded like magical powers showing up out of the blue. One belief all of witch-kind shared was the need to keep their existence a secret, and so no one who'd been raised in a clan would ever do anything to jeopardize that secrecy.

But a witch or warlock who didn't even know what they were...well, obviously, that kind of person might not be quite so careful.

Once they had a working business plan—and Jeremy had specified the kind of equipment and resources they'd need—Jake had brought the project to Connor. Honestly, he hadn't been sure whether the *primus* would really be on board or not. It was going to be an expensive proposition... not that the Wilcoxes ever needed to worry about money.

But Connor had given his approval, and now here they were. Just finishing up the last odds and ends, and then the next morning, Jake and Jeremy and Laurel would start looking for those proverbial needles in the haystack.

"Well, good luck with it," the *primus* said, and gave another look around the place. "But have you really thought about what you're going to say to these people if you do manage to track them down?"

"Yes," Jake said without hesitation, knowing he'd mentally rehearsed that speech more than a hundred times. Maybe he was being over-confi-dent, since, as the saying went, no plan ever survived the battlefield. He knew better than to mention such doubts to Connor, however.

Voice firm, he added, "First, we have to find them."

1

I SAT ON MY BED AND STARED AT THE ENVELOPE clutched in my hand. Although it didn't take too much effort to figure out what the letter was all about—the return address clearly said "Utah State University" and it had been sent to me, Adara Grant—I still wasn't sure I wanted to open it. For the past month, I'd been going back and forth with the financial aid office at U of U over my grants, and although they'd assured me on the last go-round that everything had been straightened out and the funds would be in place in time for me to enroll for my senior year, I wasn't sure I believed them. Enough had gone wrong in my life that I had a hard time thinking something might finally work out for once.

A warm wind played with the curtains, and

the air that drifted into my room was rich with the scent of dry grass and pine needles. My mother and I had only lived in Kanab for a little more than eighteen months—we never stayed anywhere for very long—and yet I felt more at home there than many of the places we'd landed. We'd rented a cute little house on the outskirts of town, and my mom had gotten a job waiting tables at one of the more popular local restaurants. No, Kanab wasn't exactly a party town or anything, but it got a steady stream of tourists coming through, thanks to its proximity to Bryce Canyon and Zion National Park, and so business at the local restaurants and hotels tended to be brisk most of the time. And because U of U had a satellite campus in Kanab, I was able to live at home and wait tables part-time at the restaurant where my mother worked, and try to save us money that way.

My mother paused at the doorway to my room. "You going to open that, or just sit there and stare at it?" she inquired, a slight smile lifting her lips. She was in her early forties, but looked at least ten years younger. With her bright blonde hair and big blue eyes, she tended to attract attention wherever she went, which might have been part of the reason why she never had a problem getting waitressing jobs, no matter how much we moved around.

I didn't look much like her. Maybe there was some shared resemblance in the shape of my mouth or nose, but I had brown hair and eyes that couldn't decide whether they were gray or green. Probably, I took after my father, but since I didn't know much about him, I didn't have any facts to go on, only gut instinct.

However, that wasn't because my mother had ever deliberately hidden things from me. No, she'd always been pretty blunt about how, twenty-five years earlier, she'd decided to go on an extended skiing trip with a college friend, starting out in Aspen with a layover in Flagstaff before heading toward their final destination in Tahoe.

Except they never made it to Tahoe. Their second day in Flagstaff, my mom's friend fell and broke her leg, and my mother had been left to amuse herself while Daphne was stuck in traction at the hospital. During that time, my mother had met the man who became my father in a bar in Flagstaff's historic downtown district. They'd spent two nights together, and then Daphne was released from the hospital and the two girls left, returning home to Westerville, Ohio, which was home.

Daphne's leg healed up...and then my mother discovered she was pregnant. My grandparents—whom I'd never met—were prominent members of the community and their Baptist church, and basically threw her out of the house. Because she'd been working part-time as a waitress in addition to going to school, she stuck with waitressing to provide for herself, working up until pretty much the moment I entered this world. That kind of life would have worn down a lot of women, but my mother still looked fresh and pretty and like the sort of country-club PTA mom she might have been if she'd finished college and gotten married to a doctor or lawyer, then gone on to have a picture-perfect family.

I never asked her why she didn't get married. There had been a few men over the years, but none of those relationships seemed to last very long. And then once I turned ten and the trouble started, there really wasn't anyone at all.

"If I just stare at it and don't open it, then it still has the possibility of being one thing or another," I said. "But as soon as I see what's inside, then it's all over."

Her neatly plucked brows drew together as she appeared to puzzle over that remark. My mother was a smart woman, and more capable than she probably had ever thought she would need to be, but I had a feeling she didn't know much about the Schrödinger's cat paradox or quantum mechanics. Not that I pretended to really understand them, either.

"You know what happens," I went on, my tone lowering. "When I get upset, I mean."

At once, her lips pressed together. We'd had this discussion before, but things had been quiet for a while, and I had a feeling she was doing her best to tell herself that the worst was over, that the storms in our past were no indicator for what the future might hold.

"You don't know that for sure, honey," she replied reasonably. "Actually, you don't really know that at all. It's just been...coincidence. Bad luck."

I didn't reply, only turned the letter over in my hands again. Maybe she was right. After all, it was pretty far-fetched to think that every time something went horribly wrong in my life, the weather turned absolutely foul, but if it was all coincidence, then I was batting nearly a thousand. When we were living near Durango, Colorado, I fell off a tree swing on my tenth birthday and broke my arm. At the same time, a small tornado had appeared out of nowhere and flattened a barn on the outskirts of town. Neither of us had thought anything of it, except that it seemed pretty weird for a tornado to set down in such hilly country. That had been the opinion of the locals, too—none of them could recall such a phenomenon ever occurring there before. It had been so out of the ordinary that the National Weather Service had dispatched a team to investigate. The damage was extensive enough for them to declare that yes, it had been an F-1 tornado, but even they couldn't explain why it had appeared there, of all places.

Strange, but it wasn't until one of the boys at school pushed me down on purpose during a rough game of dodgeball and an enormous thundercloud appeared directly over the school, sending a bolt of lightning down which nearly struck the little bastard, that I began to wonder if something very odd was happening to me. But when I told my mother what had occurred, she'd only shaken her head and said my imagination was playing with me, and of course, it was just a coincidence.

As were all the other "coincidences" that followed. Part of the reason why we'd moved so much over the past fourteen years was that it only took a couple of those bizarre occurrences for people to start to stare at us darkly and grumble about how those things had only begun happening after we'd shown up in town. After a while, though, my mother and I didn't even bother to discuss what was going on—she'd shut me down enough that by the time I was thirteen or fourteen, I realized she didn't want to acknowledge that there was something very strange going on with me. The excuses always were that she'd heard she could make more money in such-and-such a place, or that the manager in her latest job was way too handsy and she didn't dare report him. Just whatever it took to get us away to a new town where we could start over and pretend that the trail of calamity which appeared to follow our little family was nothing more than simple bad luck.

I turned the envelope over once again. "We've had a lot of it, then."

"Not since we moved here," she pointed out, and I didn't quite sigh.

She was right about that. We were outsiders in Kanab, but we'd been welcomed all the same. I'd been patching together my studies as best I could, taking classes here and there, managing to get an associate of arts degree eventually. When we settled in Utah, I applied for financial aid at Utah State University and got it, and had a completely uneventful junior year there, despite the constant undercurrent of worry that something was going to set me off and a tornado would descend and destroy half the pretty little town that was our new home.

Nothing like that had happened, though. People were friendly, but I also got the vibe—especially from the guys—that since I wasn't Mormon, I wasn't going to get asked out on dates, and I wasn't going to be a part of the local social life. Which was fine by me. It seemed safer to hold myself apart. In a way, being an outsider was all I really knew, since I'd spent my whole life having it be only my mother and me, no father, no grandparents...just the two of us drifting from place to place in a desperate attempt to find somewhere that could be home.

In Kanab, I thought we might have finally found that home, and I didn't want to screw it up.

"Anyway," my mother went on, "even if you don't get financial aid for this semester, it's not the end of the world. You can work and save up, and maybe get a loan—"

"No loans," I said. I'd heard enough horror stories about people graduating with mountains of debt that I would rather have not gotten a degree at all than be saddled with such a burden just as I was starting out in the world. "But you're right...if I'm not in school, I can work full-time for a while. That way, I can just pay for my final year outright and not have to worry about student aid."

My mother nodded, looking relieved that I was being so reasonable...but also a little sad, as if she wished she had the kind of money where paying for my college wouldn't even be an issue. It wasn't her fault, though; she'd done her best, and probably far better than most people would have expected her to.

I never asked why she'd never gone to my father and asked for child support. Maybe she was too proud, or maybe she thought he wouldn't give it to her, and so it wasn't worth the time and effort. However, that didn't make much sense, since the little bit she'd told me about him made it sound as if he had a lot of money. He'd driven a Mercedes and had gotten an expensive hotel room for their trysts, although he apparently had a big fancy house. But he had two boys at home —"he was a widower," my mother always hastened to add, as if she needed to make sure I knew she hadn't been sleeping with a married man—and hadn't wanted to try explaining her to them. An older man, but supposedly very handsome, with near-black hair and piercing dark eyes.

Maybe she'd avoided asking for child support

because she feared my biological father might try to take me from her.

"Whatever you want to do, sweetheart," my mother said then. "Just know that I support you —just like I support you going out there and taking the world by fire once you do have your degree."

Somehow, I kind of doubted I was going to set the world on fire with a bachelor's degree in business administration, but her confidence in me warmed my heart anyway. I wanted to make her proud, even as I secretly feared that I'd been nothing but trouble for her from the day I was born.

"I won't leave you, Mom," I said, and she just gave me a sad, knowing smile.

"That's what kids always tell their parents," she replied. "But I don't expect you to stay in Kanab your whole life. There isn't much here."

"It's a cute town," I said, feeling a need to defend the place, even though I knew she was right.

"There are a lot of cute towns in the world. And big cities. I hope you get to travel the world, see all the places I never got to see." Her expression was wistful, and I secretly vowed to do what I could about making that particular dream come true. Honestly, we'd moved around so much that

I was all right with the idea of sticking to one place, once I knew it was *the* place, but there was no reason why I couldn't one day buy my mother a trip to Paris, or a cruise to Mexico, or a sightseeing tour in Egypt.

Well, except all those kinds of expeditions cost a lot of money, and I'd never made anything more than minimum wage plus tips. That was all right, though. My mother had taught me a lot of things, and how to save money on a shoestring budget was one of them.

"Maybe," I allowed, not wanting to promise more than that. I knew if I told her that I'd rather pay to send her on the vacation she'd never had, she'd protest and say I didn't need to be so extravagant, that she'd rather see me take the vacation instead. "First, I need to graduate, though. And so...."

I turned the letter over one more time, then forced in a breath and told myself to just do it. After all, even though the past year or so had been a placid one, that didn't mean I hadn't had my share of minor upsets. A grabby customer— some jackass tourist who thought he'd cop a feel and instead got a plate of fries dumped in his lap —a car that wouldn't start because the battery had died—a jerk professor who'd taken half a grade off one of my papers because I hadn't used the correct font—all those aggravations had come and gone without a single crack of thunder, not one lightning bolt out of a clear blue sky. Maybe whatever it was that had afflicted me from the time I'd turned ten was now going away, like some kind of weird allergy that eventually disappeared as I got older.

Well, a girl could hope, anyway.

Jaw set, I slid my finger under the flap of the envelope, then drew out the folded piece of paper inside.

My eyes didn't scan any further than, *We regret to inform you that....*

I didn't need to read anything else.

Overhead, thunder growled. My mother startled and stared at me, giving the slightest shake of her head, as if some part of her realized the thunder and my upset were connected, despite her protestations to the contrary. "What is it, Addie?"

"They denied my financial aid," I said, my voice toneless and bleak. "Want to read it?"

She didn't reply, only reached for the piece of paper I held. Another wince as thunder rumbled again, echoing off the sandstone rock formations that surrounded the town. The day had been bright and blue, relentlessly sunny as only June in the Southwest could be, with at least a month before the monsoon rains returned and brought much-needed—and beloved—moisture to the area. But the light coming in through my bedroom window was darkening rapidly, and I didn't need to look outside to know clouds were converging on Kanab, turning day into night.

Somehow, I could feel those clouds, knew they were racing across the skies, converging on one central point like iron filings being drawn to a magnet.

Stop it, I thought, closing my eyes and trying vainly—once again—to prevent what I had unwittingly begun.

As if in mockery of my inner plea, thunder cracked again, this time so loud and so close, I winced in pain at the noise, could feel the hair on the back of my neck lifting in response to the charged air.

"Adara," my mother said then, using my given name, as if she thought that might shock me into making the whole thing go away. "You need to stop it."

So much for coincidence. She knew those phenomena were connected to me, even if she didn't want to admit such a thing out loud.

I didn't tell her I'd tried and failed utterly. No, I only gave her a very small nod and then breathed in again, telling myself I needed to be calm. Everything was going to be okay. Thousands and thousands of kids in worse situations than mine somehow managed to get through school without financial aid. It wasn't the end of the world. There was absolutely no reason for me to be overreacting like this.

Unfortunately, those calm, measured inner words didn't seem to change much of anything. Outside, lightning crackled, and the air stank of ozone. My mother cried out in alarm, and I jumped off the bed and looked outside. The bolt had struck one of the cottonwood trees on the property, and the poor thing was now ablaze, flames racing along its branches.

"Call the fire department!" I yelled at her, and she hurried away, white-faced, following my orders as if I were the parent and she the child.

Rain, I thought then. *Please, just rain. Put out the fire. Save my tree.*

All right, it wasn't *my* tree exactly, since the house was a rental, but I didn't want the poor thing to perish just because I'd had a flare of panic and anger and had somehow made the very heavens respond to my emotions.

And the storm-black skies opened up, and the rain came down in a deluge, drowning the fire, causing the yard to run wet with little rivers of moisture, pounding down on my mother's old

Subaru where it was parked in the driveway. I watched the blessed rain, watched it obliterate the fire, saw with relief how only one limb had burned and the rest of the tree seemed to be all right.

Somehow, I'd brought the rain as well, and done what I could to repair the damage I'd caused.

I just couldn't begin to understand how.

2

"WE'VE HAD A PING, SIR," ONE OF THE ANALYSTS told Agent Randall Lenz.

He immediately set down the tablet that held the report he'd been skimming and walked over to the analyst's workstation. Not quickly, because he wanted to make sure he always looked in control no matter what the situation, but inside, he couldn't quite repress a twinge of excitement. The search had been very quiet lately, and he'd begun to wonder if he was going to get called in front of his superiors to once again justify his budget, even though he believed it had more than paid for itself with the subjects he'd collected over the past few years. Unfortunately, most government agencies seemed to operate on the principle of "what have you done for me lately?", making Lenz even more eager to obtain a new candidate to add to the group already housed here at the facility.

The division he worked for had a purposely vague title. Technically, he and his support staff operated under the umbrella of Homeland Security, but their mission had very little to do with protecting the country's borders. No, he was far more interested in the enemies within.

"Target?" he asked Agent Dawson, the analyst who'd addressed him.

She glanced up from her screen. With a little more polish, she might have been pretty, but since she wore little makeup and always had her pale brown hair pulled tightly back into an unadorned ponytail, she mostly reminded Lenz of a schoolgirl masquerading as a government agent. "Adara Grant," Agent Dawson said.

Interesting. Ms. Grant had popped up on the division's radar two years earlier, but there had been no further incidents, and Lenz had thought it most likely that she'd triggered a false positive, rather than possessing any of the special talents he was seeking. But if she'd reappeared again after being dormant for nearly eighteen months....

"Details," he said, making sure his tone remained brisk and businesslike, betraying nothing of the excitement that had begun to surge within him. Agent Dawson typed a command into her keyboard, bringing up a screen with a photo of the young woman in question, along with a string of previous addresses and contacts.

"Kanab, Utah," the agent told him. "There was a call to 911 after lightning struck a tree on the property her mother, Lyssa Grant, is renting."

On the surface, the report didn't seem particularly conclusive. Lightning struck thousands of trees every year. However, Adara Grant's file had been flagged so it would send out a ping any time a strange weather event occurred in her known location, meaning this probably hadn't been any ordinary storm.

After all, odd weather seemed to dog the young woman, no matter where she went. He supposed it was a good thing that she'd never traveled to the South or the eastern seaboard, or those regions might have been plagued with even more hurricanes than usual.

"Weather?" he asked.

"Forecast for Kanab, Utah, called for clear skies and highs in the upper eighties, with light winds. Zero chance of precipitation."

"Yet there was a storm."

"Yes, sir." Agent Dawson typed in another

command, and immediately feeds from local traffic cameras filled her screen. Lenz could see that the skies over Kanab had been fiercely, brightly blue, making the red sandstone rock formations that flanked the town stand out in sharp contrast. As he watched the videos, he saw the sky darken, fierce thunderheads boiling up apparently out of nowhere to blanket the area. Lightning stabbed downward from those clouds, although the video he watched didn't reveal where it struck.

Those images all looked promising, but he knew he couldn't jump to conclusions. While he wasn't overly familiar with the weather patterns of the American Southwest—he'd lived his entire life on the East Coast—he did know that Utah and Arizona and New Mexico could get pounded by some fairly spectacular thunderstorms during the summer months.

"Typical monsoon storm?" he inquired, playing devil's advocate, and at once, Dawson shook her head, fawn-colored ponytail bobbing slightly.

"No, sir. My research tells me those storms aren't due to begin until the end of the month at the earliest. Also, there were absolutely no clouds in the area before this storm began. It just...came out of nowhere. Our models give this particular incident an eighty-seven percent chance that it was somehow caused by Adara Grant."

Why now, when things had been quiet for so long, when he'd mentally moved Ms. Grant from his very short list of possible subjects down to the also-rans, those people who might have been dogged by strange coincidences but who didn't seem to show any special abilities after all? Agent Lenz had no idea, but he thought it was time to find out.

"I'll need the jet," he said, and Agent Dawson nodded.

"On it, sir." She glanced up at him. "Approximate flight time is three hours and forty-five minutes. There'll be a car waiting for you at Kanab Municipal Airport when you land."

"Thank you, Agent Dawson," he said, and she nodded but didn't smile.

"Anything else, sir?"

"Have Adara Grant's updated file sent to my computer," he told her.

Another nod, and the analyst went to work. Agent Lenz left her workstation and headed back to his office to retrieve his laptop and briefcase, along with the duffle bag he always kept packed and ready in case he needed to head out on a moment's notice.

As he went, he found himself smiling slightly.

The young woman in question had managed to stay under his radar for quite a while, but now he thought he might finally have her within reach.

He couldn't wait to start exploring the limits of her peculiar abilities.

Jake's brother Jeremy sat bolt upright at his workstation, then started hammering away at the keyboard. The burst of activity made Jake look away from his own computer screens, where he'd been scanning through headlines from Phoenix papers and TV outlets, hoping against hope that something might stand out from the usual noise and signal any possible witch or warlock activity. In reality, that sort of task was already being handled by Jeremy's various algorithms—and it was unlikely that the de la Paz *prima* wouldn't have detected the presence of someone not of her clan in the greater Phoenix area, even if Zoe's gifts in that area were nowhere near as strong as her grandmother's once were—but mostly, Jake had just been trying to appear busy.

However, Jeremy's machine-gun typing seemed to indicate something was up.

Jake rose from his chair and went over to the

workstation where his younger brother was assaulting the keyboard. "Find something?"

"I don't know. Maybe." Jeremy hadn't bothered to glance up as he spoke, but kept typing away. "A weather anomaly that fits a pattern flagged by one of my algorithms."

That comment made Jake fold his arms and send a narrow look down at his brother. "You didn't tell me one of your algorithms had caught something."

"Because a flag is just that—a flag. It still needs closer examination." At last, Jeremy lifted his hands from the keyboard and settled back in his office chair, one hand running through his dark hair and thus turning it into a shaggy mess. "But I added a set of parameters to that particular flag...and this is what I got."

He pointed at the large cinema display of his Mac Pro, where a series of glowing red concentric circles emanated outward from a point on the map, appearing like the wave pattern of a seismic event.

"Earthquake?" Jake asked, since that was what it looked like to him.

"Nope. Unexplained weather event." Jeremy leaned forward again and hit a few keys, zooming in on the point in question.

Jake frowned as he stared at the screen. "Kanab, Utah?"

"Yes. Thunderstorm that came out of nowhere. A couple of downed power lines, one tree that caught fire."

"Thunderstorms aren't that big a deal, you know," Jake remarked, earning him a dubious look from his brother.

"A month from now, no, but this one—well, I can't even say it came out of nowhere, because it didn't seem to come from *anywhere*."

The screen shifted, showing what Jake thought must be feeds from local traffic cameras, along with security footage from various businesses in the area. All of them appeared to show the skies overhead darkening in what looked like the space of a few seconds, with bright bursts of lightning occurring just seconds later.

Watching all this, Jake rubbed his chin. It looked pretty suspect to him; even when desert thunderstorms appeared to boil up out of nothing, that wasn't really the case. The clouds always came from somewhere, although thunderhead creation could sometimes happen in less than an hour, clouds churning up as the desert air heated under the brutal sun. An hour was fast, but not this fast. Kanab had gone from clear blue skies to thunderstorms and torrential rain in literally less than a minute.

"Weather-worker?" he asked, and Jeremy nodded.

"Sure looks that way. I started another filter, going through Kanab's current residents and cross-checking them with instances of extreme or sudden weather behavior over the past five years." He started typing again, and the feeds from the traffic cameras disappeared, replaced by a driver's license image featuring a pretty but unsmiling woman a few years younger than Jake, with long brown hair and big greenish eyes. "I think this is who we might be looking for."

"Adara Grant?" Jake said as he read the name off the license.

"I think so." The screen split then, leaving the driver's license on one side, and sliding in a list of addresses and associated phenomena on the other. "Tucumcari, New Mexico—tornado. Cheyenne, Wyoming…multiple tornadoes. Logan, Utah, tornado. Durango, Colorado—tornado yet again."

Frowning at the list on the computer screen, Jake asked, "Isn't Durango too mountainous for tornado activity?"

Jeremy grinned. "Well, it should be, but if

we're dealing with a rogue weather-worker here, then that doesn't matter so much, does it?"

With a shake of his head, Jake returned to reading the list, which contained more than a half-dozen towns in New Mexico, Utah, Colorado, and Wyoming, all of which experienced strange, unexplained weather events during the times when Adara Grant had been a resident. "She moved around a lot, didn't she?"

"Looks that way. Maybe she was trying to get away from the bad weather, not realizing that she was the source of it all along."

"Maybe," Jake agreed. The list seemed to indicate the woman in question had been in Kanab for more than a year, during which time there hadn't been any incidents...or at least, none that Jeremy's algorithm had noted. Which meant there probably had been none. Jeremy was too thorough to let something like that slide. "It's what, three hours to Kanab?"

"About three and a half," Jeremy replied. "Think it's worth a look?"

"I'm not totally sure, but I can be there and back before dark, so I might as well head out and see what's going on." Jake tried to sound nonchalant, but inwardly, he could feel his heart rate speed up ever so slightly. This was why he'd dreamed up Trident Enterprises in the first place, to track down any witches or warlocks who didn't even realize what they were, and bring them into the witching world. Maybe he was giving Jeremy's algorithms too much credit and this would all turn out to be a wild goose chase...but he didn't think so.

At least he wouldn't have to worry about stepping on the toes of any witch clans in the area, because Utah was one of the few places in the United States that witch-kind had always avoided. Their existence depended on staying hidden, on not allowing the general population to know who or what they were, and there was too high a risk of detection in a place like Utah, where the close-knit Mormon communities there would be much more likely to detect something odd about the strangers living in their midst. The U.S. was big enough that there didn't seem to be much reason for settling in a place so fraught with problems, and so the witch clans had given Utah a wide berth.

For all Jake knew, Adara Grant's current location was part of the reason why her presence hadn't been detected by any other witches or warlocks. Because whenever someone of witch-kind met another magically gifted person for the first time, they experienced a tingle, or a ringing in their ears, or some sort of physical reaction that told them they were in the presence of someone like themselves. It only worked when you were within a yard or two of that person, but since there were no witches or warlocks in Utah, that wouldn't have happened to her. As for all the other places Adara had lived, well, witch clans tended to pick a spot and stay in it, and not move around a lot. No one had ever done a census of witch-kind in the U.S., but Jeremy had commented once that his calculations made their number around twenty or thirty thousand at most. That might have sounded like a lot of people, but it was still only a drop in the ocean compared to the country's overall population of more than 325 million.

Anyway, the why of how Adara Grant had managed to live all her twenty-four years without ever crossing paths with another witch wasn't the issue. What was far more important was to find her, determine that she truly was a witch and not just someone with the bad luck to be followed by crappy weather wherever she went...and then convince her that she needed to come back to Flagstaff with him so they could try to figure out which clan she belonged to.

That last would be the hardest part. Jake knew he'd be able to tell right away if he was in the presence of a witch, but even if Adara felt a tingle or a shock or a humming in her ears when she met him, she wouldn't have the context to understand that those signs were telling her she'd met someone who shared her witch blood. All she'd see was a stranger appearing out of nowhere and coaxing her to cross state lines with him, which for almost anyone would be a non-starter.

Well, one step at time. "This is the reason why we started this whole thing," he told his brother. "What's the point in getting a hit if we're not going to investigate?"

"True," Jeremy responded. His gaze moved back to the computer screen. "What do you need me to do?"

"Just keep monitoring the situation, I suppose." As he spoke, he wondered if that remark had sounded completely pompous, like he was trying to impersonate a federal agent or something. While some members of the Wilcox clan were part of the local police force—what better way to escape notice than to have people in an official capacity doing their best to make sure law enforcement wasn't paying any attention?—Jake wasn't one of them. No, he was a regular guy with a degree in forest management from Northern Pines University...a guy who just happened to be a warlock with a crazy idea about tracking down the world's witchy "orphans."

However, if Jeremy thought his older brother was play-acting as a cop, he didn't give any outward indication of it. A slight lift of his shoulders, and he said, "Sure. I can keep an eye on her cell phone calls, let you know whether she's made any sudden moves or left the area."

Jake didn't bother to ask how Jeremy could do all that. When they were in the planning stages for Trident Enterprises, Jeremy had provided a laundry list of surveillance and data-mining capacities that he'd be able to provide, and added that while he could try to explain how he was able to do all those things, there wasn't much point. "Just take it on face value," he'd added, and Jake had given a mental shrug and agreed. His brother's talent for computers and data hacking truly was just as supernatural as Adara Grant's apparent ability to summon tornadoes and make thunderheads appear in a sky that had been clear moments earlier, and really didn't require much analysis. Either you went with it, or you didn't. And since Jake was a warlock and had been around this sort of thing his entire life, he didn't see any reason to ask questions. He doubted he would have understood the answers anyway.

"Great," he said. "Contact me via the sat phone, though—a big piece of that route goes through Navajo lands, and I won't get any kind of cell signal out there."

"No problem." Jeremy reached over to pat one of their sat phones, which sat in its charging cradle on his desktop. "It's safer, anyway—the feds don't generally tap into sat phones the way they do cell transmissions."

"You're expecting the feds to be watching us?" Jake asked with a grin. The idea was sort of ludicrous; the Wilcox clan had always made sure to dot every "i" and cross every "t," just because the last thing they wanted was to attract any attention from the authorities.

"Not really," Jeremy replied. "I'm just paranoid."

"That's probably smart. I'm going to head out —let Laurel know what's going on when she gets back."

Because she wasn't there on that particular morning, had asked for a few hours off so she could go with one of their cousins to help her pick out her wedding gown at a boutique down in Scottsdale. Jake had wanted to shake his head at the request, thinking it seemed kind of silly to drive all that way to look for a dress, but he'd reminded himself that just because he'd been denied his own chance at happiness didn't mean he needed to be a Grinch about the whole thing. Besides, Trident had been up and running for almost a week, and they hadn't encountered a single possible hit in all that time. It was just bad luck for Laurel that she was away when something finally happened.

"Sure," Jeremy said easily. "She's probably going to be bummed that she missed out on this."

"Well, she won't have missed out on the whole thing, since it's going to be at least seven hours before I get back." Hopefully, with Adara Grant along for the ride, but Jake knew he would just have to see what happened. He was already mentally rehearsing what to say to her, how he could convince her that he wasn't some sort of creeper who'd decided she was easy prey.

"True. Aren't you forgetting something, though?"

Jake cocked an eyebrow at his brother. "What?"

"Her address. Twenty-two East 300 North."

"That's an address?"

"It is in Utah," Jeremy replied.

"Got it. I'll keep you posted."

Jeremy gave him a thumbs-up and turned back to his screen.

No reason to delay any further. Jake made a brief stop at the refrigerator to get himself a couple of bottles of water, then headed out to the driveway, where his new Jeep Gladiator pickup truck was parked. Good thing he'd filled up just the day before.

He had a long road in front of him.

3

I LAY ON MY BED AND STARED UP AT THE CEILING. My mother had wisely decided to leave me alone to brood, probably not wanting to provoke another thunderstorm. She'd met the firemen at the door, all apologies, telling them that the rain had put out the fire and that she was sorry to have bothered them. Of course, they'd told her it was no problem at all, and left after exchanging a few comments about what an odd storm it had been and how they'd never seen anything like it before.

Unfortunately, I'd seen plenty like it.

Neither my mother nor I was due at work until three, so I still had about an hour before I had to get over my funk and pretend to be the happy, cheery waitress the customers at the diner expected. For some reason, minor annoyances at work never seemed to be enough to invoke the turbulent emotions that preceded the outbreak of one of my strange storms. I supposed I should be glad about that, or I would have left a lot of flattened restaurants and injured patrons in my wake.

For the moment, I could only lie there in my room and do my best to stay calm as I went through a list of possible options to solve my tuition woes. The first was to get on the phone with the U of U financial aid office and plead my case, but I'd already spent months doing that and had gotten nothing but a bunch of promises that turned out to be mostly hot air. Okay, so I'd take a semester off and save up to pay for my final year. I was already behind the curve, twenty-four years old and only beginning my senior year of college, but because of the way my mother and I had moved around so much, that hadn't been exactly by choice. Still, I was already older than half my classmates, so what difference would another six months even make?

Probably not much in the grand scheme of things. It was more that I had already been chafing to be done with college so I could move on to the next stage of my life. I couldn't help feeling that I'd always be defined as my mother's daughter while I was still in school and living at home. That didn't mean I didn't love my mother —of course, she was the most important thing in my world, and I'd always be proud of her for giving so much of herself while raising me. At the same time, though, I wanted to be *me,* wanted to know who Adara Grant really was. My entire life, I'd felt as if there was some piece of me that was missing, and I needed to discover what it was. It was entirely possible that a shrink would have told me that feeling was simply because I'd never known my father, never known much of anything about him.

I wouldn't ever know, since we sure as hell couldn't afford to have me see a psychologist.

Sighing, I rolled over and propped myself up on my elbows so I could look out the window. The sky was serenely blue again, with not even a couple of clouds drifting by to prove that the storm had really happened and wasn't just a figment of my imagination. Only the blackened stub of the one tree branch the lightning bolt had hit was proof of the tempest, proof that my anger and disappointment had somehow conjured a thunderstorm from nothing.

If that was even what had happened.

Back to the problem at hand. The one thing I absolutely would not consider was dropping out of school entirely. This was a setback, and nothing more. Several times as we'd moved around, I'd had people ask me why it was so important to go to college at all, that it would have been more responsible for me to work full-time after I graduated from high school so I wouldn't be a burden on my mother. Not that people actually said the word "burden," but it didn't take a mind reader to figure out what they probably meant.

I supposed the easy answer would have been to say college was important because I didn't want to end up like my mother, working one waitressing job after another because she didn't have the education or skills to do anything else. But that wasn't the entire truth—for one thing, I'd also done a lot of waitressing, and I knew it was hard work and required a decent amount of brains to be any good at it. Besides, I was definitely unlike my mother in that I'd made damn sure there wouldn't be any "surprises" like I'd been for her. Moving around put a real damper on romance, and although there had been a couple of guys I was interested in, I'd never met anyone I thought was worth the risk of having sex. All right, I knew the pill was pretty reliable as long as you were careful and didn't forget to take your daily dose, but still, after seeing what my mother's life had turned out to be, I didn't see the point in taking the chance.

And once we landed in Utah, well, let's just say it was a lot easier to be celibate there than in some of the other places we'd lived.

Another glance at the clock. Two-thirty. Time to stop moping, get up, and go put on my game face. Not too much makeup, since Kanab was a conservative town, but just enough to look as if I'd put a little effort into my appearance.

I went in the bathroom and dutifully applied mascara, blush, and lip gloss, then brushed my hair and pulled it back into an elastic band. Luckily, the diner where my mother and I worked didn't require a real up-do, only that my hair be out of the way. I might have been able to call clouds to a clear sky, but I was utter crap at doing anything with my hair that required more work than a simple ponytail.

The doorbell rang and I started slightly, wondering who the heck would be coming by in the middle of the afternoon on a Friday. Word had gone out soon after our arrival that we were a couple of heathens, or at least definitely not interested in converting, because the Mormon missionaries had long since stopped showing up on our doorstep. We hardly ever ordered anything online, so I knew it couldn't be UPS or FedEx.

"Can you get that, honey?" my mom called from her bedroom. "I'm getting changed into my uniform."

"Sure," I replied. I always left the uniform for last, just because that way there was less chance of getting makeup on it or spilling something or whatever. I only had two of them, and half the time, the second uniform would be in the hamper and not readily available in case there was some sort of accident.

Steeling myself to dispel a couple of over-zealous Mormons or maybe some Seventh Day Adventists who'd gotten blown off course, I headed to the front door. The house was small, just a little over a thousand square feet, so it didn't take me long to get there.

When I opened the door, I blinked in surprise. No, that was no missionary, but a man probably in his late thirties, wearing a dark suit. He had short-cropped dark brown hair and piercing blue eyes, and wasn't bad-looking, with his regular features and sharply angled cheek-bones, although something about him immediately sent a chill down my spine.

Maybe it was just that he felt like a cop to me, even though he wasn't wearing a uniform.

"Adara Grant?" he asked.

He'd phrased it as a question, but I had a pretty good idea he already knew who I was. Since I guessed that lying probably wasn't an option, I made myself say, "Yes, that's me. Can I help you?"

At once, he smiled, showing two rows of even white teeth. The smile didn't reach his eyes, though, which remained positively glacial. "I hope so. My name is Randall Lenz, and I'd like to talk to you for a moment, if I could."

"We're really not interested in converting, thank you," I said politely, even though I knew he was about two decades too old to be a Mormon on his mission.

That comment made him chuckle, although something about the sound felt contrived to me. "Oh, I'm not a missionary," he replied. "I work for the government."

"We always pay our taxes on time," I blurted out, and he shook his head.

"I'm not with the IRS, Ms. Grant," he said. "Really, I only need a moment of your time."

I paused, wishing that my mother would appear and get rid of him. But her bedroom door had been closed when I walked past, an indication that she probably didn't intend to emerge until ten minutes until three, the time when we'd have to leave for work. That meant there was no way she was going to come to my rescue.

"Can I see some identification?" I asked. That wasn't an outrageous request, was it? I thought I'd read somewhere that it was within your rights to ask for I.D. if someone claimed to be working in an official capacity.

His smile didn't waver. "Of course."

He reached into the breast pocket of his suit, then got out a slim leather case containing a photo I.D. and handed it to me. His face matched the picture on the card, and it said his name was Agent Randall Alan Lenz, Homeland Security.

Homeland Security?

I swallowed, and gave him back the case with his government identification. "I don't know what Homeland Security would want with me," I told him. "I'm pretty sure we don't get too many foreign operatives in Kanab, Utah."

He didn't blink, icy blue eyes still fixed on my face. "Just few minutes, Ms. Grant."

Once again, I glanced over my shoulder, but the house was quiet, my mother probably putting the finishing touches on her hair before slipping on the comfortable shoes she wore for her shift. Letting in Randall Lenz seemed like a huge mistake, but I couldn't really turn down a request from a government agent, could I? That I.D.

looked pretty damn authentic. I supposed it could have been faked, but why would someone go to so much trouble to talk to a nobody like me?

"All right," I said reluctantly. "We can sit here in the living room."

I opened the door a bit wider to let him in, inwardly thankful that the day before had been my day off, and so I'd tidied the house and dusted and vacuumed. The place wasn't anything to write home about, a small one-story cottage built in the late 1950s, but at least it looked neat and generally presentable, despite the garage-sale furniture.

"Can I get you anything?" I asked, trying to be polite. "Ice water, or iced tea?"

"Nothing, thank you," he replied as he took a seat on the sofa.

So much for that stalling tactic. I reluctantly sat down on the wing chair, perching on the edge because it didn't feel right to settle all the way back on it. "What can I help you with, Agent Lenz?"

Another of those arctic smiles, which never seemed to reach his equally cold eyes. "Did you know that you're a very special young woman, Ms. Grant?"

Now the cold was in my spine, running down

my back, making me feel as if I was going to freeze all over and then shatter into a thousand pieces. "Me?" I responded, then gave an utterly unconvincing laugh. "No, I'm pretty ordinary."

"Was what you did earlier today ordinary?"

My fingers dug into the edge of the seat cushion. "I—I'm not sure what you're talking about."

His lips lifted a fraction of an inch. "Oh, I think you know exactly what I'm talking about. A storm out of nowhere, wasn't it?" He shifted slightly so he could glance out the front window and see the charred limb on the cottonwood tree. "Close call, I would think. What if your house had been struck?"

"What do you want?" I whispered.

"I want you, Ms. Grant," he replied, the intensity of those cold blue eyes belying the crisp, businesslike tone of his voice. "Or rather, your government wants you. Talents like yours shouldn't go to waste."

I wanted to blink and pray that I'd wake up from this nightmare, that maybe I'd discover I'd fallen asleep after the tumult earlier in the afternoon and was only having a very bad dream. How could he possibly know a truth I'd done my very best to keep from everyone, to the point where I hardly dared acknowledge it to myself?

He must have been tracking me somehow—

or rather, he'd been tracking strange weather phenomena, and then had made a connection between those events and my presence in the places where they'd occurred. Nothing else made any sense.

Of course, if he'd been doing something like that, then that seemed to indicate he—or the government agency he worked for—was actively looking for people with these supposed "talents." What the government needed with a person like me, I really didn't want to know. I doubted it could be anything good.

"I don't have any special talents, Agent Lenz," I said loudly, hoping my voice would carry down the hall and right through the closed door of my mother's room. Honestly, I didn't know for sure how much she could even do to intervene, but at the very least, having her there as a sort of leavening influence might help to defuse the situation a bit. "I think you must have me confused with someone else."

His thin lips quirked a little. "No, I don't think so. There was that tornado in Durango, Colorado —and the rains that flooded out Truth or Consequences, New Mexico. Or do you want to talk about the other twister in Cheyenne barely two years ago? I'll admit that things seemed to quiet down once you moved here to Kanab. Do you want to explain that?"

I couldn't have explained any of it to Agent Lenz even if I'd wanted to. As it was, I just desperately wanted him far, far away from Kanab in general and me in particular. "Weird weather happens," I said as calmly as I could. "I honestly don't know why you would connect me to any of those incidents."

"Because you were living in all those places when those 'incidents' occurred," he replied, looking unperturbed by my protests. "And there were no reoccurrences after you moved out of the areas in question. That tells me you had to be connected to them, even if you want to deny any involvement."

"Coincidence," I said, then added, "If you don't have a warrant or anything, then I think I'll need to ask you to leave. I have to be at work in fifteen minutes."

As I'd feared, he didn't move, only sat there on the couch, still wearing that faint smile, as if he found my show of bravado more amusing than anything else. "Ms. Grant, this isn't the sort of situation that requires a warrant. It would be in your best interests if you stopped with the excuses and cooperated."

"Or what?" I returned, inwardly a little shocked that I'd had the guts to make such a response. In general—probably because I was always worried that my strange talents would flare out of control and create a mess I couldn't possibly fix—I tried to keep my head down and act like a good little obedient citizen. The world just worked better for me that way. However, something about this man freaked me out. He was too calm, too in control, as if he knew he had the upper hand and that it didn't matter what I said or did.

But...did he? If this supposed talent—or curse—of mine was what had drawn him here in the first place, couldn't I use that same talent to scare him off?

Well, maybe, except for the little part where I couldn't control my strange powers. And even if I could, calling down the lightning to strike him where he sat would only destroy part of our house in the bargain. While I wanted to get rid of him, I also didn't want to blow a hole in the roof and set the place on fire. That was the problem with my supposed gift—I never knew what kind of collateral damage it might create.

Agent Lenz shifted ever so slightly, just enough so I could see the dark shape of a gun in its shoulder holster against the crisp white of his dress shirt. "I don't want to use force, Ms. Grant," he said. "But it's always an option."

Just that small glimpse of his service pistol was enough to make a hard lump of fear lodge itself somewhere in my throat. I swallowed and pushed back a stray lock of hair with shaking fingers. "What am I supposed to tell my mother?" I asked, and a gleam appeared in his sharp blue eyes, as if he'd guessed that I probably wasn't going to put up too much more of a fight.

"Tell your mother the truth," he replied. "Your government has need of you, and you'll be going with me to the East Coast. She doesn't need to know anything else—and can't. This program is classified."

Meaning he wouldn't tell me anything more, either. Were there others like me? The existence of this "program" seemed to indicate there were. The thought was unsettling and yet oddly exciting at the same time. Ever since those strange abilities had surfaced soon after I turned ten, I'd thought of myself as a freak, as some sort of strange genetic anomaly. But if I wasn't alone...if other people existed with odd paranormal talents...then maybe I'd finally be able to figure out what my place in the world was supposed to be.

As I stood there, wavering, the doorbell rang

again. I looked at the front door in consternation, wondering who the hell it could be this time. Considering who'd been standing on my doorstep the last time I had a visitor, I wasn't exactly keen to answer the bell.

And it seemed Agent Lenz wasn't eager for me to do that, either, because he said calmly, "Ignore it. You need to tell your mother you're leaving."

"It could be one of the neighbors," I replied, although I didn't sound convincing even to myself. Neither of our next-door neighbors was the type to socialize with us; I'd always gotten the impression that they weren't too thrilled with having a couple of heathens living on their street, although they'd always paid lip service to convention by smiling when they met us or offering a half-hearted wave when they saw either my mom or me driving past in our ancient Subaru. Still, some kind of emergency could have come up, something where they needed our help.

"Or it could be a missionary," he said in that same reasonable tone. "This is Utah, after all."

The doorbell rang again.

Shit.

Then my mother's voice came down the hallway. "Addie, answer the door, then hurry up and get changed. We're going to be late."

I shot a quick glance at Agent Lenz and saw that his mouth had tightened, the smile he'd been wearing now gone. "Um, Mom—"

"Addie, answer the damn door!"

Years of conditioning propelled my feet forward. Before my unwelcome visitor could protest, I'd reached for the knob and opened the door.

Standing on the front doorstep was probably the best-looking man I'd ever seen in my life. He was a few years older than I, tall with dark hair and eyes, and a faint scruff of a beard covering his lean jaw. Stranger than the mere presence of this apparition, though, was the weird tingle I experienced at the back of my neck as I stared up into his face, as though simply being around him had evoked some odd physical reaction that I couldn't begin to explain.

"Um...yes?" I asked, noting out of the corner of my eye that Agent Lenz had gotten up from the couch and begun to move toward me...and my amazing visitor.

"Adara Grant?" he responded in an echo of the agent's words from just a few moments earlier.

What the hell was going on? I doubted the newcomer was a government agent—he was wearing faded jeans and a T-shirt with the logo of a brewing company in Flagstaff—but I also couldn't figure out why all these strangers had decided to converge on my house at almost the same time.

Unless this man had also been tracking me somehow. Obviously, the strange phenomena that clustered around me had attracted way too much unwelcome attention.

"You don't need to answer him," Agent Lenz interposed before I could begin to reply.

At once, the stranger's gaze shifted toward the agent and his mouth thinned, even as his dark eyes grew worried. He'd obviously taken his measure of the situation and wasn't happy with what he was seeing.

Well, that made two of us.

I lifted my chin and said, "I'm Adara. What's this about?"

Ignoring the glare Agent Lenz had just sent him, the man said, "My name is Jake. I need to talk to you."

"Talk to me about what?" I asked. I noticed that the stranger hadn't given me his last name, but maybe he'd only held back that bit of information because he didn't want to offer it with a federal agent standing there and listening to everything we said.

"She doesn't need to talk to you," Agent Lenz said. "In fact, she was just leaving. Come on, Ms. Grant."

He put his hand on my arm, and almost at once, anger flared in me at the unwelcome contact. At the same time, the wind picked up, rustling the leaves of the cottonwood trees, keening around the corners of the house.

"'Leaving'?" my mother echoed, and I shifted so I could see her standing in the middle of the living room, brow puckered in worry as she took in the man in the dark suit who grasped my bicep, the much more casually dressed stranger who waited on the front porch. "Addie, what in the world is going on?"

Good question. I told myself to be calm, even as the wind picked up speed and the skies overhead began to darken once again. "Mom, I—"

"Let go of her," she cut in, glaring at Agent Lenz. However, I hadn't missed the way she'd sent a frightened glance upward, as if she'd noticed the way the wind had begun to howl and knew what was going to come next if she didn't try to de-escalate the situation. "I don't know who you are, but—"

"I'm with the government," he said. "That's all you need to know."

"I don't care who you're with," Jake retorted. "But it sure looks to me like Adara doesn't want to go anywhere with you."

Agent Lenz's eyes narrowed ever so slightly, but otherwise, he didn't appear concerned by the other man's interruption. "It's none of your business, son," he said, his tone almost kind, and yet dismissive at the same time. "Let me do my job, and no one will get hurt."

Rain began to fall, pounding onto the already wet lawn, dripping off the eaves. I winced as lightning crackled overhead and the winds whipped into a greater fury.

Stop it, I thought. *Just stop it.*

But the wind only continued to howl, pulling strands of hair loose from my ponytail so they whipped wildly around my face even though I should have been protected where I was, standing just inside the doorframe. Jake gave a nod, as if he'd expected as much...which seemed to tell me that he knew something about my strange abilities, even though I had no idea how he could have learned such a thing.

My mother moved closer. "I'm going to call the cops."

"I wouldn't do that if I were you," Agent Lenz

responded, his free hand moving toward the gun in its shoulder holster.

"It's all right," I said. "I was going to go with him."

"What?" she said, even as Jake stared at me in consternation.

"You don't need to do that—" he began.

"I do," I broke in. "I don't know who you are, but this has nothing to do with you."

"Actually, it does," he said. "You just have to trust me on that."

"As she said, she agreed to come with me," Agent Lenz said then. Some rain had made it in through the door and spattered his dark suit jacket and left blotches on his pristine white shirtfront, but he affected not to notice. "Time for you to leave."

My mother came up to the door, where the wind caught her carefully styled up-do and pulled loose a few strands, which blew around her face in a flurry of gold. "Let her go."

"Mom—"

What came next happened so quickly that it was all a blur before my horrified eyes. She laid her hand on Agent Lenz's arm, and the gun slipped out of its holster as though it had been greased. At the same time, one of the hanging flower pots that decorated the front porch came flying off the nail where it had been suspended, aiming directly for his head. It connected with a crunch. He startled, and the gun went off with a bang that sounded terrifyingly loud in my startled ears.

I blinked and saw my mother stumble backward, a red stain spreading down the front of the crisp blue uniform dress she wore. At the same time, Agent Lenz let out a curse and staggered, somehow managing to maintain his balance despite the blow he'd just suffered. Before the words had even left his lips, my mother collapsed to the floor, hand to her chest, eyes staring sightlessly up at the ceiling.

Blood began to spread outward from her limp form, creating a crimson pool on the worn beige carpet.

So much blood. No one could lose that much blood and live.

Wind was swirling in the front yard, picking up leaves and scattering them everywhere...but also coalescing into a deadly funnel made of dirt and debris and dead grass. I could barely see for the tears that blurred my eyes, but it seemed that funnel was moving toward the house.

Another flower pot went flying toward Agent Lenz. He ducked, but the object still smacked the side of his head, this time sending him to the floor, apparently knocked out.

"We have to go!" Jake shouted at me.

"My mother!" I screamed back at him.

He stood there for a second, irresolute, then went and knelt down next to my mother and laid a finger against her blood-spattered throat. Despite the howling of the wind, everything seemed to go horribly quiet as his dark eyes met mine. In his gaze, I saw sorrow, coupled with a terrible urgency.

"I'm sorry," he said, the words barely audible above the commotion of the unnatural storm shredding the front yard, and yet they still sounded a knell in my aching heart. He sent a quick glance at Agent Lenz, who was already beginning to stir, one hand feebly moving toward the visible swelling at his temple. "And we have to get away from here. Unless you really do want to go with him."

With the man who had just killed my mother? The words swirled around in my brain, not quite making sense. Or maybe it was that I didn't want to acknowledge what had just happened, that if I could prevent the horrible reality from penetrating my brain, I might be able to go back to a time a few minutes earlier...to a time when my mother was still alive.

"No," I said dully. "I don't want to go with him."

"Then come with me," Jake said, and extended a hand.

For a few seconds, I could only stare at his outstretched fingers, wondering what I should do.

Then realization flared.

Jake's hand was a lifeline...and I needed to take it.

I reached for him, felt his fingers clasp mine. And then we were running, dodging the angry, whirling tornado in the front yard as we headed for a big shiny black truck that was parked at the curb. He let go so I could climb in, and I did, then leaned my head against the seat back and felt my eyes begin to burn.

We pulled away, the truck leaping forward with an angry growl. I tilted my head toward the window, saw the tornado descend on the house, shredding the porch, tearing through the clapboard siding like tissue paper.

I couldn't see anything after that, because I was crying too hard.

4

JAKE HAD REMAINED SILENT WHILE HE PILOTED THE Gladiator through Kanab's quiet streets as quickly as he could without attracting any attention from the local cops. His heart ached for the woman who sat in the passenger seat, but even though she'd stopped sobbing just as they reached the town limits, her head was still slumped, and he had a feeling that anything he said would have been horribly, woefully inadequate.

So he stayed quiet, even as his mind buzzed.

Who the hell had that guy been? A government agent, but where had he come from? Had Adara's latest display of weather magic drawn him to Kanab, just as it had drawn Jake himself there?

Probably, but he knew the questions would have to wait. For the moment, the most important thing was to get as far away from Kanab as possible. He didn't know how anyone could have survived the whirling maelstrom that descended on the modest one-story house where Adara had been living with her mother, but on the off chance that the mysterious government agent had somehow survived the collapse, Jake figured it was better to head in the opposite direction than he'd planned.

Which was why they were now traveling southbound on Highway 89 so he could pick up the westbound 389. From there, they'd wend their way through far northern Arizona before going back up into Utah in order to pick up Interstate 15. Then they could take the interstate down into Nevada and, with any luck, lose themselves in Las Vegas.

That was the plan, anyway. Jake had formulated the contingency just in case anything went sideways and he needed to be sure he couldn't be tracked back to Flagstaff and Wilcox territory.

And man, had things gone sideways.

He hadn't thought the agent would reach for his gun. Jake had only intended to send one of the flowerpots flying at the man to knock him off balance so he'd let go of Adara. But even though the flowerpot had done exactly what Jake had meant for it to do—his talent allowed him to move much larger objects than a simple clay pot, and so he'd figured the scheme should be effective—what he hadn't figured on was the agent's finger reflexively pulling the trigger and firing the fatal shot.

It had been almost like something out of movie, but the scene had been horribly, horribly real, so real that he knew it would be burned into his brain until the day he died.

And now Adara was alone in the world.

No, Jake told himself then. *She's not alone. She has her clan, even if she doesn't know about us yet.*

"Where are we going?" she asked then, her voice clear and cool, almost painfully precise, as if she needed to exercise what control she could on something—anything—in her life.

"Las Vegas," he said. "It seemed safer to take the long way home."

"Where's home?"

"Flagstaff."

That reply seemed to stir some life into her eyes. They were reddened with weeping, but he remembered what they had looked like when he first saw her step out on the porch, green-gray, with endless shifting depths, like moss agate. He knew he'd seen eyes like that before, but at the moment, he couldn't compel his racing brain to remember where.

"Who are you?" she asked, and he let out a breath.

"Jake Wilcox. I'm a friend."

That reply made her sit up a little straighter. Voice wondering, she asked, "Are you *related* to me?"

Startled, Jake glanced away from the road to see Adara staring at him with something like astonished speculation in her expression. Once again, he got the feeling she was doing her best to focus on anything except the terrible scene they'd left behind them.

"I don't know," he allowed. After all, there was a very good chance she came from some other witch clan. She'd been born in Columbus, Ohio, which was a very long way from northern Arizona. "Why would you ask that?"

Her fingers, slender and pale, knotted in her lap. "Because my father's last name was Wilcox. Or at least, my—my mother told me it was. And she met him in Flagstaff."

Jake hadn't missed the slight hiccup as Adara stumbled over that mention of her mother, but he supposed it was good that she'd been able to utter the word at all. At the same time, a rush of triumph surged through him, tempered as it was by the loss he knew she had just suffered. "Then yes, we're probably related somehow," he said carefully. "Can you tell me anything else about your father?"

A long hesitation, during which she sent him a considering glance. Damn. Maybe he shouldn't have been so quick to press her for more information. What if she decided to stonewall him?

Then you let it go for now and ask again later, he told himself. *The woman just saw her mother gunned down in front of her.*

To his surprise, however, Adara spoke then.

"I don't know much," she said. One hand lifted to push a lock of heavy brown hair away from her face. "My mother met the man she said was my father in a bar in downtown Flagstaff. He told her he was a widower with two boys."

At hearing those words, Jake felt his heart give a weird thump. As a general rule, witches and warlocks didn't lose their spouses at relatively young ages, which meant there couldn't have been too many warlocks who matched the description Adara had just given him. Yes, he supposed that the man Adara's mother had met all those years ago had lied to cover up his philandering, but again, witches and warlocks were generally faithful and didn't go looking for relationships outside their marriages.

"His name?" he asked, hoping his voice didn't sound too strained.

"Jackson," she replied. "Jackson Wilcox. Do you know him?"

Jake's fingers clenched on the steering wheel. The woman had just lost her mother, and now he was supposed to tell her that her father had been dead for more than twenty years?

At the same time, his brain was working feverishly, trying to make sense of what she'd just said. How was it even possible that Jackson Wilcox, Connor's father, had been able to father another child, and a daughter at that? The curse that had ruled the *primuses* of the Wilcox clan for more than a hundred years until Connor and Angela finally broke it several years ago had stipulated that the men of Jeremiah Wilcox's line would only have one son, and that they would never be able to know happiness in their marriages. Then again, Connor himself had been a mystery, a child who shouldn't even have been born, and therefore maybe it wasn't so strange that Jackson had somehow managed to father a third child.

Well, that particular conundrum was for greater minds than his to puzzle out. At the moment, the most important thing was to make sure he kept Adara far away from anyone who wanted to use her powers for ill. She was even more important than he'd thought.

Since she was staring at him, obviously expecting a reply, Jake said, "Jackson Wilcox passed away when I was just a kid. I'm really sorry."

"So I am alone," she responded in a murmur he guessed she hadn't intended him to overhear.

"Not completely," he said quickly, wanting to offer her whatever good news he could think of. "You have a half-brother—Connor Wilcox. And he and his wife Angela have three children. That doesn't include all the rest of us Wilcoxes, either."

Adara's eyes widened. "I'm an aunt?"

"Yes. Ian and Emily are seven—they're twins. And Miranda is three."

"Wow." Adara was quiet for a moment, apparently absorbing that information. When she spoke again, her tone was musing. "And we're...cousins?"

"Distant cousins—our great-great-whatever grandfathers were brothers, but that's seven generations back."

"You said 'the rest of us Wilcoxes.' How many are there?"

Good question. It was his cousin Marie's job to keep track of all the Wilcox family members, to keep an eye on all the various lineages to make sure cousins who didn't have at least three degrees of separation were carefully kept away from each other. Connor also had access to that database, but he seemed content to let Marie manage that side of things. "Around five hundred or so, mostly in Flagstaff, but we've got branches of the family ranging across northern Arizona, from Williams out to Winslow and into Holbrook."

"Five hundred?" Now Adara sounded vaguely aghast.

Jake supposed it would have to be something of a shock to think you were completely alone in the world, only to discover you had so many relatives—distant or not—that it would be almost impossible to keep up with all of them. "Give or take. We Wilcoxes have lived in the area since the late 1870s, so we've had plenty of time to be fruitful and multiply...so to speak."

She took in this piece of information without comment and fell silent again, gaze fixed on the desert flashing by outside the windows of his Jeep pickup. Although he'd been thrilled to buy the vehicle, wanting to put it through its paces on the rough 4x4 trails in the forests that surrounded his hometown, now he found himself thinking it might have been smarter to buy something a little less flashy...and rare. The Gladiator had only recently come to market, and there weren't many of them in Arizona, let alone out in the hinterlands where he planned to travel. The silver Toyota Tundra pickup he'd traded in to buy the Gladiator would have been far less conspicuous.

"We shouldn't have left like that," Adara said then, gaze still apparently fastened on the rocky landscape moving past them at a brisk seventy-five miles per hour. "I should have stayed and called the police."

"And been there when Agent Whoever woke up?"

"Lenz. Agent Lenz." Her lower lip wavered for a moment, but then she pulled in a breath and blinked, hard, as if doing her best to make sure she wouldn't begin crying again. "Just because he's a government agent doesn't mean he's above the law."

Jake didn't bother to tell her she was being naïve. It would be good to think that this Agent Lenz might face some sort of punishment for what he'd done, but people like that very rarely were forced to deal with the consequences of their actions. If he'd been in Kanab to fetch

Adara, then that probably meant he worked for some anonymous agency which operated by its own rules. Far more likely, he would claim self-defense—even though Adara's mother hadn't been armed—and walk away from any investigation by the local police.

No, Jake figured the best possible outcome was that Lenz had still been unconscious when the tornado Adara had called descended on the house and tore it to shreds. That seemed like a nice, biblical piece of justice, and probably about the most they could hope for.

"I'm sorry," he said quietly. "That wasn't—that wasn't supposed to happen. I was supposed to go there and see you, tell you who you really were, who your family was...and then hope you'd come with me back to Flagstaff."

"Why would I leave everything I knew to go to Flagstaff with you?"

Good question. On the surface, he supposed that it would seem strange for him to expect her to drop everything and take off with a man she didn't even know.

"Because of who you are," he said.

Her fingers clenched around themselves again. Blue glinted on her right hand, and he realized she was wearing a silver band set with turquoise stones on her middle finger. "Who am I...really?"

The highway around them was empty and straight, and so Jake figured it was safe enough to glance over and hold her gaze as he delivered the news. "You're a witch from the Wilcox clan. Your father Jackson was the clan's *primus,* or leader. That's probably why your gift is so insanely strong."

For a second or two, she didn't respond, only stared at him as if she wasn't sure she'd heard him correctly. Then one corner of her mouth twisted, and she shook her head. "Okay, seriously...witches? This is no time for jokes."

No, it wasn't, but he hadn't been joking. "It's the truth," he said, then returned his attention to the road. "I know this may be hard to believe, but there are witch clans like the Wilcoxes all over the world. Maybe not as big and prosperous as ours, but witches and warlocks are real. We each have our particular talent, a gift that usually starts to appear when we're ten or eleven."

That revelation seemed to surprise her, or maybe it was simply that he'd explained something she'd been wondering about for years. Even as her eyes widened again, she gave the faintest of nods, as if acknowledging something to herself. "Why can't I control it, then, if it's something that just naturally happens to us witches?"

"You didn't have anyone to show you the ropes, so to speak," Jake replied. "I mean, yes, our powers develop naturally enough, but we still need someone to help us learn how to work with them, to figure out their parameters."

She tilted her head at him. "And yours—your power is telekinesis? You threw those flowerpots at Agent Lenz?"

"I was hoping to distract him. I didn't mean—that is, I would never have done it if I'd thought he would—"

"It's all right," Adara cut in. Her mouth tightened, and she shook her head, as though correcting herself. "I mean, no, it's not all right, but it's not your fault. Agent Lenz shouldn't have been waving his gun around a bunch of unarmed civilians."

Despite the seriousness of the situation—the horrors they'd left behind them—Jake couldn't quite keep his lips from twitching in an unwilling smile at her choice of words. She must have caught the shift in expression, because she frowned at him, her next words positively icy.

"Did I say something funny?"

"Sorry," he said immediately. "It's just that 'civilian' is the word witch-kind uses to describe regular people who don't have any magic. In that context, it's Agent Lenz who's the civilian, not either of us."

"Oh." Adara mulled that explanation for a moment, then nodded slightly as she twisted the ring around on her finger, gaze drifting once more to the landscape outside the window. "I suppose there are a whole lot of things I'll have to learn."

Jake wished he knew her better, wished he had the courage to reach out and pat her on the arm, or offer some other reassuring gesture. However, he got the impression she was just barely holding it together—which was completely understandable—and so might not react all that well to even a hint of intimacy.

"There are," he said. "But it's okay. We'll be there for you."

"All you Wilcoxes."

"Exactly."

She went quiet again, the bright sunlight catching a glint of tears in her eyes. Jake thought he'd better buy her some sunglasses when they stopped for gas. It was fiercely bright out there in the open desert, the sun just beginning to move toward the west, and the glare would only get worse as the afternoon wore on. He supposed he should be relieved that none of Adara's storms had followed them here, that however roiled in spirit she must currently be, her inner torment hadn't translated into thunder and lightning or gale-force winds.

About all he could do was hope she'd be able to keep things under control until they were safely back in Flagstaff.

Randall Lenz sat in the motel room he'd rented for himself, an ice pack pressed against his throbbing temple. His team had converged on the house and pulled him out of harm's way just as the tornado Adara had called began to tear off pieces of the roof, and had tried to load him into their van before any of the neighbors ventured out to see what was going on. However, even with the considerable resources he had at his disposal, Lenz knew it would be difficult to completely cover up Lyssa Grant's death, and so he'd ignored their offers of first aid and had run into the kitchen, turned on the gas in the stove, and lit one of the candles he'd spotted sitting on the small round table in the dining area. Sure enough, even as the van sped away and the tornado began to dissipate, the gas ignited, blowing the little house into splinters.

They'd still find Lyssa Grant's body, but there wouldn't be enough left for them to ever discover her true cause of death. Nor would they have any reason to look beyond the obvious. Accidents like that happened every day.

He did his best to push away the image of the sudden shock and pain on her face, pretty features contorting in terror. An accident, but he wasn't supposed to make mistakes like that. It was clumsy, a rookie's error.

A breath, and he forced himself to focus on the here and now. What he really needed to do was figure out who the hell that stranger was, the man who had appeared so unexpectedly and ruined everything. He'd said his name was Jake, which gave them something to go on...but not much.

Still holding the ice pack against his head, Lenz got his phone out of his jacket pocket and called HQ. A woman's voice came through the speaker.

"Agent Dawson."

"Dawson, it's Agent Lenz. Things went sideways in Kanab."

"Sorry to hear that, sir." A pause, and she said, "Satellite surveillance picked up an explosion. What happened?"

"I'll debrief you when I get there. For now, I

need you to go over the satellite footage frame by frame, starting at roughly 13:35. A man came to the house. See what you can discover about what he was driving and where he went. He took the target with him."

"Yes, sir. Let me take a closer look and get back to you."

"Waiting."

He ended the call there and dropped the phone on the bed, then leaned against the padded headboard. His skull hurt like a bitch, throbbing like someone was banging a drum inside his temple, but he hadn't wanted a medic to look at him, had only wanted to get himself hidden away in an anonymous motel at the edge of town so he could regroup and figure out what to do next. Heading back to Virginia had been out of the question; even though he'd lost Adara Grant for the moment, Lenz wasn't about to admit defeat this early in the game. All he needed was for Agent Dawson to analyze the satellite footage and give him the make and model of the vehicle this "Jake" had been driving. After that, simple scans from traffic cams along the highway would provide the data he needed to figure out which direction they'd gone. Not that you had a lot of choices in that part of the world —they could have gone east toward Page, north into Utah, or west toward St. George and the interstate. Even so, going off half-cocked in the wrong direction would serve no purpose. It was better to sit and wait to see what Dawson had to tell him.

With a slight groan, he got up from the bed and went into the bathroom. A splash of cold water on his face helped slightly, but he knew it was going to take more than a few minutes' rest to recover from that blow to the head. How had it even happened? He supposed the winds Adara had summoned were strong enough to pull that flowerpot free from the nail where it had hung, and yet it almost felt as though the thing had been flung at him on purpose.

Well, maybe her powers were stronger than he'd thought, although manipulating physical objects seemed to be an entirely different talent than conjuring storms. None of the other subjects they'd tested seemed to possess more than one supernatural ability, although several of them could unlock doors and summon fire with their minds—a modest flame, though, enough to light a candle and no more. Why some of the subjects should have those particular gifts in common, he didn't know...and neither did any of the people involved. They'd always had those powers, they claimed...or at least, had possessed them since the time they were ten or so years old.

Yet another puzzle. For the moment, though, Randall Lenz wanted to force his aching brain to focus on Adara Grant. She was by far the most powerful of all the gifted individuals he'd brought into the program, and he refused to admit that some stranger had managed to tear her from his grasp. Eventually, he'd find her again.

And this time, he'd make sure there weren't any more mistakes.

5

WE PULLED INTO LAS VEGAS A LITTLE BEFORE FIVE. The sun still blazed down, bright and unrelenting, and at that time of year, it would be hours before full dark arrived...if it arrived there at all. Even in full daylight, the town's neon signs and marquees blazed away, advertising the million and one ways to keep yourself entertained in that faux oasis in the desert.

The whole place made my brain hurt. No, actually, I realized that all of me hurt, muscles and mind alike aching in the aftermath of what had happened in Kanab just a few short hours earlier. I didn't want to think about it, but it seemed as soon as I shut my eyes, I could see that horrible scene all over again—the raised pistol, the billow of smoke from the barrel...the shocked flare of my mother's blue eyes as the bullet hit her, shattering her ribcage, knocking her backward under the force of the impact.

No, I wasn't sure whether I'd ever be able to forget that sight, no matter how long I lived.

"I thought we'd stop at a drugstore or something, get you some stuff before we check in at a hotel," Jake said as he shot a concerned glance in my direction. I hadn't said much since we'd stopped in St. George for some gas, where he'd bought me a pair of sunglasses and some bottled water at the convenience store. His was an off-hand sort of kindness, as if he wasn't quite sure how to handle me.

Not that I could blame him. I wasn't sure how to handle me, either.

"Sure," I said drearily. It wasn't until we'd made our stop in St. George that I realized I'd run out of the house with absolutely nothing— no purse, no phone, no I.D. I literally had the clothes on my back and nothing else. Considering what had happened, it was probably a good thing that I hadn't already changed into my waitress uniform. The situation was bad enough already, but it would have been even worse if I'd been wearing that damn thing instead of the jeans and T-shirt I currently had on.

Jake pressed a button on the steering column

and said in a distinct voice, enunciating clearly, "Drugstores."

For a second, I wondered what the heck he was doing. But then a crisp female voice came out of the truck's speakers. "CVS, 3300 South Las Vegas Boulevard," it said, even as the display on the nav centered on the address in question.

Talk about the future. Sure, I knew car navigation systems were a thing, but this was the first time I'd actually seen one in use. My mother's beat-up Subaru certainly didn't have that kind of technology.

"I don't have any money," I blurted. "I left my purse behind at the house."

Jake shook his head. "That doesn't matter. I'll take care of it."

"But—"

"It's fine," he said. A pause, and then he went on, "I know you've been through a lot, Adara—"

"Addie."

He blinked.

"Addie," I repeated. "That was what my mother always called me. 'Adara' is for job applications and interviews with my high school counselor."

That comment made him smile, and I realized once again how really good-looking he was. Maybe I shouldn't have been noticing such a thing when I'd just lost my mother to unexpected violence earlier that afternoon, but at the same time, it sort of helped for me to focus on the fine shape of his jaw, the friendly crinkles at the corners of his dark eyes, the bright blaze of his grin. If I was thinking about all those things, then I wasn't thinking about the way my life had changed in the flash of a second as Agent Lenz's gun went off.

"Okay, Addie," Jake said. "Money really isn't going to be an issue. Every member of the Wilcox clan gets a stipend, a sort of monthly allowance to supplement whatever we make from our jobs."

"How much of a stipend?" I asked. Possibly, that was a crass question, but it just sort of slipped out. Right then, I didn't have much of a filter.

However, Jake didn't look offended by my query. "Six grand a month."

Six.... Holy hell. Even pooling our incomes, my mother and I had never earned even half that much. It hadn't mattered most of the time, because she was a genius at locating inexpensive houses to rent and clipping coupons and doing whatever it took to make a dollar stretch around the block, so to speak, but still. And now, just because I'd turned out to be a Wilcox witch, I'd get six thousand dollars every month without doing anything at all?

"That's...a lot of money."

His shoulders lifted. Without responding, he followed the instructions on the nav, moving to the right so we could get off the freeway at a street called Spring Mountain.

"We're getting close," Jake said, eyes narrowing behind his sunglasses as he glanced over at the display on the dashboard. "We'll go to the CVS, buy a few things for you, and then see about finding a hotel room."

Well, that particular task shouldn't be too hard in a place that appeared to be wall-to-wall hotels. But even though the logistics of getting a place to crash for the night probably weren't going to be difficult, part of me still shivered a little at the thought of sharing a hotel room with Jake Wilcox. I'd never been alone with a guy in a hotel before. Hell, I'd barely been alone with a guy, period. A few dates here and there, and that was it.

I tried to reassure myself that Jake wasn't going to put any moves on me. Not when tragedy had just descended on my life, not when we were on the run from a government agent who apparently didn't give a shit who got in the way of his mission. Besides, Jake and I were cousins.

Distant cousins. Very, very distant cousins. When shared blood got that attenuated, I was pretty sure it really didn't count anymore...at least not in terms of making sure you didn't end up like the Hapsburgs or something.

The CVS turned out to be right on the corner by the Treasure Island Hotel. Jake somehow managed to maneuver into the parking garage at the last minute, where we ended up on a lower level.

"We can check for a room here," he said, sounding a little too matter-of-fact. "It would simplify things. Sound okay?"

"Sure," I replied, also knowing that my tone was probably too casual. "It's not like we're here on vacation or something."

At once, his expression sobered. "I know. I'm sorry. And we'll be in Flagstaff tomorrow. But it would have been a long haul to try to get there today, and with everything that happened, I didn't want to be driving at night."

I supposed I could see his reasoning—I didn't think I'd want to be out on the interstate some-where in the dark, not knowing whether Agent Lenz or his minions were hot on my trail. At least in daylight, we'd be able to see him coming...hopefully.

"No, I get it," I said. "So, let's see about that room, and then we can head over to the CVS."

"And maybe the mall," he added. "I noticed there was one across the street."

"Sure," I responded. I'd seen the mall on the map as well, but I hadn't wanted to presume that Jake might want to take me there. Yes, I was supposedly entitled to some Wilcox money, and yet none of that seemed real at the moment.

Even though it was a Friday night, the hotel still had a few rooms with two queen beds available. Jake paid cash, sliding a couple of hundred-dollar bills across the counter to the girl at the reception desk. She didn't bat an eyelash, which told me that it wasn't too unusual for someone to be flashing around that kind of cash in Vegas. But I could see why he was being careful; although I didn't think he'd given his last name when he introduced himself to me, Agent Lenz had been standing there and would have heard everything. No point in advertising our presence in Las Vegas by using credit cards.

After we checked in, we took the elevator to the twentieth floor, where the room was located. I'd never been that high up in my life, and found the view outside the plate-glass windows to be positively vertigo-inducing.

Turning away from the window, I went and

picked up one of the complimentary bottles of water that had been placed on the dresser. My mouth felt dry, and I took a long swallow.

"I need to make a call," Jake said as he set down the duffle bag he'd scrounged out of the back seat of his fancy Jeep pickup. "We'll go out after that."

"Sure," I said. "Do you need some privacy?"

At once, he shook his head. "No, I'm just calling my brother to check in."

He got a heavy, odd-looking device out of the duffle bag and sat down on the bed. I realized as he lifted the thing to his ear that it must be a satellite phone, although I'd never seen one in real life before. A good way to stay off the grid, I supposed; I'd watched enough TV to know that the government could track people through cell phone usage, but I didn't know whether satellite phones could be policed the same way.

"Jeremy," he said as I sat down in the chair near the foot of one of the beds and sipped again from my bottle of water. A pause, and he added, "Yeah, I know. Things got crazy. I—" Jake broke off there, brows drawing together as he listened to his brother's interruption. "No. No, we're fine. We got away clean, as far as I can tell. But you need to check on this Agent Lenz. I don't know where the hell he came from, but he definitely had an interest in Adara's abilities. Um...." He stopped again and looked over at me. "Do you know Lenz's full name?"

"Randall Alan Lenz," I supplied. "I saw his I.D."

Jake gave me an approving smile and relayed that information to his brother, then said, "We'll be in Flagstaff midday tomorrow. Then we can start to figure all this out. Just get back to me with anything you discover—and let me know right away if there's even a hint that they're headed in this direction. Okay. Yes. Got it. Okay."

He ended the call, and I lifted an inquiring eyebrow, thinking that Jake would fill me in.

However, his expression was heavy, and he replaced the phone in the duffle bag without saying anything. "Are you hungry?"

Food had been just about the last thing on my mind. I'd had a salad for lunch, and figured that would hold me until dinner. And it was barely five.

Besides, how was I supposed to eat when I'd just witnessed my mother's murder less than four hours earlier? Right then, I was more numb than anything, as if my brain had deliberately pushed my grief somewhere in the background because it knew I had to keep functioning.

"I'd rather shop first," I said frankly.

"Okay," Jake replied. His expression was one of relief, as if he'd been worried that I wasn't going to agree to shopping until he'd told me what he and his brother had discussed.

However, I could see that he didn't want to talk, and honestly, I was okay with that. I'd been hit with enough blows that day that it would feel good to just focus on purchasing a few necessities. Once we were done with that, well, maybe Jake would feel more like talking...and I'd feel more like eating.

We went back down in the elevator and headed outside. The heat felt like a blast furnace even late in the afternoon, so much hotter than Kanab, which at least had the leavening influence of lots of mature trees. Here, everything was concrete and asphalt and glass, and the glare made me squint behind the cheap sunglasses we'd gotten at the gas station in St. George.

But it wasn't too far to the CVS, where I loaded a shopping basket with a toothbrush and toothpaste, deodorant, travel sizes of shampoo and moisturizer. Thank God I'd had my period a week earlier, so at least I didn't have to ask Jake to pay for tampons, and I avoided buying any makeup except for some tinted lip balm. I also picked up an oversized "I <3 Las Vegas" T-shirt, figuring it would be good to sleep in.

"That should do it," I said after Jake had paid for my purchases and we were headed back outside.

He looked dubious. "You're sure? You didn't get very much."

It had felt like a lot to me. But then, I'd always had to mete out my purchases, spacing them through the month so they wouldn't take up a disproportionate amount of any one paycheck. "No, I'm fine."

"Not even a change of clothes?"

My gaze strayed to the mall located across the street from the spot where we stood outside the drugstore. That mall was unlike anything I'd ever seen before, a conglomeration of disparate buildings with a huge oval sunshade suspended from a tower in the middle, making it look as though a UFO was hovering over the shopping center. I could probably count on one hand the times in my life I'd been inside an actual mall; my mother and I had shopped at Walmart and Family Dollar and the local thrift stores in whichever town we were currently inhabiting.

Sorrow flared again as I remembered how my mother had tried to turn our shopping into a game, how we'd try to hunt for the biggest bargains, the greatest deals. I'd known we were poor, but somehow, it hadn't seemed to matter so much. We always had a roof over our heads and food on the table. Maybe it wasn't the sturdiest roof or the fanciest meal, but we'd always managed to get by.

"Hey," Jake said, and I blinked to see him watching me with concern in those velvety dark brown eyes. "We don't have to go over there if you don't want to."

I drew in a breath, resolving to make the best of the admittedly shitty hand the universe had dealt me that day. There was nothing I could do to bring my mother back, but I knew if she could still somehow see me, was maybe looking down to watch over her daughter, then I needed to make sure I didn't disappoint her.

"No," I told him. "It's okay. Let's go."

And I headed over to the pedestrian walkway that connected the little shopping area where we stood to the much grander mall on the other side of the street, chin high.

I knew I had to consider this the first day of my new life.

Of course, my "new life" didn't include bleeding Jake Wilcox dry by shopping at Neiman Marcus —I wasn't quite that detached from my former existence. No, I went to Macy's, which still felt way above my pay grade, and found two pairs of jeans on sale for fairly reasonable prices and a couple of tops. I was wearing my favorite pair of flats, so I didn't see the need for new shoes. However, while Jake waited off by the escalator, I also added a bra and a few pairs of underpants to the pile, figuring it was probably smart to get a couple of extra things, since I had no idea what would await me when I got to Flagstaff.

He'd given me cash to pay for my purchases, so at least I didn't have to suffer the humiliation of having him stand there at the register and see what I was buying. Once everything was safely hidden in an anonymous shopping bag, I went over to him.

"All done," I said.

"That was fast," he remarked.

"I didn't need much."

One eyebrow lifted, but he apparently decided not to comment on my frugality. "Hungry yet?"

By that point it was nearly six, maybe a little early for dinner...especially in Vegas...but I thought I could eat something. Or at least, the idea of food didn't make me vaguely nauseous the way it had earlier. Something felt wrong about eating, and yet I knew that starving myself wouldn't accomplish anything. My mother would want me to eat, so I would.

"Sure," I said. "You can decide where—I'm not picky."

"Let's go look at the directory," he suggested, so we left Macy's and went in search of one. Luckily, there was a kiosk not far away from the store entrance, and we paused there while Jake perused the offerings. "Let's try the Capital Grille."

I glanced down at the red T-shirt, jeans, and black flats I was wearing, then shot him a dubious look. "That sounds fancy."

"I thought you said you weren't picky."

"I'm not...but I also don't want to go to some four-star restaurant wearing this."

He opened his mouth, as if he wanted to protest, then seemed to stop before the words could leave his lips. Most likely, he was reminding himself that I'd been through a lot that day, and there was no point in squabbling over where we were going to have dinner.

"California Pizza Kitchen?"

That sounded a lot friendlier. "Okay."

Looking relieved, he led me away from the kiosk and toward the restaurant in question. It actually wasn't all that far, and because we'd only barely nudged past six o'clock by that point, we were able to get a booth without even having to wait.

The waitress who came to take our order seemed way too cheerful, although I told myself that of course she couldn't possibly know what I'd suffered through that day. Jake ordered a beer, and I—feeling somewhat reckless—asked for a glass of merlot. I knew next to nothing about wine, but I figured merlot sounded somewhat safe.

After she'd brought our drinks and took our orders for our meals—barbecue chicken pizza for me and a meat-laden Sicilian for Jake—she disappeared again. I reached for my glass of wine and sipped from it, not sure how I felt about the taste but damn glad of the relaxing effect it had as it slipped down my throat.

"Better?" Jake asked, and I nodded.

"A little."

His expression was sympathetic. "I can't even imagine what you've had to deal with today."

Another sip of wine, mostly because I didn't know how I was supposed to respond to that statement. "I'm surviving," I said, my tone flat, letting him figure out that I wanted to leave the topic behind. "What did your brother say?"

Jake set down his beer, his gaze slipping past me. I could tell he didn't want to make eye contact. Still, he startled me by saying, "Your house is gone."

"What?" My fingers had started to tremble, so I put down my glass of wine as well, then clenched my hands in my lap where they couldn't be seen. "What do you mean, it's gone?"

"There was an explosion soon after we left. The fire department's preliminary report was that the gas was left on and a candle burning nearby ignited it...but we both know that's not what really happened."

I swallowed, even though the lump was back in my throat. "Agent Lenz?"

Jake nodded. "I'm sure he did it to cover up your mother's death. In a place like Kanab, nobody's going to dig too hard into something that looks like a tragic accident. But your mother was...recovered...and is in a local funeral home."

Well, that was something. A cold piece of reassurance, yes, but it still helped to know that my mother was now resting someplace where people would treat her with dignity. "And me?"

"They're still trying to figure that out. They don't think the fire was hot enough to completely incinerate a human body, but if you were in the kitchen when the gas ignited...it's possible. That's the theory right now. How else to explain your disappearance?"

How else, indeed? I was sort of surprised that no one had seen me take off with Jake, since our street had several stay-at-home moms, and you'd think that one of them might have spotted something out of the ordinary. Then again, maybe the crazy weather had made them stay inside, and they hadn't emerged until the house blew up and rocked the neighborhood.

If nothing else, the explosion and my disappearance would provide a piece of gossip that should keep people busy for the next few weeks.

My mouth twisted in a lopsided smile. "So... I'm dead?"

"Not officially. But I think it's safe to say that no one's going to come looking for you."

"Except Lenz."

Jake picked up his beer and took a sip. "Except him," he admitted with some reluctance. "However, Jeremy said he hadn't detected any coordinated efforts at pursuit, so it sounds like we're in the clear for now."

"And Lenz?"

"Satellite shows a van pulled up to the house moments before it exploded. He left with two other men."

So, the bastard hadn't died in the explosion. I hadn't really expected to get off that easily, which was why I'd continued to think of him as a threat, but it sure would have been nice to know I didn't have to worry about Randall Lenz any longer.

I leaned against the back of the booth and said, "'Satellite'? Are you Wilcoxes running some sort of spy operation?"

Jake chuckled. "Not really. I set up a small organization dedicated to looking for people like you—people born to a parent with...gifts. My brother runs the tech side of things. Computers are his talent."

Definitely a much handier power than mine. I knew I'd much prefer hacking surveillance satellites to inadvertently destroying property with tornadoes that blew out of nowhere every time I got angry about something.

"So...these talents don't seem to have much rhyme or reason to them," I remarked.

"None that we've been able to find. It's not like you have all healers in one branch of the family or whatever. No one's really been able to figure quite why our gifts manifest the way they do. And even though I said that you're really powerful because your father was, that's not necessarily how it works, either. Sometimes a really strong witch and warlock can have a child whose gifts are pretty weak by comparison." He shrugged and picked up his beer, then added, "It's sort of a crap shoot."

"'Crap' being the operative word," I said, and his mouth twitched slightly.

"I wouldn't go that far. Weather-working is a very desirable gift. It's just that you've never had a chance to train yours."

We had to stop talking then, since the waitress came by with our pizzas and asked if there was anything else we needed. There wasn't, so we thanked her and she went off to leave us alone with our food. It actually smelled wonderful, and my stomach woke up and told me it probably could do with some fuel right about then. For a few minutes more, Jake and I both remained quiet as we ate and washed down bites of food with beer and wine. Eventually, though, he settled against the back of the booth and offered me another of those smiles that made me think I might possibly be able to get through my current nightmare after all.

"We have a weather-worker who can help you," he said. "And we'll take care of anything else you need as well—a place to stay, a new bank account, new I.D. I know it's going to feel strange at first, but we'll do what we can to ease the transition."

"Thanks," I replied, even though I knew the word was completely inadequate to the situation. If I'd suddenly been gifted with the ability to travel in time, then I knew I would have gone right back to the moment when Agent Lenz's gun had fired, would have jostled his arm so the bullet discharged harmlessly into the ceiling. But since it sounded like I was stuck with this one dubious talent, then I couldn't deny that it was a huge relief to know I wasn't going to be left stranded, that there were people who were willing to give me a place to land.

"You're welcome," was all Jake said, but I had a feeling he was able to guess at what I'd been thinking.

After that, we finished our meals, and he asked if I wanted to walk around the mall or go look at the sights. On any other day, I would have said yes immediately. Las Vegas had always been on my bucket list—not because I had any desire to gamble, but simply because I'd always wanted to see its glittering lights, to take in all the various theme hotels and attractions and shows.

That night, though, my heart was far too heavy for those sorts of diversions. I told Jake I was tired, and he only nodded and said it was probably better for us to hang out in the hotel room and then go to sleep early, since that way we could get on the road before much of the morning had passed.

It was sort of strange to plunk down on our

respective beds and watch the latest Marvel movie on the in-room HBO...but at the same time, I was glad of the chance to sit there and make myself focus on the film and not what had happened earlier that day. When the movie was over, we both got ready for bed—to my relief, Jake wore a T-shirt and a pair of sweats, and so was pretty much covered up—and slipped under the covers after a hasty, awkward shared "good night."

I lay there for a long while, staring at the ceiling. While the room was supposedly sound-proofed, I could have sworn I was still able to hear the traffic on the street so many stories below. Or maybe it was my imagination manufacturing those sounds, since otherwise the room felt far too quiet. I thought Jake was asleep; his breathing seemed regular enough, even if he wasn't snoring.

Stupidly, I was jealous of him, jealous of his ability to pass peacefully into slumber. Then again, his life hadn't been torn apart. He hadn't mentioned anything about his parents, but I got the impression that they must be still around, that—despite all of them being witches and warlocks—his family was a pretty normal one.

My mother's face flashed into my mind's eye —the laughing, pretty features of the woman who'd always been my entire world. She didn't deserve what had happened to her. If she'd only come out into the living room a minute later....

I didn't even realize I was crying until the first tear slipped down my cheek and dripped, ticklish and warm, into my ear. At once, I raised a hand to wipe it away, and for some reason, the mere act of doing so made a sob burst from my throat, even though I was doing my best to keep quiet.

Obviously, I hadn't done a very good job of it, because Jake seemed to sit up immediately, the bedsprings creaking faintly as he moved. His voice came to me in the darkness. "Addie? Are you all right?"

"Uh-huh," I responded, but the "huh" came out as a sort of hiccup as the next sob seemed to tear its way out of me.

Sheets rustled, and then my bed squeaked as he sat down on it. No words, only strong arms going around me. Just that simple human presence was enough to open the floodgates, and I burrowed my face in his shoulder and wept stormily, no longer trying to hold back, somehow knowing that the best thing to do was cry myself out.

Poor Jake. He sat there in silence, holding on to me as I sobbed, until at last the storm seemed to pass, and the tears gradually dried themselves.

I lifted my head. By then, my eyes had adjusted a little to the darkness, although the room was still very dim, and his face was only a pale blur. "I'm sorry," I said.

"Don't be." He'd stroked my hair a few times while he held me, but now he shifted slightly on the bed, as if realizing it was probably a good idea to put a little distance between us. "Don't ever apologize for feeling something. It's when you try to close it all off that it hurts the worst."

For a second, I only sat there, pondering his words, thinking about the quiet tone of his resonant voice as he spoke in the darkness. The way he'd talked made me think that maybe he was no stranger to this kind of suffering.

At last, I said, "You lost someone?"

He didn't answer right away. I heard a soft sound that might have been a sigh, and then he said, "Her name was Sarah. We were engaged."

"I'm so sorry." An automatic reply, but I was sorry for him. No one should have to endure that kind of pain.

"Thank you." Another pause, and he went on, "It's been almost three years. Most of the time, I'm okay. Then something comes along that reminds me of her, and it's as if I've just heard the news for the first time."

"What happened?" Maybe I shouldn't have

asked the question, but I had to wonder what would have taken a woman who could only have been in her early or middle twenties at the most. If witch clans had healers, then I doubted his fiancée could have been suffering from some kind of terminal illness.

"An accident. She went camping with some cousins. They were kayaking on the Colorado River. A monsoon storm came through, and the river flooded. They lost control of the kayak. The other two in the kayak survived, but Sarah... didn't."

Oh, God. I'd seen streams and rivers during monsoon storms, had seen how fast they could rise. It was probably a miracle that only one person had perished, but I wasn't about to say such a thing to Jake.

Instead, I murmured, "I'm sorry" again, but I wasn't sure he heard me. In a low voice, he continued.

"I sometimes wonder if I might have been able to help her if I'd been there. Maybe I could have used my gift to push the kayak to shore, or moved the boulder that shattered it out of the way...." The words trailed off, and this time I was the one to reach out and offer comfort, to lay a hand on his arm. I didn't say anything, only hoped the presence of another person might reassure him. I didn't know how successful I was, but I heard him pull in a breath. His hand covered mine for a second or two, warm and heavy. Then he withdrew it, and said, "Anyway, you're probably trying to second-guess yourself as well. Don't. There isn't anything you could have done."

"I know," I said in a very small voice. That was the horrible truth. Maybe I couldn't have answered the door, but the truth was, Agent Lenz probably would have just broken in if I'd ignored his knock. We'd been set on a collision course, and now the only thing I could do was try to pick up the pieces as best I could.

Jake patted me on the shoulder, then pushed himself up from the bed. "Try to sleep. We need to head out early tomorrow."

"Okay." I lay back down, and a moment later, I heard him settle himself on his bed, a rustle of sheets as he pulled the covers back up.

Silence fell. I didn't know whether he dropped off to sleep again right away...or whether he lay there as I did, both of us straining against the darkness as we tried to come to terms with our pain.

6

T<small>HEY</small> <small>SKIPPED</small> <small>THE</small> <small>BREAKFAST</small> <small>BUFFET</small> <small>AND</small> <small>GOT</small> bagels and coffee to go from the coffee shop in the hotel, and were on the open road by nine o'clock. Jake was relieved to see that Addie seemed subdued but calm enough that morning as they packed up their few belongings. She made no mention of the confidences they'd shared the night before, and he decided it was better not to bring up the subject. If she wanted to talk, he would be there for her, but he also understood how hard it could be when someone kept trying to force a dialogue when you didn't want one. Her grief was still fresh and raw, and yet it seemed to him as though she was doing her best to come to terms with the loss of her mother and the way her world had abruptly shifted on its axis.

Saturday morning, and traffic was thick. Luckily, though, most of it was headed into Las Vegas rather than leaving it, and so once they were outside the city proper, he was able to get up to speed quickly enough. At that rate—and barring any accidents on the highway—they'd probably make it to Flagstaff around one o'clock.

While Addie was in the shower, Jake had called Jeremy to make sure there still was no sign of any pursuit, and also to ask if Laurel could go ahead and get housing set up for their newfound relative. Jeremy assured him that all was still quiet—"it's kind of hard to make out any details about a vehicle when the satellite signal is being scrambled at the source"—and that their cousin was already over at the little cottage down the street from Jake's house, which had been purchased specially for this very purpose.

"How is she?" Jeremy had asked, surprising Jake somewhat. Half the time, Jeremy was so buried in computer code that he barely seemed to realize the people around him were breathing, let alone having emotional reactions to the events in their lives.

"She's okay," Jake replied. "Shaken up, but I

think she's going to be all right. We just have to make sure she stays safe."

"Not a problem. I took a copy of his image and posted it on the family bulletin board, so everyone will be keeping an eye out and will let me know if they see anything."

"Thanks," Jake said, relieved that his brother had been so proactive. He didn't bother to ask where Jeremy had gotten a photo of the agent in question; his brother was very good at digging up useful information. And one good thing about being part of a witch clan that depended on family cooperation to keep everyone's identities secret was that you never had to worry about someone saying the wrong thing to the wrong person, or questioning why it was so important to stay on the lookout for suspicious people. The Wilcoxes would do their best to prevent Agent Lenz from slipping into their territory undetected. Jake knew that some *primas* had the ability to detect when an interloper entered their domain, but Connor didn't seem to have that gift, which was why they needed everyone to step up and keep an eye out.

"So, see you in a few hours, I guess," Jeremy told him, signaling that he wanted to end the call and get back to monitoring his computers.

"Right. I'm going to take Addie straight to the cottage, so I'll call once we're there."

"Sounds good."

They'd hung up then, and not long after, Addie had emerged from the bathroom, combing her damp hair, face bare. Not that she really needed makeup; her fair skin was pretty much flawless, and her full mouth seemed to be naturally rosy.

At the time, Jake had told himself he probably shouldn't be paying attention to those sorts of details. Now, though, as they drove south on the highway and the sun streamed through the car windows, casting a golden glow on her face and awakening warm highlights in her long, dark hair, he realized that was going to be harder than he'd thought.

She wasn't just pretty; she was beautiful.

To distract himself, he told her about their destination in Flagstaff. "There's a cottage a few doors down from my house that we bought for any 'guests' we might find. That's where you'll be staying. Eventually, of course, you'll probably want to get your own place, but there's no rush on any of that. You can take as much time as you need to get settled."

Addie looked almost surprised. "I never really thought about having a house. I just...." The words trailed away, and she gave a rueful shrug. "I guess because my mom and I were always renting, I never believed I'd ever be able to have a place that I owned. So, you own your house?"

"Yes," he replied. "Most of us do. Of course," he added, wanting to reassure her that he knew the situation looked a little unusual to someone unfamiliar with the way the clan did business, "it helps to have other Wilcoxes approving the loans and doing the paperwork."

"Mortgage broker witches?" Addie said, her expression now almost amused.

It was the first time he'd seen a real light in her luminous gray-green eyes, and Jake wanted to do whatever he could to make sure it wasn't extinguished, that she'd always have a reason to light up like that. "Yes, and lawyers and teachers and electricians and small business owners... we're sort of all over the place. Anyway, with Wilcox cousins handling the loans, it's a lot easier to skate by with our 'nontraditional' income."

"Convenient," she remarked. "I guess there must be all sorts of perks to being in a witch clan."

"Quite a few. But you can learn more about that as you get settled in."

She nodded, but something in her face

seemed to shift, as though it had really started to get through to her that this wasn't some game of "let's pretend," that she actually was going to have to restart her life in a brand-new place surrounded by people who were strangers to her. Yes, technically, they were related to her, but since she'd never met any of them—hadn't even known they existed until he'd told her about them the day before—their shared blood probably didn't count as much as he wanted it to.

Jake resolved that he'd do his best to make the transition as easy as possible for her. Hopefully, she'd think it a good thing that his house was only two doors down from the cottage. He wanted her to feel as if she could reach out to him with any questions or problems, and being on the same street made it easier for them to get together...but not as creepy as it might have felt if she'd been staying in a guest house on the property or even next door.

"One step at a time," he assured her. "But I know Connor will want to meet you as soon as you feel up to it."

"My half-brother," she said, her tone now one of bemusement, as though she was still having a hard time wrapping her head around the concept of having a sibling after an entire life spent believing she was an only child.

"Right." Jake purposely hadn't reached out to Connor with the news, figuring he might as well wait until he and Addie were safely in Flagstaff. How the *primus* was going to take the revelation that he had a sister, Jake honestly couldn't begin to guess. In general, Connor was pretty easygoing —especially in contrast to his late brother, the strong-willed former *primus*. But it wasn't as though long-lost sisters came out of the wood-work every day...especially when the sister in question technically shouldn't even exist, at least according to the dictates of the curse that had ruled their family's life for generations. "But again, we'll get all that figured out after we're home."

The word slipped out before he could stop himself, and Jake winced inwardly, wondering if Addie was going to take the comment the wrong way. Of course, he didn't believe that she would start thinking of Flagstaff as "home" right away, but he did hope she'd allow herself to ease into it. Surely, being around her relatives when she'd always thought of herself as being pretty much alone in the world had to count for something.

Or maybe not. He barely knew her, and he honestly had no idea if she'd ever even thought of herself as being alone, or whether having a small family that included only her mother and herself had always been plenty for her.

But Addie only tilted her head to gaze out through the truck's windows, and gave a very faint nod. "Sure."

Partway through the trip, she actually dozed off for a bit, her chin drooping to almost touch her chest, and Jake experienced an unexpected and not completely welcome surge of tenderness as he glanced over at her, at the way her dark hair fell around her face, almost but not quite obscuring her delicate features. He'd fallen asleep again quickly enough the night before, but maybe Addie hadn't been so lucky. If she'd remained wakeful, no wonder she was tired.

However, she woke up as he guided the truck off the southbound 93 and onto I-40 east, passing through Kingman. She blinked, and he smiled at her.

"Welcome to Arizona."

A quick glance out the window, and then she looked back over at him. "It just looks like more desert."

"Well, true." Kingman had never been his favorite place, used as he was to the ponderosa forests that surrounded his hometown. "But we'll be in the trees in about an hour or so."

"'Trees'?" she repeated, clearly not sure what he'd meant by that statement.

"Flagstaff is surrounded by the biggest continuous ponderosa pine forest in the world," he told her, thinking he probably sounded a little too much like a tour guide. "It's really beautiful. And you're coming at a great time of year—summer in the high country is a little piece of heaven."

Her mouth lifted slightly, as though she was trying to picture it in her mind. "Sounds like Durango."

"It probably is...a little," Jake said. "I've never been to Colorado, so I wouldn't know. In general, we witches and warlocks don't travel much."

"Oh?" Addie said then, sounding genuinely curious. "Why not?"

"Because it's sort of a tradition that each clan stays in its own territory and doesn't go into another clan's territory without permission."

"Did you get permission to come to Kanab?"

He shook his head. "No. There aren't any witch clans in Utah—didn't want to compete with the Mormons, I suppose."

That remark made her smile outright. "No, it's probably not the best place in the world if you're trying to maintain a secret identity. What about Vegas, though?"

"There's a clan in Nevada—the Delmonicos —but most of them live in the northwest part of the state, up around Reno and Lake Tahoe, places like that. Because Las Vegas gets so many tourists, I guess they've decided it's not worth policing. That's why I didn't worry about getting permission to go there."

Addie seemed to absorb that piece of information, then shrugged a little as she settled against the back of her seat. "So...the Wilcoxes are in northern Arizona. What about the rest of the state?"

"The McAllisters are sort of in the middle, though they tend to mainly live in the Verde Valley—Jerome and Cottonwood and Clarkdale. But they also have branches of the family in Payson and Prescott and Wickenburg. And then down south, from Phoenix all the way to the Mexican border, are the de la Pazes." Jake paused there before deciding to add, "Connor's wife Angela is a McAllister."

"So, you're all friendly with each other?"

That innocent question made him smile, although he knew Addie wouldn't have seen the irony in it. "We are...now. It's kind of complicated. A lot of things have happened in the past seven years or so."

"Like?"

The last thing he wanted to do was explain how, up until the time Damon Wilcox passed away and Connor took over leadership of the clan, the other Arizona clans had viewed the Wilcoxes with distrust, if not outright enmity. They had a bad reputation going all the way back to the time when Jeremiah Wilcox settled in Flagstaff with his three brothers, his sister, and their assorted spouses, and before Connor, none of the Wilcox *primuses* had done much to disabuse anyone of the notion that the rules didn't apply to them. No, if anything, they'd encouraged it. Jake hadn't even realized how much the McAllisters had thought of the Wilcoxes as the "big bad" until he'd hung out with some of them in recent years. It was sort of like thinking you were one of the good guys in *Star Wars,* and then discovering you'd actually been part of the Empire all along.

"Plenty of time to talk about that later," he said. From the way Addie's brows drew together slightly, he could tell she didn't think much of his evasive response, although she didn't push back, and instead gave a little shrug.

He really didn't want to get into all that ancient history right then. Maybe later, after she'd had time to meet some of her family, to see that they really were a bunch of nice, normal people—well, mostly—then he'd go into some of the Wilcox history. At some point, someone would have to. Jeremiah Wilcox was Addie's great-to-the-seventh-power grandfather, and it wouldn't be fair to keep the truth from her.

For the moment, though, they had far more pressing matters to worry about. Jeremy had said that Agent Lenz didn't appear to be an issue...for now...but Jake didn't see how that state of affairs could continue for much longer.

He knew very little about the man in question, but he could already tell one thing.

Randall Lenz didn't seem like the type of guy who would give up easily.

His head still ached, and he wondered if he should see a doctor after all. Not the team's medic; the men had already returned to their various regular postings once it was determined that their quarry had somehow managed to give them all the slip, leaving him alone as he decided what to do next. However, Kanab probably had a walk-in urgent care clinic where he could have a doctor or nurse practitioner check to make sure he didn't have a concussion.

Lenz scowled and pushed the thought aside.

He didn't want to admit to such weakness. Probably, what he really needed was a cup of coffee.

For all he knew, his headache could be directly blamed on what a clusterfuck this whole endeavor had turned out to be. Agent Dawson had gotten back to him and told him—sounding hesitant and worried, as if she feared he was going to blame her for the fiasco even though she couldn't have had anything to do with it—that the feed from the satellite had been corrupted somehow and was nothing more than a mass of static for the hour preceding his arrival at Adara Grant's house and approximately twenty minutes afterward. The traffic camera footage likewise had been corrupted.

Coincidence?

Randall Lenz didn't believe in coincidence.

On the other hand, he had a hard time believing that someone like Adara Grant—a young woman with no family, no connections, not even a college education—could have pulled off that kind of sophisticated hack, or even knew the sort of people who might be able to accomplish such a feat. A far more likely culprit was some sort of associate of the mysterious "Jake" who'd shown up on her doorstep. However, even though Lenz had given the man's name and the details of his appearance to Dawson in the hope she'd be able to locate someone matching his description, he knew that was a long shot at best. If the person in question didn't have a criminal record, it would be difficult to track him down.

Which meant that Adara was with a stranger of unknown origin and motivations, someone who wanted her for...what? The same thing he did?

Randall Lenz didn't like that idea very much. However, he wasn't naïve enough to think there weren't governments out there who wouldn't be very, very interested in capturing someone with Adara Grant's abilities. This Jake person didn't look or sound Russian, but he supposed he could have been. Or an independent operative working for the Saudis...or the Iranians or the North Koreans, although he had to admit those two latter possibilities were long shots. Russia seemed to be the far more likely culprit.

Well, if the man who had appeared out of nowhere on Adara Grant's doorstep had ever been identified as a Russian asset, then Agent Dawson would make the connection soon enough. And if she did, that would solve that particular puzzle.

But not, unfortunately, the larger problem of where "Jake" had taken Adara. Inquiries would be made, asking if people along any of the probable routes they might have traveled had seen a couple matching the description of the two fugitives, of course, and yet, those sorts of investigations tended to be unwieldy and time-consuming. There was no guarantee that he would find any leads...and if he did, the trail might very well be ice cold by the time he was finally able to get an actionable piece of information.

The motel room he was renting didn't have a coffeemaker, so he showered and got dressed, then headed out in search of some caffeine and breakfast. Just down the street was a retro-looking diner, so he went in there and sat down at the counter.

A plump woman with unnaturally brassy blonde hair asked if he wanted any coffee. He said yes, noting as he did so that her eyes looked red and tired, as if she'd cried recently. And when she returned with the pot and poured him a cup, he noticed the black ribbon pinned to her name badge, which let him know her name was Tammy.

Apparently, Tammy saw him looking at the ribbon, because she let out a sad little sigh and said, "Yesterday, we lost one of our waitresses and her daughter—who worked here, too. So, we're all a little down right now."

"Oh, I'm so sorry," Lenz replied, hoping he sounded appropriately somber. It didn't take much deduction to guess who his waitress's co-workers had been. What was interesting was that she'd said they'd "lost" Adara as well, although Agent Dawson hadn't reported to him that local law enforcement considered her another casualty of the explosion at the house. "That had to be quite a blow."

"It was." Tammy reached into the pocket of the apron she wore and pulled out a Kleenex, then dabbed her eyes with it. "We're all still sort of shell-shocked. They weren't locals—they'd lived here for about a year and a half or so—but everyone who works here is treated as family. And to go like that...."

"A car accident?" he asked, figuring that would be a natural assumption.

Another dab of the Kleenex at the corner of her eye, and then the waitress returned the tissue to her pocket. "No. A gas explosion at their house. Burned the place right to the ground with both of them in it. And if it had happened only five minutes later, they would have already left for work and been completely safe. Such a tragedy."

"That it is," Lenz agreed, feeling inwardly relieved by these revelations. If Adara was presumed dead as well, that made the whole thing much easier. If—*when,* he corrected himself—he caught back up with her, there would be no need of a cover story to explain her disappearance from the world. She was already no one, a ghost.

Perfect.

"We're taking a collection to pay for the funeral," Tammy went on, nodding toward a jar that sat on the counter. It had the words "Grant Memorial Fund" on it in a cursive font, the words surrounded by hearts. Clearly, someone had put the graphic together on their home computer and printed it out on a color inkjet printer. "Poor things didn't have much to their name, but the town wants to do right by them."

"That's very kind of you," he said. He reached into his pocket and brought out his wallet, then dropped two twenty-dollar bills into the jar, where they lay on top of the collection of fives and ones that already rested there. Part of him wanted to contribute even more, but he pushed back on that impulse, knowing that doing so would attract too much attention.

Although he knew guilt was an unwieldy emotion at best, he was still troubled by what had happened to Lyssa Grant. He'd never intended to shoot her, only intimidate her and her daughter into cooperating with him.

The waitress's eyes widened a bit. "No, that's very kind of *you*, sir. Thank you so much." She looked as though she wanted to tear up again, but managed to gather herself and add, "And what would you like for breakfast?"

He asked for a Denver omelet and a side of hash browns, and sipped his coffee as the waitress walked away to take the orders from an older couple who'd just sat down in a booth across from the counter. The coffee seemed to be easing his headache, or maybe it was simply that the news he'd just received had somewhat improved his outlook on life.

After all, no one was going to go out of their way to rescue a dead woman....

7

JAKE PULLED INTO THE DRIVEWAY OF A SMALL house on a quiet, tree-lined street of historic homes. Just looking at the place made me feel a bit better—it was painted off-white with dark red shutters, and had a small front porch and cheerful flowerbeds filled with pansies and snap-dragons and Icelandic poppies in shades of red and orange and yellow.

Parked out in front was a new-looking slate-blue Jeep Renegade. Did everyone in the Wilcox clan drive shiny new cars?

My companion tilted his head toward the Jeep and said, "Looks like Laurel is still here. Come on—I'll introduce you."

Nervous butterflies fluttered in my stomach. It was one thing to be around Jake—after spending more than twenty-four hours in his company, I viewed him as almost familiar—but I didn't know whether I was mentally ready to meet other members of this family I hadn't even known I had.

I nodded and tried to tell myself that it could be worse. At least I was only meeting one person this time, rather than a large group of Wilcoxes. And Jake had said that Laurel worked with him on his witch-finding project, which meant she must have mentally prepared herself for the eventuality of long-lost relatives popping up out of the blue.

We got out of his truck, pausing only to collect my bags of purchases from where they sat on the back seat. The air outside was warm but definitely not hot, smelling of fresh-mown grass and a clean, spicy scent that might have come from the ponderosa pines that covered the mountainsides all around the town. A small breeze tugged at my loose hair, friendly, as if inviting me to come closer and explore.

Following Jake, I went up the porch steps. He paused at the front door and gave a single knock, then called out, "Hey, Laurel—it's Jake and Addie. We're coming in."

Without waiting for a reply, he opened the door and stood aside so I could enter. The house didn't look much bigger than the one my mother and I had rented in Kanab, but it was about a hundred times nicer. All the windows were open, letting in more of that delicious air, and filmy curtains billowed in the breeze. The walls were painted a cheerful butter yellow, and the floor and the window frames and the beams in the ceiling overhead were all the same rich dark oak, mellowed with time. Everything had been decorated in a sort of shabby chic cottage style, from the overstuffed couch and matching chair in a friendly teal and yellow print to the picture frames in various shades of rubbed seafoam green and yellow and white.

From down the hallway I heard footsteps, and a moment later, a girl around my own age appeared in the doorway. Like Jake...and myself...she had dark hair—I was starting to get the impression that most Wilcoxes were dark—but her eyes were an interesting warm hazel, almost amber as the light shining through the open windows caught in them and reflected the golden flecks within. And she was very pretty in a sort of fresh, unfussy way, like someone who would have been hired to model in skin care commercials. Looking at her, I felt the same little tingle I'd experienced when I first met Jake. Nerves, or something else?

"Addie, this is Laurel," Jake said, and I raised a hand and gave a small wave, not sure whether this was the kind of situation that warranted a hug.

Laurel, however, didn't seem to harbor those sorts of reservations, because she came forward and wrapped her arms around me, giving me a quick but enthusiastic embrace. "Hi, Addie," she said. "It's so exciting to meet a cousin I didn't even know I had."

"Same here," I replied, even as I inwardly reflected that I wished the circumstances of our meeting had been a little different.

Something in my expression must have tipped her off that I didn't exactly share her enthusiasm, because her smile faded a little and she said, "And I'm so sorry to hear about your mother. That's not—I mean, we didn't plan—"

"It's okay, Laurel," Jake cut in. "We all know this wasn't anything we wanted to have happen. Does Jeremy have any updated information on the situation?"

"Not really," she said, looking subdued. I felt a little sorry for her; the last thing I'd wanted was to make her feel awkward. "But in a way, I suppose that's good news. There's no sign that you've been followed, or that anyone was able to tell which direction you went when you left Kanab."

Thank God. Even though I'd dozed off a little on the drive to Flagstaff, I'd still been on edge, unsure whether I'd look over my shoulder at some point and see a cavalcade of black unmarked SUVs converging on Jake's truck. If that was even what Agent Lenz would use to pursue us—I didn't know what actual government agents did in situations like that, and was only going on what I'd seen on television or in the movies. Come to think of it, I hadn't even seen a strange vehicle parked on my street in Kanab, so I didn't know how Randall Lenz had gotten to the house. Maybe he'd popped up straight from Hell.

"Good," Jake said. He looked over at me. "Want a little tour?"

"Sure."

Laurel glanced at her cousin, as if trying to get a read on his current state of mind, but he looked pretty impassive to me. Then again, it wasn't as if I knew him well. Someone who'd been around him his whole life might have been able to pick up a few tells that I'd overlooked. "I'll get going, then. Jeremy wanted me to go by Best Buy and pick him up another spool of fiber-optic cable."

"For what?" Jake asked. "I thought he had everything pretty well hooked up."

She shrugged. "I've learned not to ask. But he's always fiddling with something. Will you be coming in tomorrow?"

A pause, and then he said, "I'm not sure yet. It depends on when Addie and I are going to be meeting with Connor. I'll let you know."

For a second, she looked slightly confused, as though she wasn't sure why it was necessary for me to meet the clan's *primus* so soon after my arrival. But then her shoulders lifted again, and she said, "Okay. Have a good one, you two."

She went over to pick up a black fringed purse that sat on the small round dining room table, then headed out. After she was gone, I looked over at Jake.

"You didn't tell her about my father?"

"No," he said. "Or Jeremy. I thought it was better that Connor learned about your father first. Right now, my brother and Laurel just think you're a Wilcox cousin of some sort, and nothing more than that."

I supposed he had a point. If it turned out that I had a half-sibling I didn't know about, I probably wouldn't have been thrilled to have that person's identity bandied around the family before I had a chance to learn such a piece of important information for myself. "Makes sense," I replied. "Are you going to call him today?"

"Yes," Jake said without hesitating. And though I wasn't sure how much I looked forward to that meeting—after all, finding out your father had unprotected sex with a college girl half his age had to be awkward at best—I did appreciate the way Jake had answered my question so quickly. That meant he wasn't trying to hide anything from me, wasn't playing any games. Probably, the only reason he hadn't called Connor already was that we'd been on the road the entire time and he didn't want to have that conversation while he was driving. "But let's get you settled first."

"Sounds like a plan."

After that, he showed me around the cottage. Not that there was all that much to see—it had two bedrooms and a bathroom, and a small but extremely modern kitchen with quartz counters and a subway-tile backsplash. Everything looked new and basically untouched, as if no one had actually lived there yet.

Which turned out to be the case. Oh, the house had had its share of inhabitants over the years, since Jake explained that it had been built in 1910, but he'd bought it some six months earlier and had spent the time ever since renovating the place. So, in a way, I would be the first person to live there in its new incarnation.

"This is just temporary, though," he added hastily, as if not quite sure what to do about my silence as I followed him around the house. "Like I said, you'll want to get your own place once we get all the money sorted out."

I slanted a look up at him. "I thought you said I'd get some sort of stipend."

"Oh, you will," he reassured me. "I'm not talking about that. I'm talking about the money from your father's estate. He was a very wealthy man. Damon and Connor inherited everything—"

"Damon?" I cut in. I didn't think I'd heard Jake mention that name before, although maybe he had and I'd just missed it.

For a second, he appeared very uncomfortable, gaze sliding away from mine. But then he looked back at me and said quietly, "Damon was Connor's—and your—older brother. He died about seven years ago."

More questions immediately rose in my mind. Had Damon met with some sort of accident, the way Jake's fiancée Sarah had?

Something in his face was telling me not to ask. I didn't know what had happened, but I could tell I needed to let it go for the moment. "Oh," I said.

An awkward pause, and then Jake pulled in a breath and went on, "Connor's been managing all of the money ever since then. But you're entitled to some of it."

"I don't know," I said, my tone dubious. Right then, I didn't know whether trying to lay claim to an inheritance I hadn't even known existed was the best course of action. I didn't want to step on any toes. "It's really not that big a deal. I'm sure I can manage just fine with the stipend."

Jake leaned against the countertop and shook his head. "You're Jackson Wilcox's daughter. That's kind of a big deal. And you'll get your part of the inheritance. Connor's a really honest guy —he's not going to try to cheat you out of anything. Really."

His eyes met mine, earnest, as if he needed me to acknowledge that I had nothing to worry about from this unknown half-brother of mine. And maybe I didn't...but I also wished I could convince Jake that the stipend alone was far more money than I'd ever had in my entire life. It was becoming more and more obvious to me that the Wilcox clan operated in a sphere so different from my own, they might as well have been on another planet. Not just the whole witch thing, although that was hard enough for me to wrap my head around. No, it was clear that they had a lot of money, and were used to throwing that money around. Most likely, my thrift-store and coupon-clipping existence would be utterly alien to them.

Even the house we stood in—I didn't know much about real estate, but I had to guess that even a small place like that had to have cost a couple hundred thousand, considering the neighborhood where it was located. Add in the cost of all those renovations, which couldn't have been cheap, and it seemed to me that Jake must have sunk at least a quarter million in making sure it was ready for its first guest. But as far as I could tell, he didn't see anything terribly strange about spending that kind of money for a place that might not even end up being used.

"Okay," I said quietly. "I believe you. I just wanted you to know that I hadn't even thought about any kind of inheritance. I mostly...." The words trailed away, and I crossed my arms, even though it was certainly warm enough in the house. "I mostly just want to meet my brother."

Because once I knew Connor was real—and if I was able to see any kind of resemblance between the two of us—then maybe I'd start to feel more connected to this place, wouldn't feel so adrift. I'd continue to mourn my mother, of course, but at the same time, I might begin to feel there was something I could hold on to.

"Of course," Jake said. His tone was gentler, as if he understood why I was so focused on Connor. "And I'm going to call him soon. Are you okay to be by yourself here?"

Good question. The events of the day before would be seared into my brain until the day I died, but at the same time, I'd had Jake with me through all of it. Would I be able to manage once he left me alone, or was his presence the only thing preventing me from completely falling apart?

"Sure," I replied, with a confidence I certainly didn't feel. "You're just two doors down, right?"

"Exactly. Here—I'll show you."

He led me back out to the front porch, then pointed up the street, in a direction I thought was north. "See that big green Victorian house? That's mine."

It was hard to miss. The cottage where we stood was probably the smallest house on the block, while Jake's was definitely the biggest. It stood an imposing two and a half stories tall, and had a turret on the front and a massive stone front porch.

"All that house for just you?" I blurted, and the faint smile he'd been wearing disappeared.

"We bought it when we—well, when Sarah and I got engaged."

With the intention of starting a family there, I supposed. Ouch. There was no way I could take back the words, and so I glanced away from him and murmured, "I'm sorry."

"It's okay," he said, although a certain tension to his jaw told me that no, it really wasn't. "I suppose it does seem like kind of a big place for one person to be rattling around in. I've thought about selling it, but I just never got around to starting the process. Anyway," he went on, making an obvious attempt to lighten his tone, "if you start to feel weird being here by yourself, just come on over. I'm only going to be making a few phone calls and making up to Taffy."

"'Taffy'?" I repeated, wondering if I'd heard him correctly.

"My dog," he explained. "She's probably got her nose out of joint about being abandoned for the past day, even though Jeremy went by and fed her and took her on her walks."

For some reason, learning that Jake had a dog made me like him that much more. I'd always wanted one, but because my mother and I had moved around so much and so many rentals wouldn't allow pets, that was a dream forever unfulfilled.

"Well, go take care of your dog," I told him, realizing I was smiling as I spoke. "I'm just going to get settled here. If I need to, I'll come by."

"Sounds good." He hesitated for a moment, as though unsure whether he should give me a hug, as Laurel had, or whether he should just leave. But then he seemed to decide on an awkward pat on the shoulder, because that was what he did, just before he headed down the porch steps and began walking toward the big Victorian he'd pointed out to me.

I stood on the porch for a minute after he disappeared into his house. Maybe that was simply because it felt good to stand there and feel the breeze play with my hair, or maybe it was because once I went back into the cottage and started to put my things away, I'd be agreeing to take this next step in my life.

Then again, what else could I do?

Frowning slightly, I went inside. Even though I was now alone, I didn't feel strange about being in the cottage by myself. There was something so warm and friendly about the place—had Jake chosen all this furniture, or did Laurel help him? —that I knew it was going to be okay. Not good, because it was going to take me a while to get to that place, but okay was a start. Okay was better than where I'd been the day before.

Hanging up my two shirts and putting away my few toiletries in the bathroom took all of two minutes. I went back out to the living room and sat down on the couch, glad to feel how comfy and soft it was, as though someone had gone to the trouble of breaking it in. Or maybe that was just how it had been constructed. I wouldn't know, since my mother and I had never owned a brand-new piece of furniture.

It was very quiet. I could tell this was the sort of street that didn't get much traffic, except for the people who actually lived there. A bird sang in one of the trees outside, and I felt something tight and hard and painful within me begin to let go, as if someone had loosened an invisible knot.

Oh, it still hurt. I didn't know how easily I'd ever be able to let go of that hurt, or whether I'd even want to. Not completely, anyway. I would never forget what Agent Lenz had done to my mother, how a single moment of recklessness had torn her from this world. At the same time, though, I also had to recognize that she wasn't coming back, and that I needed to focus on making sure I made the most of this new chance at life I'd been given.

I felt safe there. Maybe I was being too confi-dent in the abilities of the Wilcoxes to shield me from Agent Lenz and the organization he worked for, but was even a government agency any match for hundreds of witches and warlocks?

That probably depended on what their individual talents happened to be. All the same, the mere fact that this new family of mine had lived in this place for more than a hundred years, growing and prospering and yet still managing to keep their true natures hidden, spoke to their resourcefulness. Jake's actions alone had already showed me a little of what they were capable of.

Jake. That little pat on my shoulder had been meant to be encouraging and nothing more, but it still seemed as though I could feel the weight of his hand against my flesh. At the same time, I recalled the way he'd held me the night before, had let me cry into his shoulder when the burden of my sorrow became too much to bear. While it was happening, I hadn't thought much about the embrace except that I was glad of the human contact, but now I remembered so much more—how warm his arms had been, how the steady beating of his heart had reassured me I wasn't as alone as I thought. He'd smelled good, too, of something that reminded me of pine needles but might have just been his aftershave.

A strange warmth went through me then, a

sensation so novel, I had to pause for a moment and try to identify what it was.

Need...desire.

Okay, and that was just crazy. I barely knew the guy. Plus, he was my cousin.

Distant cousin, I reminded myself, even though I tried to push the thought away. I shouldn't be thinking about him like that. He was watching out for me because I had no one else, but I knew I shouldn't mistake his casual thoughtfulness for anything more than what it actually was.

And even though I wanted to go to him, I made myself stay there on the couch. I pulled in a breath and watched a small puff of a cloud move across the sky beyond the window, and I didn't move again until the impulse had passed.

Even so, I knew I'd turned a strange corner in that moment of need...and had absolutely no idea what to do about it.

8

THE ENTRY IN HIS CONTACTS LIST FOR CONNOR'S cell phone stared up at him, even as Jake stood in the kitchen and gazed down at his phone. He knew he needed to make the call, but for some reason, he hadn't yet been able to make himself touch the screen and initiate the contact.

Taffy nudged him with her nose, and he leaned down to scratch her behind the ears, grateful for the excuse to delay phoning Connor. The dog's wiry reddish-brown body wriggled in delight, feathery tail beating against his leg. As he'd thought, she'd been a little miffed about being abandoned, but since Jeremy had fed her and walked her and taken her home with him the night before so she wouldn't be alone, it wasn't as though anyone was going to call him out for animal cruelty or something.

Jake still didn't know exactly what kind of dog she was—his veterinarian cousin's best guess had been a mix of papillon, chihuahua, and pomeranian—but he'd found her hiding behind the trash cans at his former condo, barely more than a puppy, starving and scared. He'd coaxed her out with food and the lure of a peanut butter–scented tennis ball he got at the local PetSmart, and ever since that day four years ago, she'd been his constant companion. Sometimes he'd wondered if he might have gone crazy with grief after Sarah's death if it weren't for Taffy's comforting presence.

For a moment, Jake's thoughts went to Addie, who was currently suffering a different kind of loss, if no less painful. Maybe it hadn't been a good idea to leave her alone. But he reassured himself that she knew to come over to his house if she started to feel hinky about anything, and besides...he really wanted to be able to make this call without worrying about her listening in.

Of course, that meant he actually had to make the damn call.

Setting his jaw, he touched the screen and lifted the phone to his ear. A few rings, and he prayed the damn thing wouldn't go to voicemail.

This wasn't the sort of news he wanted to leave in a message.

However, just before the fourth ring, he heard Connor's voice. "Jake?"

"Hi, Connor. Hope I wasn't interrupting anything."

"Not really. Anthony and I were just going over some numbers, but I was about to call it quits and head up to Jerome for a late lunch with the family. What's up?"

Jake ran his free hand through his hair and pulled in a breath. *You can do this.* "We've already found one."

"An orphan witch?"

He wanted to wince at the term, but then, he was the one who'd first started using the phrase to refer to witches or warlocks who'd been born outside a clan. Connor couldn't know that the witch in question was an orphan in every sense of the word.

"Yes. A weather-worker. She was living in Kanab, Utah. Um...there were some complications. Federal involvement."

A pause. Then Connor said, "Shit."

There's an understatement. "I know. It got a little dicey. Addie's mother was shot."

"Addie is the witch?"

Jake didn't miss how Connor hadn't bothered

to ask who was doing the shooting. They'd decided at the outset that Jake wouldn't be armed, even if he might be going into questionable situations in his quest to locate those clanless witches and warlocks. His telekinetic power was its own weapon, one that was effective, if not necessarily lethal.

He cleared his throat and said, "Yes. Adara Grant."

"She's okay?"

"She's fine. Shaken up, as you can imagine. She's at the cottage right now."

"Alone?"

"It's two doors down," Jake said patiently. "She's fine. There's no sign that anyone followed us when we left Kanab. But I'd like you to meet her."

"Well, sure," Connor replied, as if that should be obvious. "I suppose I should welcome her to Wilcox territory. Any idea who her clan is?"

Here we go. "Um...she's one of us."

"Seriously?"

"Yes. She says her father's name was Jackson Wilcox."

Dead silence. Jake pulled the phone away from his ear, wondering if the call had been dropped, although deep down he knew that wasn't the real reason why he hadn't heard the *primus's* response.

Then Connor said, his tone flat, "That's impossible."

"I wanted to think that, too, but she says her father met her mother in Flagstaff when she was here for a skiing trip. Says he told her mother that he was a widower with two boys. The stories line up."

"Except for the part where there's no way the curse would have allowed my father to have a daughter."

Since Jake had thought much the same thing, about all he could do was shrug. However, because Connor wasn't there to see the gesture, he said, "I know it seems impossible, but...how could she make up a story like that and get so many details right?"

"I don't know," Connor replied. Now he sounded troubled, as if he'd begun to realize that just because he didn't want to admit that Addie's story was possible didn't mean it wasn't true. "Shit. This is just...I don't know what to do with this, Jake."

"Meet her," he said at once. "She...she looks like one of us. Her magic is really strong. How it happened, I have no idea. When I first visualized

Trident Enterprises, I never imagined this sort of scenario occurring."

"Guess you should have." Now Connor's voice was wry. "I mean, when you're out there tracking down clan-less witches and warlocks, there's a good chance they're in that situation because their witch or warlock parent was running around on someone."

Jake supposed he was right. "Your father wasn't running around on anyone, though," he pointed out. "Addie's twenty-four, so your mother had been gone for quite a while by the time he met Lyssa Grant."

Another long pause, during which Connor was probably doing some mental calculations. "Right. I guess I would have been around fourteen when they got together. My father wasn't with us for much longer after that, though. I'm surprised he had the energy for a fling."

Jake wasn't sure how to respond to that comment, so he decided it was better not to say anything. Jackson Wilcox had passed away from a heart attack when Jake was just a little kid, and he honestly didn't remember much about the man who'd occupied the *primus* position before Connor's older brother Damon took over.

"Anyway," Connor went on, apparently guessing correctly the reason for Jake's silence, "can you bring her down to Jerome? We've been planning to get back up to Flag, but that probably won't happen until the end of next week at the rate we're going, and I doubt you want to wait that long."

No, definitely not. Jake didn't know whether Addie would be too enthusiastic about another car trip so soon after arriving in Flagstaff, but he figured he would do what he could to make the drive interesting. Maybe take the back way overland through Williams and down into Perkinsville to reach Jerome via country roads. If nothing else, it would be a good way to stretch his new vehicle's legs, so to speak.

"Sure," he replied. "We'll grab something to eat here in Flagstaff and then head to Jerome. Expect us around four or so."

"I will—and I'll let Angela know." Connor let out a gust of breath that was clearly audible on the phone's speaker. "This is going to be fun to explain to her. But we'll be ready."

"Thanks, Connor. See you then."

Jake ended the call there and looked down at the phone to check the time. A little after one. Not too late for lunch; he'd had it in the back of his head that he needed to do something about getting them some food, but it wasn't until he'd been talking to Connor that he realized he really couldn't haul Addie down to Jerome without taking her to lunch first.

Since he'd already fed Taffy and refilled her water bowl, he bent to pet her again, saying, "Sorry, girl—I need to go out for a few hours."

Her brown eyes met his, and one ear cocked slightly. Seeming to sense that she was about to get abandoned again, she went up on her hind legs, dancing around, trying to show what a good dog she was and how she wouldn't be any trouble.

"You're way too good at the whole guilt thing, you know that?" he inquired as he scratched her behind the ears again. Then he said, "Okay, okay. You can come, too." He knew that Connor and Angela had a dog, but if the two animals didn't get along, he could just leave Taffy in the yard or whatever. Besides, judging by the way Addie's beautiful eyes had lit up when he mentioned his dog, he had a feeling she would like to meet his pet.

Taffy immediately dropped to all four paws and began circling him, tail wagging furiously, as he went to the table in the foyer where he kept her leash. After clipping it to her collar, he led her outside and locked the door behind him, then went down to the cottage.

When she opened the front door in answer to

his knock, Addie looked surprised to see the dog. However, she smiled almost immediately and kneeled down to pet Taffy, whose tail went a mile a minute as it swept some dust from the wooden boards that made up the porch floor.

"Looks like you brought me a visitor," she said, and Jake grinned.

"Well, I kind of got guilted into it," he admitted. "Anyway, I talked to Connor, and he wants us to come down to Jerome."

"Now?" Addie asked, looking somewhat aghast. She glanced down at herself, at the floral short-sleeved blouse and jeans she was wearing. "Like this?"

"You're fine," he told her. "Connor and Angela are pretty casual people."

This piece of information didn't seem to reassure her. "I don't know...."

"It's going to be okay. Connor really wants to meet you." Something of an overstatement, but Jake didn't want to make the situation any more awkward than it already was by telling Addie that Connor was more shocked than anything else by the sudden appearance of a heretofore unknown half-sister. "And we can get lunch in town before we head down to Jerome. I figure you must be hungry."

She appeared vaguely startled by the

mention of food, as if such a thought hadn't even crossed her mind. "What about your dog?"

"Not a problem," he answered easily. "It's nice weather—there are lots of places in Flagstaff with pet-friendly patios. What're you in the mood for?"

"You pick," she said. "You know the town, and I don't."

Fair enough. He had a place in mind, something relaxed and low-key but with great food and a nice little slice of Flagstaff history. "Okay," he replied. "I'll take you to Tourist Home."

"That's the name of the restaurant?" she asked, now looking almost amused.

"Don't knock it until you've tried it," Jake said. "Let's go ahead and lock up here, and then we can head out."

"You'll have to do it," Addie told him. "You didn't give me a key."

He grinned at her. "You're a witch—you don't need a key."

That remark only made her blink. "Excuse me?"

"Watch."

He reached over and closed the door, then touched the latch. At once, it made a soft *click* as the tumblers settled into the locked position. "Try it."

She reached over and pressed down. Naturally, nothing happened. Eyes wide, she looked back at him. "How did you do that?"

"It's something all witches and warlocks can do. Go ahead—try it. Unlock the door."

"I don't know how," she replied, tone exasperated.

"You don't have to know how," he said. How was he supposed to explain something that should have been second nature to her? But then, he'd been raised in a witch clan. He'd always known he could do such a thing because he'd seen other Wilcoxes lock and unlock doors with nothing more than the power of their minds ever since he was a little kid. Addie had no such context, no reason to believe he wasn't asking her to do the impossible. "Just...think it. Think about the door unlocking when you touch the latch. That's all you need to do."

For a few seconds, she hesitated. But then he watched her breathe in, as though steeling herself to make the attempt. She reached out and touched the latch...and it pressed down as soon as she made contact.

Her eyes flared wide with astonishment. "It worked!"

"I told you it would," he replied. "Now, try locking it."

Seeming a little more sure of herself this time, Addie reached for the latch again, laying her fingers on it for just a few seconds. The *click* of the latch was clearly audible.

"How...?" she began, then paused, as if she wasn't sure exactly what she'd meant to ask.

"Like I said, it's something all witches and warlocks can do. Same thing with fire—we can't all summon fireballs or anything quite so spectacular, but pretty much all of us can point at a candle and have it light, or do the same thing to logs in a fireplace." Jake smiled, thinking of all the times he'd used that particular talent to get a fire going in the winter. It definitely beat fussing with kindling and wadded-up newspaper. "You can try that later...it would be a little conspicuous if you lit the porch on fire or something."

Her mouth quirked, pretty and full. "Like I'd do anything like that to this house. It's way too cute."

He was glad she approved of the place. While it wouldn't be her permanent home, she still might be staying there for a while, and he wanted her to be comfortable.

"Good to know," he said. "And now you've proven to yourself that you can control one of your talents. When you start training with our weather-worker, it won't seem so strange."

That comment made her expression shift to something thoughtful, as if he'd suggested something she hadn't considered before. However, her tone was noncommittal as she replied, "I suppose so. When will that be?"

"Probably tomorrow," Jake said. Although he knew exactly who he wanted to guide Addie through coming to terms with her weather-working gifts—while it was a fairly common talent in most clans, the Wilcoxes only had one person who'd been born with it—he hadn't reached out to the witch in question yet. He knew she wouldn't say no, but there might be some logistics to get worked out. "For today, though, it's all about meeting your family."

"'My family,'" she repeated, looking a little sad. He could tell that she must have been thinking about her mother, and he wondered if he should reach out and offer some kind of reassuring gesture. But then something about the set of her shoulders seemed to stiffen, and she added, "I'm looking forward to that. Let's head out."

And she made her way down the porch steps, Taffy pulling at her leash so she could tag along. Jake watched both of them for a second, then followed them down the stairs.

He wished he knew Addie well enough to guess whether she'd been telling the truth.

~

Randall Lenz picked up the phone before it rang a second time. "You have something for me?"

"I think so," Agent Dawson responded. "Surveillance video in a convenience store in St. George picked up a couple who look as though they could be Adara Grant and her companion. Sending it over now."

St. George was located roughly fifty miles west of Kanab and would have been a likely destination. If the footage truly proved the couple had been there the day before, then he stood a good chance of figuring out where they'd headed after that. His instincts about those sorts of things had always been good; in fact, it was the hints his intuition had provided that allowed him to be so successful in his work. Maybe that was part of the reason why the whole Adara Grant debacle had rankled so much. He wasn't used to making those sorts of mistakes.

"I'll take a look," he said, not bothering to thank Dawson. After all, she was only doing her job. "If it checks out, then I'll go investigate in person."

"Got it. Good luck, sir."

She hung up, and his phone beeped, indicating that he'd gotten a new message. He clicked on it, determined it had come from Agent Dawson, and watched as the grainy black-and-white footage began to play.

On a screen that size, Lenz couldn't make out a lot of detail, but he saw enough. A slim woman with long dark hair entered the convenience store, accompanied by a tall dark-haired man in a T-shirt and jeans. The woman inspected the kiosk containing sunglasses for sale, selected a pair, and then went to meet her companion at the counter. He took the sunglasses from her, had some sort of dialogue with the clerk, and then handed several bills to the man, although the images were muddy enough that Lenz knew he'd never be able to tell exactly what denominations those bills actually were.

It seemed the man was canny enough to use cash, which meant that tracking him down would be more difficult. Not impossible, of course, but it would have been much easier if he'd left a paper trail of credit card transactions in his wake.

But apparently, he wasn't quite that much of an amateur. Once again, Lenz wondered just who the hell he was, and how he'd managed to appear out of nowhere at exactly the wrong moment.

Those mysteries would be cleared up at some point. For now, it was far more important to get moving before the trail turned too cold.

He went outside to his black Ford Taurus. All he had was the one duffle bag, which contained toiletries and several clean shirts and changes of underwear, and he tossed it in the trunk before sliding behind the wheel.

It felt good to get out of Kanab. He hadn't liked staying there, since it kept reminding him of his failure to collect Adara Grant, but leaving hadn't been an option, either, not when she might still be somewhere in the area. True, she'd disappeared nearly twenty-four hours earlier, and yet he refused to accept defeat. She might not have gone all that far.

He hoped.

The drive took longer than he would have liked, mostly because the highway dipped to the south before turning north toward St. George. However, within the hour he was pulling into the outskirts of the community, which was also flanked by reddish sandstone formations, although the landscape felt more bleak there than it had back in Kanab, which had a surprising amount of greenery for a desert town.

He pulled into the parking lot of the Shell station, which was located only a block or so from I-15. It seemed fairly busy, and he hoped the clerk who'd been on duty would remember enough about that particular pair of customers that he would be able to offer a few tidbits of valuable information.

Someone was at the counter, paying for a couple of sodas, so Lenz waited off to one side until the transaction had been completed. Once the woman had collected her drinks and gone back outside, he approached the clerk. A quick flick of his I.D., and he said, "I'm with Homeland Security. Do you recall seeing this woman?"

He held up his phone, where he'd stored a screen grab from the surveillance video. It showed Adara Grant glancing over at her companion as she set a pair of sunglasses down on the counter.

"Oh, yeah," the clerk replied. He was in his mid-twenties, with short-cropped reddish-blond hair and the sort of ruddy complexion that the desert sun hadn't been very kind to. "She came in yesterday afternoon. Had some guy with her."

The appreciative gleam in the clerk's eyes told Lenz that the man probably remembered her because she was pretty and around his own age. "Did she say anything?"

"No. She seemed worried about something, or maybe upset...I don't know. The guy did all the talking."

"What did he say?"

The clerk reached up to scratch the back of his neck. "He wasn't exactly talkative, either. Bought some sunglasses in addition to the gas, thanked me, and then left."

It had probably been too much to hope that someone on the run from federal agents would pause to engage in idle chitchat with a convenience store clerk. "Did you see what he was driving?"

That question elicited another gleam in the man's pale blue eyes, although for a completely different reason. "Oh, yeah. It was one of those new Jeep trucks. Black. Sweet ride."

The note of envy in the clerk's tone was obvious. Although Randall Lenz didn't make a habit of assessing the cost of every new vehicle that came on the market, he guessed that someone working minimum wage in St. George, Utah, probably couldn't afford the kind of truck he'd just described. Not that he cared. What he cared about was that he now had a valuable piece of information about the two fugitives.

"Did you notice the license plates?"

"Nope. They parked at the far pumps, and

you can't really see something like that from this angle."

It had been a long shot, but Lenz couldn't quite prevent a stab of disappointment from going through him. "Did you see which way they headed when they left?" he asked.

"They turned left onto 100 North, but that makes sense if they were heading back to the highway," the man replied. "But I couldn't tell you where they went after that."

Meaning they could have either headed north on I-15, going deeper into Utah, or turned south toward Nevada. Lenz supposed that depended on their final destination...if they'd even had one in mind when they stopped for gas. They could have just been doing their best to put as many miles between them and Kanab as possible.

However, while Adara Grant was probably inexperienced about a great many things, he hadn't gotten the impression that she was a fool. He knew if he'd been on the run, he would have headed someplace where he could lose himself among the population, a location where he'd be inconspicuous. And the vehicle the clerk had described sounded like it was anything but inconspicuous. It would have stuck out like a sore thumb on a Utah highway.

But not too far away was a place where a truck like that probably wouldn't merit a second glance. It was just a hunch, but his hunches very rarely failed him.

He thanked the clerk and went back out to his car, then sat behind the wheel as he got out his phone and made a call.

"Dawson," his assistant said. "Did you find something, sir?"

"Possibly," he replied. "Start pulling traffic footage in Las Vegas, Nevada. We're looking for a late-model black Jeep Gladiator."

"Plates?"

"Unknown. You'll have to do what you can with the information I've provided."

"Working. I'll get back to you when I have something."

"Got it. I'm going to head to Vegas."

Randall Lenz ended the call and slid the phone into his pocket before touching his finger to the ignition button. As he pulled back onto the road in front of the gas station and pointed the Taurus toward I-15, he found himself smiling slightly.

Las Vegas was a big town...but he didn't think it would be big enough to hide Adara Grant.

9

JAKE HAD EXPLAINED TO ME THAT HE WAS GOING TO take the back way into Jerome...but I hadn't realized just how "back" that route actually was until we left the southern edge of Williams, a small town about twenty miles west of Flagstaff, and headed off into the trackless wilderness.

All right, it wasn't completely trackless. We were following a dirt road, one that seemed to be fairly well-traveled. However, since I'd never gone four-wheeling in my life, it definitely felt like we were out in the middle of nowhere.

"This route is really going to take us to Jerome?" I asked as we bounced along. In the back seat, Jake's little red-brown dog with the extravagant ears was sliding around on the leather surface every time we hit a particularly nasty bump, but, judging by the doggy grin she wore on her pointy face, she was having the time of her life.

"Yes," he said. "This road has been here since the town's mining days. I guess they used to transport livestock and lumber along here. And it keeps us from having to cut through Sedona, which can be a real mess on the weekend."

I thought I'd vaguely heard of Sedona but couldn't remember much about the place. "It's a tourist destination?"

A chuckle. "To put it mildly. And it's really beautiful—lots of red rock formations, super picturesque. But it's a lot less beautiful when you're crawling down 89A at roughly two miles an hour. Traffic can back up halfway through Oak Creek Canyon during peak tourist season."

That didn't sound fun at all. No wonder Jake had decided to take this decidedly off-the-beaten-track approach to get to Jerome. Not that I really had any idea where Jerome was located—my knowledge of Arizona geography had been pretty much limited to knowing how to find Phoenix on a map. I reflected then that it was interesting how my mother had avoided coming back to the state, even in all our wanderings. Had she been worried that she might somehow bump into Jackson Wilcox again, that he, with all his money and power, might try to take her daughter away from her?

I supposed it had been a reasonable fear. She couldn't have known that my father had passed away while I was still a tiny child. How old had he been? Not that old...I sort of doubted my mother would have hooked up with someone old enough to be her grandfather. As with so many other things, she hadn't gone into a lot of detail, had only told me he'd been older but very good-looking. And I read between the lines to guess that she'd been caught up in the excitement of a fling with someone attractive and successful and worldly, and had been all too willing to lose herself in their whirlwind courtship.

And while it might have been easy to blame her for being careless, she claimed that she'd been on the pill at the time, and had thought it would be perfectly safe to be with him. All my life, I'd thought I was just one of those "accidents," the little statistical blips that arose from the three percent of a medication that was supposed to be ninety-seven-percent effective. Now, though, I had to wonder whether there had been other forces at work. Supposedly, my father was a very strong warlock. Had he done something to make sure the pill would fail my mother?

I couldn't know. The man in question had

been dead for more than twenty years, and he'd taken his secrets with him to the grave. Possibly, Connor might have some answers for me, but I wouldn't let myself count on that.

Jake's glance slid toward me, as if he expected some sort of response to his comment about Sedona's traffic, so I made a noncommittal sound as I clung to the "Jesus handle" above my head and hoped the road wouldn't be a rutted mess all the way to Jerome. And it wasn't, really—we encountered sections that were almost smooth, including a bridge that crossed over a slow-moving river, its banks thick with the bright green of cottonwood trees.

The last leg of the journey was actually the worst, because there we crawled along a gravel road that was cut into the side of a cliff face, a lane so narrow that we had to hug the rock wall whenever another vehicle came from the opposite direction. Through the swirling dust, I thought I saw a red rock formation far off in the distance to the east.

Jake must have caught the direction I was looking, because he said, "That's Sedona—or part of it, anyway."

"It's beautiful." And it was. Even from miles and miles away, the red rocks fairly glowed against the bright blue sky. No wonder the town's streets were choked with people wanting to get closer to that beauty.

"Then we'll go sometime...on a weekday," he added with a smile.

I smiled back at him, even though I could feel my expression start to falter. It felt beyond weird to be making plans for a future sightseeing trip when my life had fallen into ruins just the day before. Shouldn't I be mourning my mother?

And yet...I knew I was. The ache of her loss was like a heavy weight in the pit of my stomach. It hurt, and hurt all the worse because I knew there really wasn't anything I could do about it except hope the passage of time might begin to ease that ache. At the same time, I hoped she would want me to go on, to try to put my life back together in this new and strange place.

If that meant spending time with the man who sat in the driver's seat and expertly piloted his four-wheel-drive truck along the narrow and treacherous road...well, I thought I might be okay with that.

Eventually, we came down out of the switchbacks, and a mile or so later, the dirt road gave way to asphalt. It still wasn't in the greatest shape, but far better than the unpaved surfaces we'd been traveling on for the past twenty miles or so. We passed a place that advertised itself as a "ghost town" but mostly looked like a hodge-podge of abandoned farm vehicles and other odds and ends, passed a large parking lot that Jake explained was overflow for the times when Jerome was packed with its own tourists, and then came out past an old-fashioned building that proclaimed itself to be the Jerome Volunteer Fire Department. Up another steep hill crowded on either side with buildings that had to have been there since the late 1800s, and then down a street with large Victorian-style homes, some of which actually had lots big enough for real yards.

We parked in front of one of those, an imposing home with a wide porch and stained glass panels flanking the front door. "This is where Connor lives?" I asked.

"One of the places where he lives," Jake replied. "I guess this was the home of all the McAllister *primas,* and so Angela inherited it when she became *prima*. They live here part of the year and then spend the other half of the year up in Flagstaff at a house they bought when they got engaged. Usually they'd be up in Flag already—they tend to bail out of Jerome when the weather gets hot—but it sounds like Connor's been busy with the vineyard and that's why they haven't gotten around to moving the family."

Yet another revelation I hadn't been expecting. "Connor owns a vineyard?"

"Yeah, he bought it about five or six years ago. He manages it with a guy who's married to Angela's best friend."

Sounded cozy. Or at least, I thought it might be nice to be such close friends with people that you were willing to go into business with them. Apparently, the arrangement was working out, or I doubted the partnership would still be active some five years or more after they'd gotten started. Wondering about the situation made me experience a little pang, one I thought might actually be jealousy. No, it wasn't that I wanted to run a vineyard or anything, but simply the idea of having close friends like that, people who'd been part of your life for years and years. I'd never had anyone I could call a really good friend...well, unless you counted my mother.

I shouldn't have let the thought cross my mind, though, because out of nowhere, my eyes stung with tears. Blinking, I pretended to be fussing with my seatbelt, but I obviously wasn't doing too good a job of hiding my emotions, because Jake spoke then in an entirely different tone.

"It's going to be okay, Addie. I know this is rough, but...you've got family here."

"I know," I replied, using my knuckles to wipe the tears away. There probably wasn't any point in trying to explain what had really made me mist up right then, so I pulled in a breath and added, "It's okay. I just...I suppose sitting here and looking at this house just made it all real suddenly."

In the back seat, Taffy let out a faint, inquiring whine, as if she'd picked up on my mood. I leaned back and patted her on the head, doing my best to let her know it was okay. When I turned to face forward again, Jake reached over and touched my shoulder briefly. "I get it," he said. "We can sit here as long as you like."

For some reason, those words made me want to cry all over again. Why was he so damn nice? I supposed there wasn't any reason why he shouldn't be, but on the other hand, I hadn't run up against a lot of nice in my life. People mostly had seemed indifferent, wrapped up in their own problems. And then there had been uncaring bosses and downright mean landlords—and let's not forget about the lecher in Tucumcari who tried to get my mother to sleep with him, then directed his attentions toward me when she turned him down—and gossipy girls who made snotty comments about my thrift-store wardrobe, and basically, a whole world that didn't seem to have a lot of room in it for someone like me.

"I'm okay," I said, giving Jake a wan smile. "It's going to look weird if we stay parked here and don't go inside."

His brown eyes met mine, worried. "You're sure?"

"I'm sure."

That almost sounded convincing. Not totally, but it would have to do.

We got out of the truck, pausing so Jake could clip on Taffy's leash and help her down from the back seat. Then he went over to the gate in the honest-to-God white picket fence and opened it for me, following a pace or so behind in order to let the dog smell around a bit. The yard was very neat, with a manicured green lawn and beds of roses bordering the brick walkway that led to the front porch.

At the foot of the porch steps, he caught up with me so we could walk the rest of the way next to one another, Taffy dancing along on his other side. We paused at the front door, as if Jake knew I needed a moment to gather myself. I noticed that the stained glass panels that flanked the door were even more beautiful up close, shimmering in shades of blue and green and red and amber.

After taking a quick glance at me, Jake leaned over and pressed the doorbell. The Westminster chimes sequence echoed somewhere deep within the house, and a minute later, the door opened.

The man standing there was tall, around Jake's height, and probably in his mid-thirties, with the same near-black hair, although the stranger's hair was much longer, pulled back into a ponytail away from his handsome, cleanly chiseled features. But even though he was extremely attractive, it wasn't his overall looks that caught my attention. No, instead my gaze was caught by his eyes, a translucent gray-green, seeming to shift from one color to the other even as I stared at him.

My eyes.

From the startled flash in those eyes, I got the impression that he'd realized pretty much the same thing at almost the same moment. Then he seemed to recover himself, and extended a hand, saying, "Hi, Addie. I'm Connor."

"Hi," I said, knowing how awkward that one limp syllable sounded. On the other hand, I was sort of glad he hadn't pulled me into a hug the way Laurel had. That would have been even more uncomfortable.

"Come in," he said next, then stepped out of

the way so Jake and I could enter the house, the dog tagging gamely along. I hadn't missed the way Connor had glanced down at Taffy, but apparently he'd decided not to comment on her presence.

The interior of the house was just about as impressive as the exterior, although not as fussily Victorian. I didn't know a lot about interior decorating, but it was pretty obvious that the place had been redone in the not-so-distant past, maybe when Angela took over as *prima*. Connor guided us into the living room, which was furnished with oversized leather couches and several burnished-wood accent tables that looked as though they'd come from local artisans. The same with the paintings that hung on the walls—they were all originals, and probably from locals, if the subject matter of juniper trees and golden landscapes and Sedona red rocks was any indication. Taffy looked around, nose twitching, but she seemed to understand that she needed to be on her best behavior, because she went over by the hearth and plunked down on the rug there, her chin on her front paws as she gravely watched the rest of us.

"Go ahead and have a seat," Connor told Jake and me. "I'll get Angela—she's upstairs with the kids."

Even as he spoke, I heard some high-pitched giggles that must have come from several small children, followed by a pattering sound that was probably the kids tearing down the upstairs hall. I listened to those noises, so ordinary, and realized that those were my nieces and nephew running around up there.

"Thanks," I said, since I felt like I needed to say something, and he left the living room in search of his wife. A few seconds later, I could hear his much heavier tread on the stairs.

Once he was gone, Jake looked over at me. "Still doing okay?"

I nodded. In a way, I did feel better now that I'd met Connor, as if the worst was over. Maybe I was being entirely too hopeful about the situation, and yet I wanted to believe everything was going to be all right. "I'm fine, Jake."

His hand touched mine, gave my fingers an encouraging squeeze. The same warmth I'd felt before went through me, and I looked away, not wanting him to see the way I'd reacted to his touch. I knew he was just trying to be friendly and give me the emotional support I desperately needed, and so the last thing I should be doing was responding to him in any way that wasn't equally neutral and friendly.

Somehow, I managed to smile, and then the

uncomfortable moment had slipped past, because Connor returned to the living room with Angela at his side.

She was very pretty, dark-haired and with the most spectacular green eyes I'd ever seen in my life. When I got up from the couch to greet her, she reached out and gave me an impulsive hug, just as Laurel had earlier that day. As Angela's gaze met mine, she gave an involuntary little gasp.

"Wow!" she exclaimed. "I mean, it's just that I wasn't expecting...." Her words trailed off, and she glanced up at her husband before looking back over at me. "I guess I wasn't expecting you two to look at all alike. Connor and Damon didn't resemble each other very much."

"It's okay," I said quickly. "I know what you mean."

And honestly, feature for feature, we probably wouldn't have been mistaken for brother and sister, since I looked a lot like my mother, although my coloring was completely different from hers. But if someone just glanced at Connor and me, saw the dark brown hair and the gray-green eyes, then they'd probably assume there had to be some sort of family connection.

Angela's gaze appraised me for another minute, as if trying to gauge how shaken I was by this whole thing. Right then, I was thinking that I seemed to be handling it better than Connor, since he still just stood there in front of the other couch, as if he'd forgotten that it was meant to be sat upon. Angela tugged at his hand and went to sit down, and he followed her.

"Sorry," he said at last, as she poured iced tea from the pitcher that sat on the table in front of us and handed a glass to Jake and me. "It's just—I guess I'm trying to figure out how this could have happened."

Angela raised a finely arched eyebrow as she gave one of the remaining glasses of iced tea to her husband. "Um, Connor, I'm pretty sure I can explain it to you if you're having a hard time with the concept."

Her remark made him let out an uneasy laugh. "That's not what I meant. It's more that with the curse...how was it possible?"

Curse? What the hell were they talking about? I glanced over at Jake, and he looked almost sheepish. Well, he had said there were things he didn't want to get into right then, that we'd have time to talk later, and apparently this "curse" was one of those things. Part of me wanted to laugh at the mere notion that a curse could be a real thing, but I supposed once you accepted the truth of witches being real, then you just sort of had to roll with whatever other punches came after that.

"What curse?" I asked, doing my best not to sound accusatory.

"It's a really long story," Connor replied. "But basically, Jeremiah Wilcox, the *primus* of the clan when the Wilcoxes first came to Flagstaff, had a Navajo wife. She was a very strong magic-worker. They became estranged, and she fell ill, and when she was on her deathbed, she cursed him and all the men of his line so they'd never know joy in their marriages, and that they'd have only sons, no daughters."

"Which is why we can't quite figure out how you were born," Angela put in. She'd also poured tea for herself, but she held the glass resting on her knee, as if she wasn't sure whether she wanted to drink any of it or not. "You're the first female born to Jeremiah's line since the mid-1800s...well, until my daughter Emily came along."

"But she was born after the curse was broken," Connor reminded her, and for a moment, their gazes caught and held. A lot of history there, obviously, a huge chunk of story that I might or might not learn one day.

Angela nodded. "Right. And the curse was

very definitely still active when Addie came along."

Put that way, it did seem very strange. Yes, I had to accept the curse and all its ramifications, but even with that necessary suspension of disbelief, I couldn't quite wrap my head around the concept of a family having generation after generation of sons but no daughters.

Next to me, Jake shifted. He leaned forward to set his glass of tea down on a coaster, then said, "But Connor, you were an anomaly, too. None of your grandfathers had more than one son."

"True." Connor rubbed a hand over the dark scruff that covered his chin, expression abstracted. I got the impression that he'd puzzled over that particular conundrum more than once in the past. "We still don't know if that was because the curse was finally beginning to weaken a little, or because there were other forces at work."

Clasping her hands on her knee, Angela leaned forward slightly, green eyes intent on the two of us, although I had the feeling she was watching both of us because she didn't want to seem as though she was staring solely at me. In a way, I could understand why she would want to stare, would want to analyze my features one by one to see if she could detect other, more subtle points of resemblance to her husband. When she spoke, though, it was only to pick up the thread of Connor's comment.

"Magic isn't science," she said. "There are rules to it, but those rules aren't always as hard and fast as we'd like. Like Connor said, maybe the curse was finally starting to loosen its grip on the Wilcox clan. Or maybe there were ripples in time and space that made it possible for you to be conceived, Addie. In the end, what really matters is that you're here now, and we're going to do whatever is necessary to make sure you feel you're part of this family."

From the way she spoke, I got the feeling that she and Connor had discussed all this pretty much as soon as he hung up the phone from talking to Jake. Which made sense; it was better to present a united front and act as though we were all one big happy family, no matter what he might have privately thought about having a long-lost half-sister turn up out of the blue.

"Exactly," Connor said then. Something about his posture seemed a little more relaxed, making me think it wasn't that he objected to me personally, but had only had some difficulty trying to figure out how the curse had even allowed me to exist in the first place.

A sudden notion occurred to me, and I said, "Maybe the curse couldn't affect my mother's pregnancy because she left Flagstaff so soon after she was—well, so soon after she slept with our father. She was gone within two days."

Angela lifted an eyebrow as she considered my suggestion. "That's possible. It can take up to five or six days for fertilization to occur." She stopped then, giving a rueful shake of her head. "Sorry—I know that sounded totally clinical. But it's definitely a possibility."

Actually, I didn't mind that she was being clinical. It was easier to analyze the situation in cold scientific terms than to think about my mother, barely twenty-one, enjoying herself with her handsome older man, never realizing that the little fling she'd embarked on would end up changing her life forever. So many times, I'd wondered what she would have made of herself, who she could have become, if she'd never met Jackson Wilcox, had never been burdened with a child before she even had a chance to finish college.

Of course, if she'd ever actually heard me use that word, she would have told me in no uncertain terms that I wasn't a burden, that she could have decided not to have me, or to give me up for adoption. Because—for whatever crazy reason—she'd wanted me.

And because of me, she was now dead.

No. I shoved that thought aside with as much mental force as I could muster. She was dead because of Agent Randall Lenz. He'd come to Kanab in search of me, but that wasn't my fault. I had no control over his actions. And I knew I needed to repeat that hard fact to myself as many times as necessary to make myself understand and believe it.

"It's a very good theory, actually," Connor said. "Because when Nizhoni—Jeremiah Wilcox's Navajo wife—cast that curse, I have a feeling she was thinking of the way the clan had made its home in Flagstaff. Witch clans tend to stay put. I doubted it entered her mind that someone might be carrying a child of Jeremiah's line and actually leave the area."

Angela pursed her lips slightly, her expression dubious. "I don't know—she was so ill with a fever when she made up that curse, I'm not sure she was thinking that rationally. But for whatever reason, it didn't stick in this particular case." She smiled at me then, adding, "And we're all very glad of that."

Through all of this, Jake had remained silent, possibly because although he was a member of the Wilcox clan, he wasn't immediate family to either Connor or me, and therefore thought he shouldn't be weighing in on the situation. However, he'd apparently decided it was time to reenter the conversation, because he said, "I'm going to have Joanna train her, if that's okay."

"Perfect," Connor responded. He glanced at me and went on, by way of clarification, "Joanna is the Wilcox clan's weather-worker. She'll be able to get you on the right path."

I hoped so. My emotions had been up and down enough that day that I'd been worried I might stir up an unwanted thunderstorm, but apparently, my unsettled mental state hadn't been unsettled enough to warrant that sort of a response. Anyway, Jake had made it sound as though it really wasn't that difficult to get a grasp on your inborn witchy powers once you knew what you were supposed to be doing, so with any luck, a couple of training sessions with this Joanna person might be enough to prevent any future unintended tornadoes.

If I stopped having crazy weather follow me wherever I went, I'd be a lot harder to find. Maybe the universe would finally decide to be kind and make sure Agent Lenz had no further way to track my movements.

"And," Connor went on, "even though you're

staying at the cottage now, I assume at some point you'll want something a little more permanent. Once we can get you new identification and a bank account, I'll transfer your share of the inheritance to you."

Even though Jake had hinted this sort of thing was probably going to happen, my newfound brother's matter-of-fact statement made me stare at him, not sure I'd heard his words correctly. Just like that, he was going to hand a bundle of money over to me?

"You don't have to do anything right away," I said quickly. "I mean, there really isn't any actual proof that I'm even your sister."

Connor didn't smile, only looked at me straight on, those eyes that were so like mine fixed on me. When he spoke, his tone was gentle...but also very firm. "I think I'm looking at the proof right now. You're obviously a witch—and I think it's pretty clear that you're a Wilcox. Too many details in your story line up with what I already knew. He tried to keep it from Damon and me, but we both knew that our father hooked up with civilian women from time to time. The curse prevented him from remarrying after our mother died, and I suppose he figured that was the safest way to scratch his biological itch."

I couldn't quite prevent myself from wincing in response to that remark. Although I could tell he noticed—his lips thinned slightly—he didn't bother to apologize. What was the point? While I might have wanted to paint the situation as some sort of doomed May/December romance, I knew that my mother had only been looking for some casual sex to amuse herself, and clearly Jackson Wilcox had harbored pretty much the same intentions.

"We can do a DNA test, if you want," Connor continued. "But I don't think it's necessary. Honestly, I'm glad to give you the money. I don't need it."

His words had the ring of truth, and yet, I still had a hard time believing what he was telling me. Did money matter so little to him?

As I sat there on the couch and stared at my brother, it began to sink in that it wasn't so much that money didn't matter...more like he had so much of it, giving a chunk to me wasn't going to make any difference in his life.

Obviously trying to defuse the tension between us, Angela said with a grin, "He doesn't need it because he married a rich chick."

He put a hand on her knee, matching her grin with one of his own. "That's right. This probably feels strange to you, Addie, but we're more about making sure the money we have enhances and enables our lives than worrying about how much we actually have. When I say it won't make a difference to me to give you your share of the inheritance, it's only the truth. Whereas I know it will make a huge difference in your life."

"All right," I said reluctantly. Then, partly because I was honestly curious and partly because I wanted to know what I was getting myself into, I added, "So...how much money *are* we talking about here?"

Connor rubbed a tanned hand over the stubble on his chin. "Mmm...about two and a half million, I think. Or maybe closer to three million. I haven't checked the latest statement from my stockbroker."

That might have been the first time in my life I'd ever been rendered truly speechless. I sat there, staring at this man who'd turned out to be my half-brother, and thought I had to have misheard him. No way in the world was I about to have two million dollars—or possibly closer to three—dropped into my lap like that.

Jake shifted on the couch next to me. Although I couldn't say exactly how I knew, I got the very strong impression that he wished he could reach over and take my hand, let me hold on to him as I did my best to deal with this latest shock. But while he'd offered such a gesture of encouragement not too much earlier, I guessed he didn't want to offer that sort of comfort in front of Connor and Angela. Probably a good thing; I was already having a hard time sorting out my thoughts about Jake Wilcox, and better not to wrestle with that particular issue in front of an audience.

At last, I blurted, "What am I supposed to do with that kind of money?"

"Anything you like," Angela said, her full mouth curving a little at the corners. "Finish college...buy a house. Spend a week at a Scottsdale resort getting pedicures and massages. Whatever works for you."

I'd honestly never even thought about spa treatments—who had the time for those sorts of things?—but yes, definitely go and get my degree. A house...sure. But I vowed whatever I ended up doing, it would be after soberly analyzing my options and deciding what would be the best return for my investment. I wanted to make sure that whatever my future plans turned out to be, they would have met my mother's approval...if she'd only lived long enough to see them for herself.

"Northern Pines University is right in Flagstaff," Jake offered. "Most of us Wilcoxes go to college there. But there's Arizona State University down in Tempe, or the University of Arizona in Tucson. You'll have lots of options."

More options than I'd probably know what to do with. In that moment, though, I resolved inwardly to go to Northern Pines. After all, I'd only just discovered this side of my family. Why would I want to travel to the other end of the state to go to college when I had one right there in Wilcox territory?

"And you don't have to decide anything right away," Connor told me. "Work with Joanna first to learn how to control your talent. Get settled in Flagstaff and meet more of your cousins." His eyes met mine, and I saw sadness in those mossy depths. "Give yourself time to grieve."

His words were enough to bring back the lump in my throat, and I reached for my iced tea and made myself drink some, hoping that might help. I wasn't sure whether it really did, but at least doing so made me focus on something other than how much I really didn't want to cry in front of this newfound family of mine.

When I thought it was safe to speak, I asked, "And what about Agent Lenz?"

Connor's mouth tightened. Voice brisk, he said, "We'll take care of that. The Wilcoxes are a force to be reckoned with. If he comes snooping around, he's going to regret it."

Looking at the man who was the head of the Wilcox witch clan, I found myself inclined to believe what he had just said. His expression had grown grim, and I fancied he looked far more like our father in that moment than he usually did.

But then he seemed to relax, adding, "Now that we've taken care of business, how about you come upstairs and meet your nephew and nieces?"

Of course, I agreed. I might have lost one family...but I'd somehow gained another.

10

In all, Jake and Addie spent almost three hours at Connor and Angela's house, some of that time whiled away as she got acquainted with the nephew and nieces she'd never known she had. Ian and Emily, the twins, had gotten a reputation in both the Wilcox and McAllister clans for being a pair of hellions, but they were on their best behavior that afternoon, clearly determined to charm their young, pretty, and completely unexpected aunt. It probably helped that the twins and their little sister Miranda were all enchanted by Taffy, and wanted to spend as much time as possible petting her and throwing her ball for her when everyone went out into the yard to stretch their legs. The family had a dog named Blue, but he was a big shepherd mix, and having a dog more their size clearly made an impression on the children.

Eventually, though, Jake and Addie were able to tear themselves away—albeit with promises that they'd be back to "play" once the family was up in Flagstaff for the summer. Taffy was pretty worn out by that point, and happily fell asleep on the back seat in the truck almost as soon as she lay down. Jake had planned to take Addie around Jerome and show her a little bit of the town, but even though the sun had begun to go down behind the mountain by that point, he thought it was a little warm to leave the dog in the vehicle. However, when they had to stop in the middle of Main Street to let someone back out of one of the parking spots in front of Grapes, Taffy perked up immediately, looking around as if ready for her next adventure.

That seemed to decide things. "Want to wander a bit?" he asked Addie. "Jerome is a pretty cool little place."

Her gaze shifted to the back seat, where Taffy was standing up, tail wagging. "What about your dog?"

"She can come with us," he said. "Lots of people bring their dogs up here. If there's a shop you want to go in, the two of us can wait outside."

For a second, it looked as though Addie

might protest. But then her shoulders lifted a fraction, and a small smile touched her beautifully curved lips. "Okay. That sounds fun."

And it was. There was something satisfying about wandering down the uneven sidewalks with Addie at his side, the dog straining at the leash as they moved from spot to spot. Once or twice, she actually did go into a shop, but he could tell she was only looking around. He supposed she couldn't do much else, since she didn't have any money or credit cards.

After the second shop, Jake said, "If you see something you like, let me get it for you."

Alarm flared in her eyes, and she shook her head. "Oh, I couldn't let you do that."

"Sure you could," he said with a smile, adding before she could protest, "I know you're good for it. You can pay me back after Connor gets your bank accounts set up."

For a second, Addie stared at him, and then she flashed a lopsided smile. "Right. I'd almost forgotten about that. I suppose money isn't really going to be a problem, is it?"

"Not really," he replied. "I mean, don't go crazy. But it would be nice to have something to remember your first trip to Jerome and the day you met your brother, wouldn't it?"

She didn't reply right away, but only stood

there next to him on the sidewalk, gaze tracking to the golden, juniper-studded contours of the Verde Valley below, moving farther to the red rocks of Sedona beyond. Her chest moved as she appeared to pull in a breath, and then she nodded.

"Yes...I would like something to remember all this."

They began to walk again, and a few minutes later, she went into a store that specialized in selling local wares—pottery, jewelry, handwoven textiles and rugs. She seemed to be inside that shop longer than the others she'd inspected, and when she came out, she was smiling.

"I found something. The woman who owns the shop—she's a witch, too, by the way—is holding it for me. I told her my friend would be in to pay for it."

"Great," Jake said, relieved that Addie had allowed herself this one small indulgence. Or maybe it wasn't so small; he hadn't yet seen what she'd picked out for herself. However, he could already tell, based on the way she'd shopped in Las Vegas, that she wasn't an extravagant person, and so he doubted she'd chosen anything terribly expensive.

He handed her Taffy's leash so he could go inside. The woman at the counter gave him a knowing smile, and he knew why—just as Addie had said, the owner of the shop was also a witch, clearly a McAllister, plump and with graying red hair.

"Visiting Connor?" the woman asked, and Jake nodded.

"Yes, we came down from Flagstaff for the afternoon."

"I could tell you were both Wilcoxes," the woman said. "I'm Rachel—Angela is my niece."

"Oh—nice to meet you," he responded. He'd vaguely known that Angela's aunt owned a store in Jerome, but he'd never heard which one. Even though relations between the two clans had become much more relaxed over the past few years, it wasn't as though members of the Wilcox family went out of their way to hang out in Jerome. This was only Jake's second visit, although he'd been meaning to come back for a while.

He could tell that Rachel was watching him with a speculative glint in her hazel eyes, probably wondering what business he'd had with Connor. Something important enough to make him drive all the way down to Jerome rather than waiting for the family to head up to Flagstaff for the summer, obviously, but Jake knew it wasn't his place to talk about Addie's true identity, or the reason why Connor had wanted to meet her right away. Most likely, Angela would let Rachel know soon enough, but that was between the two of them.

"Your friend picked out one of Angela's pieces," Rachel said, adding with a smile, "She has good taste."

Jake had heard that Angela did some jewelry design on the side—a talent she'd picked up from her father, who was a silversmith of some renown—but he'd completely forgotten that she offered those items for sale in her aunt's shop. Definitely a good choice for a keepsake, then, and he thought that Addie must have some good instincts, to select one of Angela's pieces out of everything available in the store.

"Did she?" he responded. "That's pretty cool."

Still smiling, Rachel reached under the counter and brought out a cardboard jewelry box, then laid a silver pendant on the bed of cotton padding inside. It was an intricate piece, with a rough-hewn quartz crystal in the center surrounded by grass-green cabochon stones he thought might be tourmalines.

"Does it come with a chain?" he asked, since he hadn't seen one as she set down the pendant.

"No. And I don't sell silver chains, but I do

have some nice thin leather cords for hanging pendants."

"Then put one of those in the box, too, please."

Rachel went to a different case, pulled out one of the cords in question, and then threaded the pendant onto it before she set it back in the box and closed the lid. "Ninety-five dollars," she said.

The damage could have been a lot worse. He still had a bunch of cash left over from his road trip, and so he laid two fifty-dollar bills on the counter and waited for the change. When he was done with the transaction, he tucked the receipt in his wallet, thanked Rachel, and picked up the box and went outside.

Addie and Taffy had wandered a few paces down the sidewalk, to a spot where the buildings ended and there was a stretch of open walkway with an iron railing to protect pedestrians and sightseers from the steep hillside below. The dog was sitting patiently, tail wagging, as her temporary guardian stared out at the amazing vista beyond, with Sedona's red rocks turning even redder thanks to the sun's descent behind Mingus Mountain.

"Here you go," Jake said, handing Addie the

box and taking Taffy's leash from her. "That's one of Angela's pieces, you know."

Caught as she was just starting to open the box, Addie looked up at him, startled. "I didn't know she made jewelry."

"It's sort of a hobby, I guess." Well, maybe more than a hobby, since she actually earned some money at it, but it wasn't as though the McAllister *prima* needed the cash.

"Then this makes an even better keepsake than I thought it would," Addie said. She pulled out the pendant on its thin black cord and lifted an eyebrow. "I didn't think it came with a chain."

"It didn't," he said casually. "But Rachel had the cords, and I figured you'd want to wear it right away."

"I did. I mean, I do." A faint flush tinged her cheekbones, but she didn't say anything else, only undid the clasp on the cord and fastened it around her neck. The pendant snuggled into the hollow of her throat as though it had been designed to lie there. "Thanks. I'll pay you back as soon as all the money stuff gets sorted out."

Right then, Jake mentally vowed not to take a penny for the pendant. He wanted it to be his own present for Addie, although he had a feeling she would probably argue that she hadn't asked him to buy her anything.

Well, he'd deal with her protests when the time came.

"Do you want to eat here, or head back to Flagstaff?" he asked, deciding not to respond to her comment.

Her glance traveled to Taffy, who was still sitting patiently on the sidewalk by Jake's feet, although he could tell the dog was starting to get a little antsy. "What about Taffy?"

"They allow dogs on the patio at Grapes," he replied, then pointed across the street to the restaurant in question. "It's a nice warm evening—it'll be fun."

She still looked unconvinced. "I'm not sure I want to go back along that dirt road after dark."

Actually, neither did Jake, but there was no reason for them to return to Flagstaff via the same route they'd taken to get to Jerome. "No worries. We can go home through Sedona—there won't be nearly as much traffic leaving as there was coming in earlier today. Okay?"

A pause, and then her shoulders lifted slightly. "Sure."

They crossed the street, and Jake asked Addie to hold Taffy's leash while he went inside the restaurant and checked on the availability of a patio table. Luckily, a group had just left, so he headed back out to collect Addie and the dog while the table was being wiped down, and then they went onto the patio via the little gate in the fence that enclosed the area.

As he'd assured Addie, it was a warm evening, more than comfortable for sitting outside and watching the setting sun paint Sedona redder and redder before the last of the day's light bled away. Taffy, used to the drill, curled up on the ground next to the counter-height chair where Jake sat, and Addie took the seat opposite him. She looked a little tired, but far more relaxed than she'd been earlier in the day...and seemed even more relaxed after the waitress brought them a couple glasses of wine.

"This doesn't feel real," she remarked as she took her first sip of pinot noir.

"What doesn't?" Jake responded, although he thought he had an idea of what she'd meant.

"Any of this." With her free hand, Addie gestured toward the street beyond, and Jerome as a whole. "That I met my brother today...and his wife, and their kids. Like I got this whole perfect prepackaged family in this funny little town that feels like something out of another century."

"It's a lot to take in, I suppose," he said. "But I told you that you had nothing to worry about."

She nodded, then lifted her glass of wine to take another sip. "I know. But after everything that's happened...." Her head drooped a little, and she didn't quite meet his eyes. "I guess I was just expecting the worst."

Right then, he wished she'd sat next to him, just so he could reach over and take her hand. Or maybe reaching out to her like that would be dangerous. He could feel the way he was beginning to react to Adara Grant, and he still hadn't decided what in the world he should do about it. On the one hand, he thought this awakening attraction was a good sign, because for the past three years, he hadn't believed he would ever care about such things again, that he'd be mourning Sarah for the rest of his life. Now, though, while he knew he would always love her, he wondered if it was time to move on.

But Addie had suffered her own losses, and her wound was far more raw and new. Making any kind of move right now would be horribly insensitive, wouldn't it?

"I can understand that," he said quietly. "I'm just glad everything went so well today."

"And you're really not worried about Age—" She stopped herself there, as if realizing that discussing the topic of Agent Lenz in a public place probably wasn't the best idea.

However, Jake figured he could reassure her without going into the kind of specifics that would give anything away to any nearby listening ears. "Not really. We have mechanisms in place for dealing with that kind of thing. I think the most important thing for the next few days is to just let yourself breathe and remember that you're safe now."

"'Safe,'" Addie repeated, as though trying to remind herself of what the word meant. "I'll do my best."

The conversation was halted there for a moment as the waitress appeared with the pizzas they'd ordered earlier. They shared, each of them having a little of each other's choice so they could try out the different kinds. Everything was good, although he supposed they should have maybe gotten a different entree.

"Next time we go out for dinner, I'll try to take you someplace that's not pizza," he joked, remembering their meal at California Pizza Kitchen in Las Vegas the evening before.

However, she looked at him seriously, brows drawing together in the sort of frown that made him realize he'd completely blown it. "Oh...are you planning to take me out to dinner again?" she asked.

For a moment, he could only stare back at her and wonder how to respond without completely sticking his foot in it. Then her mouth quirked, and he realized she was teasing him.

"You've got way too good a deadpan face, Addie," he said, and the twitch at the corner of her mouth turned into an actual grin.

"I suppose that comes from years of dodging gropers at the restaurants where I worked," she replied, then picked up her slice of Greek pizza and took another bite. "You never want to let them see that they got to you, you know?"

No, he didn't know, because although he'd had odd jobs working for various Wilcox-owned businesses while he was in high school and college, he'd never waited tables. And even if he had, he doubted anyone would have tried to grab his ass.

"I'm surprised you didn't drop a tornado on their heads," he told her, and her grin abruptly faded.

"Thank God I didn't," she said quietly. "I don't always know what'll set me off. But I guess simple irritation isn't major enough to set the wheels in motion."

Good to know, he thought, although he only said, "Well, you won't have to worry about 'gropers' ever again. As for the rest...." He paused for a moment, told himself to be brave, and then went on, "I'd like to have dinner with you again, if that's what you meant."

Her fingers tightened on her wine glass, but she affected a shrug as she said, "Are you asking me out on a date, Jake?"

"I don't think we need to be that official, do you?" he responded, doing his best to keep his tone light. Even so, he wanted to give himself a mental kick. This was way too soon. What the hell was he thinking? He was totally out of practice with this sort of thing, especially since a rough mental calculation told him it had been almost seven years since he'd asked anyone out on a date.

"No," Addie said after a long pause. "Let's be extremely *unofficial.*" Her gaze met his, level, not flirtatious at all. Still, he thought he could see a certain warmth in her eyes, and guessed that the invitation hadn't been as unwelcome as he'd feared. But was it true interest on her part, or only a way to distract herself from the grief she carried within her?

He supposed he'd find out soon enough. "Sounds like a plan."

They went on with their meal after that, the discussion moving to light topics such as the places he'd like to show her in Flagstaff, and Jake hoped he hadn't done anything to upset the delicate trust she'd begun to have in him. But it would be dishonest to hide his interest, wouldn't it? Anyway, if she'd shot him down, he would have accepted that she didn't share the attraction, and gone on with his life.

As it was...well, he supposed he'd just have to wait and see whether this was a good thing, or whether he'd thrown an unwelcome wrinkle into both their lives.

Hotel rooms were plentiful in Las Vegas. Randall Lenz checked into Mandalay Bay, figuring it was as good a choice as anything else, then got out his laptop and attached his secure phone to it. A moment later, Agent Dawson's face appeared on the screen. She looked both tired and cross, and he recalled that it was well past seven on the East Coast. Not that it really mattered; normal work hours were the exception at their agency, not the rule.

"Anything?" he asked, not bothering with a greeting.

Dawson tucked a stray strand of mousy hair behind one ear. "I don't know."

"You 'don't know'?" he repeated. He scowled

at the screen. "Either you found something or you didn't. Which is it?"

"I did get an image of a black Jeep Gladiator on an I-15 traffic cam passing the Cheyenne Avenue exit at approximately fifteen-thirty local time. However, when I attempted to continue tracking the vehicle at the next camera, the images were scrambled again, just as they'd been in Kanab."

Interesting. Lenz ran a hand over his chin, absently feeling the stubble there. He'd been so out of sorts that morning, he hadn't even bothered to shave. Not that it probably mattered, but he still felt annoyed with himself for being so sloppy. Normally, he would never have slipped up in such a way. He needed to make sure it never happened again.

"Where's the scrambling coming from?"

Dawson's thin shoulders lifted slightly. "I can't tell for sure. Our analysts aren't finding any obvious intrusions into the traffic-cam systems, so if it's deliberate, whoever's doing it is damn good at hiding their tracks. But we haven't given up."

"Don't. Keep trying. Whoever is doing it has to be leaving some kind of trace behind."

"Yes, sir." A pause, and then she asked, "Any idea how long you're going to be in Las Vegas?"

"As long as it takes, Dawson. Keep me posted if there are any updates."

"Yes, sir."

He closed the laptop then, severing the connection. A scowl creased his forehead as he went to the window and stared out at the city, glittering in the bright afternoon sunlight. Somewhere down there, Adara Grant and the mysterious "Jake" had hidden themselves...if they hadn't already left town. It was entirely possible that they'd only spent one night there, or had merely stopped for food before pushing on to... well, wherever it was that happened to be their destination.

For just a moment, he wondered if he'd been too hasty about destroying Adara's Kanab home. Possibly, this Jake person might have left a fingerprint on the door, or on the jamb. But no, he'd only knocked and hadn't touched anything else. Even if he had, there was a good chance he wouldn't have left a clear print anyway. Besides, fingerprints were far from a sure thing. They only existed in a database if someone had had a reason to get fingerprinted in the past, whether to get bonded, obtain a teaching credential, or get some kind of clearance...or possibly because they'd been arrested at some point. As much as Randall Lenz would have liked to think that Jake had some kind of a criminal record, he didn't seem to be the type. His clothing was plain but good quality, and he definitely didn't look like a user. His vehicle was new, and expensive.

That vehicle....

Not bothering with the laptop, he picked up his phone and sent Dawson a quick text. *Cross-reference any sales of black Jeep Gladiators over the past year with men whose first names are Jake or Jacob*, he typed. A few seconds later, her reply showed on the screen.

Working.

That seemed to be about all he could do for the moment.

Well, except one thing.

Resolute, he dug the electric shaver out of his duffle and went into the bathroom to get cleaned up. It might be a waste of his time to start inquiring about Adara and Jake when there were literally hundreds of different hotels where they could have stayed, but Lenz figured he might as well give it a try.

After all, what else did he have to do with his time?

11

I DIDN'T REALLY KNOW WHAT TO SAY TO JAKE ON the drive back to Flagstaff, so I decided to remain quiet, acting as though I was exhausted by the trip, my head leaned against the back of my seat and my eyes shut.

Actually, it wasn't much of an act. The day had turned out to be a very long one.

And yet, with all of the things that had happened during that day—meeting my brother and his family, learning that I would soon be a millionaire, discovering that I'd somehow managed to escape the curse that had haunted the Wilcoxes for more than a hundred years— one detail in particular kept preying on my mind.

Jake had asked me out on a date.

Okay, it was probably one of the most sideways invitations ever offered, but still. He hadn't seemed put off by my non-answer, had taken my comment at face value. A non-answer had been about all I could give him, simply because I wasn't sure how I was supposed to react. I could lie to myself and say I wasn't attracted to him, but what would be the point? He was definitely the handsomest man I'd ever seen in my life...and kind and tough and resourceful as well. Who *wouldn't* want someone like that asking them out?

Well, someone who'd just lost her mother, who'd just discovered she was far more than she'd ever believed, who'd learned she had a huge extended family just waiting to take her under their wing and make sure she survived this transition into her new life. With all that on my plate, I'd be crazy to even contemplate attempting a relationship.

And yet....

This was all impossible. I tried to tell myself that I hadn't committed to anything except another dinner at some hazy point in the future, but since I hadn't turned Jake down outright, he knew I was receptive, even in my current muddled state.

Sigh.

Eventually, we emerged from winding Oak

Creek Canyon and into what looked like a vast, black forest. The highway continued without interruption, and though far ahead I glimpsed the taillights of another vehicle, it nonetheless felt empty and frightening, the darkness swirling all around us. There hadn't been any sign of pursuit, not even a hint that Agent Lenz had figured out where we'd gone, but a chill still began to inch its way down my spine as I wondered if a series of black, unmarked vehicles were going to burst forth from one of the service roads that fed into the highway, or whether a black helicopter would swoop down from above and somehow scoop me up from Jake's truck.

Silly fancies, I knew, but I couldn't quite shake the feeling of foreboding, of unfriendly eyes following our progress. Only when the frontage road we'd been driving on gave way to obvious signs of suburbia—gas stations, a Walmart, a Coco's—did I finally allow myself to relax slightly. The chances of being snatched up when surrounded by people and streetlights seemed much lower.

About five minutes later, Jake turned off the main road and into the older neighborhood where his house and the cottage were located. He pulled up into the driveway of the cottage and said, "I'll walk you to the front door."

I didn't bother to protest. Maybe my silence signaled to him that I wanted to prolong our time together, but in reality, what I really wanted was to postpone the moment when I would be left alone in the cottage. It might have been perfectly safe, but for whatever reason, knowing that Jake was only two doors down wasn't enough reassurance to keep me from imagining a terrible series of worst-case scenarios.

We walked up to the front door. I hadn't left the porch light on, but he only had to look at it and it flared to life, illuminating the area—which of course was completely empty except for the same flowerpots of geraniums that had been there when we left.

"Go on," he said, and I realized he was encouraging me to use my powers on the door lock.

Even though I'd performed the same feat earlier that day, I still couldn't prevent myself from feeling a tingle of apprehension as I reached for the handle. However, my anxiety was completely unfounded, since I heard the tumblers inside click as soon as I laid my fingers on the cool metal.

"You see?" His smile seemed almost blinding in the illumination from the porch light, although that could simply have been my eyes trying to adjust to the change. "Nothing to it."

"I suppose not."

Jake pushed the door open and went inside, and I had no choice but to follow him. The lights inside flared on as well, showing that the cottage was empty, just as we had left it.

Mounted on the wall next to the door was a flat little box I hadn't even noticed before, clearly the control panel for an alarm system.

"You can arm this after I leave," he said. "It's really simple—just enter '9382' and press 'stay.' Then, if anyone tries to open a door or a window, or trips one of the motion sensors on either the front or back porch, the alarm will go off."

I supposed he thought that having an alarm system would make me feel better about being alone in the house overnight. However, as I stared at the panel, I couldn't quite prevent the little shiver that inched its way down my spine.

"Is the neighborhood not safe?" I asked.

The faintest of frowns, and then he shook his head. "No, it's totally safe. You honestly have nothing to worry about here. The alarm system is more for peace of mind than anything else."

"Oh."

That was all I said, but the single syllable was enough to deepen his frown, to make him stare down into my face. I wished I could look away; being scrutinized like that was never fun, especially when the person doing it to you was the man you'd recently realized you were extremely attracted to. However, tearing my eyes from his seemed worse than trying to look back at him as innocently as possible, and so I stood my ground.

"You don't want to be here by yourself."

It wasn't a question.

"I'm sure it's safe," I said, knowing I had to give him some sort of reply. "But...."

A long pause. He hooked his thumbs in the pockets of his jeans and rocked back on his heels slightly, clearly trying to figure out what he should do next. When he spoke, his words surprised me, since I'd just expected him to convince me that I was being silly for not wanting to stay in the sanctuary he and his team had prepared.

"Then bring your stuff over to my place," he said. "I have a bunch of extra bedrooms."

"You're sure?" I asked, relieved and apprehensive at the same time. While I knew I would feel much better not being on my own, sleeping at Jake's house came with its own particular set of problems.

They're only problems if you turn them into problems, I scolded myself. *You slept in the same hotel room with him last night and didn't turn it into a big drama.*

True, except the night before, I'd still been shell-shocked by everything that had happened in Kanab and had no idea I would find myself attracted to my rescuer...or however I thought of him. Oh, maybe in the depths of my distress, I'd still noticed how gorgeous he was, but I would have put aside the thought as entirely inappropriate. It was probably inappropriate now as well, although I'd given up on trying to ignore how much better I felt when Jake Wilcox was around.

His posture relaxed slightly, as though he was glad he'd gotten past the worst of our awkward moment and just wanted to make sure I was okay with the arrangement. "I wouldn't have offered if I wasn't okay with it," he told me. "Like I said, I've got lots of extra rooms. One of them even has a bed—Jeremy crashed there for a few weeks about a year ago when the townhouse he bought was being renovated. It's fine."

This all sounded refreshingly normal, like the sort of thing any guy would do for his little brother—at least in a family where everyone got along. I wondered irrelevantly when I'd get to meet Jeremy, then decided I had bigger fish to fry at the moment. "Okay," I said, not bothering to keep the relief out of my voice. "Just let me get my things together."

"Take as long as you need."

If he was irritated with me for so cavalierly blowing off the house he'd carefully put together for his "strays," he didn't show it. He just went over to the couch and sat down, clearly prepared to wait for however long it would require for me to pack my things.

Since my "things" consisted of the items I'd purchased in Las Vegas and nothing else, that particular task didn't take me very long. In about two minutes, I was back out in the living room. "Ready."

Jake smiled. "Okay."

It seemed silly to drive when we were only going two doors down, but since he'd parked in the driveway at the cottage, of course he'd want to move his Jeep to where it belonged. The garage sat at the end of a long driveway, and appeared to be some distance from the back door. Thinking of Flagstaff's harsh winters, I didn't feel like that was the best setup in the world, but then I realized cars hadn't even been a thing when the house was first built, and so the garage was obviously a later addition.

But it was June now, and the first snows of winter seemed a long way off. I followed Jake out of the garage and along a walkway that led to the back porch, and from there we went inside the kitchen.

I tried not to stare. Oh, it wasn't that the kitchen was all that big—I could tell the space probably retained its original proportions and layout—but everything had been impeccably updated, from the granite counters to the leaded glass on the upper cabinets and the friendly washed antique blue of the woodwork. The floor was wood, and creaked faintly.

Jake apparently didn't notice my reaction to the kitchen, because he breezed on through the space and led me down the hallway to the stairs, which had a carved mahogany balustrade. I caught glimpses of the dining room and what had probably once been the parlor and was now the living room, all with the original woodwork intact, although the walls had been painted in warm shades of brick and dark green and deep parchment rather than papered the way they'd probably been when the house was first built, and the furniture itself was relaxed and contemporary rather than fussy Victorian antiques.

"Up here," he said, and I followed him to the second floor, which had another long hallway bisecting the area, with three doors on the left and four on the right. "You can take the first bedroom," he added as he opened the door. "Sorry I haven't done much with it, but Jeremy said the mattress is comfortable."

Jake wasn't being modest; the space he'd indicated definitely wasn't as "done" as the downstairs. Yes, the same warm woodwork framed the doors and windows, and there was crown molding around the ceiling, but the walls were plain off-white and the furniture consisted of a queen-size bed with a black iron headboard, a simple bedside table with a glass-shaded lamp sitting on it, and a highboy that matched the table over in one corner.

Simple as it was, I felt immediately better knowing I'd be sleeping in that room with a warlock just down the hall, rather than in the cottage by myself...even if that cottage was guarded by an alarm system. "It looks great," I said. "Thanks."

"Not a problem. Bathroom is two doors down the hall." A pause, and then he added, "And I'm just across the hall in the front bedroom, so if you feel hinky about anything...."

The words trailed off, but I knew what he was trying to say. He wanted me to know he was right there, just in case I was seized by night terrors or needed to know reinforcements were close by.

"I'll be fine," I said.

"Okay." Looking a little uncomfortable, he went on, "I suppose I should have thought of this sooner. I mean, the cottage is probably fine under most circumstances, but after what happened with your mother...."

Again, his words faded away, as though he'd realized that maybe completing the thought wasn't the best idea. But I understood. While he'd imagined shepherding his lost witches and warlocks to sanctuary in the cottage he and his team had prepared for that very task, he probably had never imagined any of them losing a parent to an unexpected attack by a rogue federal agent.

If Agent Lenz was a rogue at all. Far more likely was the reality that his actions had been sanctioned by someone a lot higher up the food chain, a person or persons who had decided human life wasn't that important when measured against any advantages the government might gain by having supernaturally powered humans working for them.

"I'd rather not be alone," I said quietly.

For a moment, Jake didn't respond. I got the feeling that he wanted to reach out and give me a hug, or at the very least, touch my hand to let me know he was there for me, but wasn't sure how I would react to such a gesture.

I could understand his diffidence. To be honest, I didn't even know how I would react to that kind of an advance. It would have been way too easy to let him take me in his arms and have him hold me while I cried. Because those damn tears were stinging my eyes again, and I knew it wouldn't take much to make me break down again.

However, I didn't want him to come to me out of pity. Compassion and kindness, sure, but it was probably better to just put a cap on the evening and see what the next day would bring.

Maybe he got some of my vibe, or maybe he'd come to the same conclusion on his own. Either way, he said simply, "Good night, Addie," and then went across the hall to his own room and quietly closed the door behind him.

I stood in the bedroom for a moment, wondering if I'd just made a colossal mistake. But there wasn't much I could do about it at that point.

"Good night, Jake," I whispered, and shut the door to my borrowed room.

Strangely, I felt much better when I woke up the next morning. Maybe it was only that I could tell the day was a bright and sunny one out past the wooden blinds that darkened the room, or maybe it was the realization that I'd gotten a solid eight hours of sleep with no interruptions, no federal agents breaking in, no storms brought to life by uneasy dreams.

From downstairs came a faint *clank* as Jake put a kettle on the stove or performed some other early morning task in the kitchen. The thought of coffee was appealing, but I really wanted a shower first. The day before, I hadn't washed my hair, since we'd been focused on getting out of Las Vegas as quickly as we could, and it was time to get myself really clean.

Like the kitchen, the upstairs guest bath had been fully modernized, and had a large glass-enclosed shower with granite tile and a big adjustable shower head with massaging jets. It felt delicious to let the hot water knead my scalp, to use the shampoo and conditioner and soap I'd bought at Walgreens to wash away some of the residue of the last two days. I could still feel the hurt lurking inside, but that morning I felt a little better equipped to handle it, as though the extra night's sleep had done something to replenish a store of strength I hadn't even realized had been so terribly depleted.

I hadn't bought a blow dryer, and there wasn't

one under the sink, so about all I could do was comb out my wet hair and be glad that it was straight and silky and generally looked acceptable even when air-dried. Probably no point in brushing my teeth if I was just going to have coffee once I got downstairs, but I went ahead and put on a little lip gloss and some mascara, telling myself I might as well make that tiny bit of effort.

When I got to the kitchen, I saw Jake leaning against the granite counter, his own hair looking slightly damp and a dark scruff covering his chin. He also appeared far more rested—and so gorgeous that I had to actively keep myself from staring.

"Coffee smells good," I said, desperate for any kind of comment that would break the tension I could already feel building between us.

"I'll pour you a cup," he replied, then set down the mug he'd been holding and went over to the cupboard to fetch one for me. He filled it up from the fancy stainless machine that sat on the counter across from the stove, and came over and handed it to me. "Milk or sugar?"

"Both."

"Milk's in the fridge, and there's some sugar in that red bowl on the counter."

Obviously, Jake didn't see the need to play

barista for me. Or maybe he'd decided it would look weird if he tried to wait on me hand and foot. I wasn't going to complain, only thanked him and went to the fridge, where there was a quart of milk sitting on one of the door shelves. After pouring some in my coffee, I took the mug over to the sugar bowl and put in a teaspoon, and stirred it well.

One sip told me the man knew how to make coffee. I looked up from taking a second swallow and saw him watching me.

"Better?" he asked.

"Much. Thanks."

A nod. I got the feeling he was being deliberately casual because I'd been sending out mixed signals and he wasn't quite sure how to react. Well, I couldn't really blame him. I honestly didn't know what I was doing, either, other than trying to survive from one day to the next.

We drank coffee in companionable silence for a few moments. Then he said, "Laurel is going to come over in a little bit and take you shopping. I figured you'd have more fun doing that with her than you would with me."

I wasn't entirely sure about that—I'd been hoping to spend more time with Jake—but on the other hand, it would definitely be less embarrassing to shop for more underwear without him tagging along. I made a noncommittal sound, and he went on,

"And after you're done with that, you can come over to Wheeler Park to see the setup."

"'Wheeler Park'?" I repeated, not sure what a park had to do with his witch-finding efforts.

He grinned. "Our 'headquarters' are located across the street from Wheeler Park. It's just a few blocks from here. I walk there sometimes, if I don't have someplace else I need to go after I'm done for the day. Anyway, I figured you'd want to meet Jeremy and see something of the operation."

Since I'd been wondering about Jeremy, I thought that sounded like a good plan. "Sure," I said.

"I don't do much for breakfast," Jake added. "But I've got some bagels in the freezer, if that works for you."

In general, I wasn't a huge breakfast person, either, so bagels sounded fine by me. I nodded, and he went ahead and got out a couple, defrosted them in the microwave, and then put them in the toaster oven to get crispy. Once we were done eating, I went back upstairs to brush my teeth and replace my lip gloss, and by the time I was done, it was almost ten o'clock and someone was ringing the doorbell.

That someone turned out to be Laurel, looking just as cheerful that morning as she had the day before when I'd first met her. Because it was a warm, sunny day, she wore cropped jeans, a sleeveless top in a fresh, bright green, and flip-flops.

"Hey," she said as she came into the living room, apparently unfazed to find me at Jake's house rather than at the cottage that was supposed to be my crash space. I guessed that he must have called her to tell her to pick me up at his place, but still, I was a little surprised to see she wasn't at all disappointed that I hadn't taken advantage of the house they'd all worked so hard on.

She was carrying a pretty flowered reusable shopping bag, and set it down on the coffee table with a slight *thunk*.

"I have all the stuff," she said, although I had the feeling those words were directed more at Jake, who stood over by the fireplace, than at me.

"Any problems?" he asked.

"Nope. You know how good Jasper is at all this stuff."

I wondered who "Jasper" was. Another of an apparently inexhaustible supply of Wilcoxes, I supposed.

Laurel reached into the bag and pulled out a

brand-new iPhone still in its box, and handed it to me. "Merry Christmas."

"For me?" I said stupidly, even though of course the phone had to be mine. Still, I wasn't used to people giving me thousand-dollar phones as casually as handing over a stick of gum.

"Who else?" she replied with a grin. Next out of the bag was a slim red leather wallet. This time, I took it from her without question... although questions bubbled to my lips as soon as I opened it to see the I.D. inside, as well as a brand-new Social Security card tucked behind it.

I had no idea where they'd gotten the photo, but that was definitely me on the shiny new Arizona driver's license. Except....

"Adara Wilcox?" I asked, seeing that name on both the license and the Social Security card.

Jake and Laurel exchanged a glance.

After an uncomfortable pause, Jake said, "We didn't want to take your name away completely, but we also didn't want to send up any red flags by having 'Adara Grant' pop up in Flagstaff. So, we compromised."

I wasn't sure what to say. On the one hand, I understood why Jake wouldn't want to use my real name, especially if I started opening up bank accounts and renting or buying a home. On the other hand, seeing that I was no longer officially Adara Grant made me feel adrift again, as though I didn't really know who or what I was, just someone getting pushed and pulled by every change in the tide.

"And the address?" I said, figuring I'd better shift the topic to something a little less fraught.

"A mail drop," Laurel supplied. "We can update it once you have a permanent residence, but that seemed the easiest thing for now."

It was on my lips to ask how this "Jasper" had managed to manufacture what looked like a completely authentic driver's license and Social Security card, but I realized I was dealing with a clan of powerful witches, and there probably weren't a lot of things they couldn't do if sufficiently motivated. Instead, I forced a smile and said, "Thanks—this makes me feel a little more real."

Laurel's eyes crinkled at the corners. "Keep looking—I think you'll find even more to make you feel 'real'...so to speak."

Mystified, I glanced back down at the wallet. I'd been so preoccupied with the I.D., I hadn't even noticed that the section for storing bills was full of twenties. What the...?

"Just a little something to get you started," Jake said. "Now that you have your I.D., we'll get a bank account set up so Connor can start transferring funds to you, but in the meantime, you have something to go shopping with."

I honestly wasn't sure what to do about such generosity. And all right, maybe none of this had come out of Jake's or Laurel's bank account, had come from some kind of Wilcox clan slush fund or something, but still, I hadn't expected to be showered with money like that. What was in that wallet looked like more than I would have made in a month.

But my instincts were telling me it would be better to smile and accept the money, rather than protest they were being too generous. Although Connor hadn't made any remarks to that effect, I had the uneasy feeling I was being given special consideration because I was the daughter of a former *primus,* rather than your run-of-the-mill long-lost Wilcox.

"Thank you," I said, doing my best to look pleased by their largesse instead of uncomfortable at the thought that this might only be the start of the attention I could expect as Jackson Wilcox's child.

"Well, enough business," Laurel announced. She rubbed her hands together, looking delighted at the prospect of causing some serious retail havoc. "We girls have to get shopping. Do you want us to get some takeout from Taverna after we're done? We can bring it by Trident and all have a late lunch together."

"Works for me," Jake replied, even as I sent both of them an inquiring glance.

"Trident?"

"That's what we call the operation," he explained. "Trident Enterprises. If anyone asks, we're an IT consulting business—Jeremy can field any questions along those lines that might come our way, but so far, no one's really made any inquiries."

Convenient for Jake & Co., I supposed. But then, these days most people seemed inclined to stay out of each other's business. Most of our neighbors, no matter where my mother and I had landed, were only concerned that we weren't loud and didn't leave vehicles parked all over the place, and had kept the personal questions to a minimum.

But thinking about my mother only saddened me, and I pushed the thought away. It wasn't that I wanted to forget her, only that I knew I needed to focus on other matters at the moment.

"Ah, got it," I said, praying that my tone wouldn't give away what I'd actually been thinking. I picked up the wallet with the I.D. Laurel had provided, and the new iPhone as well—and hoped she would be able to show me how to work it, since all I'd ever had was my mother's hand-me-down Android phones. Summoning a smile, I added, "Let's go shopping."

12

ALL SEEMED QUIET ENOUGH IN THE MODEST TWO-story home across the street from Wheeler Park. Jake pulled into the driveway, noting that Jeremy's silver Dodge Ram truck was already parked there. Well, no real surprise; it might have been a Sunday, but Jeremy wasn't the type to take the day off. Actually, if it weren't that he'd helped his younger brother move into his townhouse not too long ago, he might have wondered whether Jeremy had started living in the Trident headquarters full-time.

Since it was just about a picture-perfect day, the sun warm but the breeze mild—one of the reasons why so many people from the Phoenix area flocked to Flagstaff in the summer to get away from the Valley's brutal triple-digit temperatures—the windows were open, letting in abundant fresh air. Jake found Jeremy in the PC center, fingers flying on a keyboard as lines of code flowed over the screen before him. Long ago, he'd stopped trying to make any sense of the sort of magic that allowed his brother to bend that code to his will, although he still couldn't quite prevent himself from staring at the endless stream of numbers and letters and symbols.

"What're you working on today?" Jake asked as he sat down on one of the spare office chairs.

"Hacking more cameras," his brother replied, not looking away from the screen. "It looks like Inspector Javert is doing his best to keep up with you, but I've thrown a monkey in his wrench."

Jake had the feeling he should have recognized the reference, but his memory appeared to be failing him right then. "Who?"

Jeremy paused long enough to throw a half-contemptuous glance over his shoulder. "Javert. From *Les Misèrables.* You know, the police inspector who keeps chasing the bread-stealing hero for years and years."

Right. Jake ran a hand through his hair and frowned slightly. "Well, let's hope our guy isn't quite that persistent."

"Seems like he is, but then, it's only been a

couple of days. He did manage to follow you to Vegas, actually."

Shit. "Wasn't the whole point of scrambling the satellites and the traffic cameras in Kanab to keep him from ID'ing my vehicle?"

Jake's tone had been faintly accusatory, but Jeremy appeared not to notice, instead giving a shrug that didn't look terribly concerned. "Yes, but if he saw your truck, then he wouldn't have that hard a time following you. I told you that thing was way too flashy."

Which it was, but Jake had test-driven the Gladiator and fallen in love, and that was the end of the story. Still, he probably should have rented a car for this particular adventure. Something boring and completely inconspicuous, like a silver Toyota Camry or a beige Hyundai Sonata. At the time, though, he'd been in a hurry, and also, he'd held the thought in the back of his mind that there was a good chance the Gladiator's not-insignificant off-road abilities might come in handy if he needed to leave the highway to shake off any pursuit. But at this point, the damage was done.

Rather than directly respond to his brother's comment, Jake said, "So, what's Agent Lenz up to now?"

"Not much, as far as I can tell." Jeremy finally

pushed away from the computer slightly, swiveling his office chair so he could face Jake. "That is, he checked into Mandalay Bay and went back out about a half hour later. Looks to me like he's going from hotel to hotel, making inquiries."

Which seemed to indicate that even if he'd made it to Vegas, he didn't possess enough information to know where his quarry had gone next. "Any pattern to his movements?"

"Well, Mandalay Bay is the southernmost of the big hotels along the Strip. As far as I can tell, he's moving slowly north. He's gone to Luxor and Excalibur so far."

Jake released a slow breath of relief. If Jeremy's observations were correct—and there was no reason to think they weren't—then it would take Agent Lenz a while to reach Treasure Island, which was near the top of the Strip. And if he made detours along the way, going to some of the smaller hotels, then his task would take even longer. With any luck, a day or so might pass before he finally got to the hotel where Jake and Adara had stayed.

"I used cash," he said, but Jeremy only lifted his shoulders again.

"Which helps, of course, but if he has a picture of Addie to show the clerks, someone might remember her."

Yes, she was memorable. Or maybe not. Jake wasn't going to deny he found her beautiful, with that fall of dark hair surrounding her graceful oval face, those amazing gray-green eyes with their heavy fringe of black lashes. But lots of beautiful women went to Las Vegas, most of whom dressed much flashier and were more likely to attract attention. Also, Addie had stayed behind him as he checked into the hotel, not directly approaching the clerk. There was a chance that no one had really noticed her.

A slim hope, but better than nothing.

"He doesn't have a picture of me, though," Jake said. "He doesn't even know my last name."

"You *think* he doesn't know that," Jeremy said darkly. "Or have a picture of you. The dude's a government agent, Jake. He has access to all kinds of resources."

"He doesn't have you, though."

The sideways compliment didn't even seem to register. Or maybe Jeremy had simply brushed it aside. He never seemed to care much about receiving praise for his work, possibly because he knew a lot of it was due to his singular magical ability, something he'd been born with rather than achieved through hard work or sheer skull sweat.

"He might have his own version of me,

though," Jeremy remarked. "And whoever he works for, it's severely locked down. I haven't been able to dig up anything about him except that he works for Homeland Security and has been employed by the federal government since 2005." His expression brightened slightly, and he added, "Oh, and he owns a house in Alexandria, Virginia. Those records are pretty easy to find."

Good for Agent Lenz. Jake wished the bastard was back in Alexandria, drinking a beer in his backyard on this fine Sunday rather than sniffing around Las Vegas, doing his best to find out where his prey had gone to ground.

"What are the chances he'll be able to track us to Flagstaff?"

Jeremy scratched his chin. Like Jake, he hadn't bothered to shave that day and was looking kind of scruffy. "Maybe fifty-fifty. I assume you didn't give the hotel a real address."

"No," Jake replied. "I'm not that stupid. I gave a fake name and a fake address in Southern California."

"A real fake address, or a fake-fake address?"

"It's a real address," Jake said, a note of irritation creeping into his voice. "But not a house. It's a grocery store in Rancho Cucamonga."

Jeremy looked almost amused by that reply. "How did you come up with that one?"

"I looked it up on my phone. I knew I'd need something to throw them off the scent but obviously didn't want to give the address of a private residence."

"Rancho Cucamonga, though?"

"I liked the name."

That response made his brother's mouth twitch, but he didn't comment on the reply, only said, "Well, the fake address should put him off for a while, I suppose. But we also need to be prepared if he does make it to Flagstaff."

"Connor's already one step ahead of you. He's put the word out. If Agent Lenz shows up here, he's going to discover he's bitten off a whole lot more than he can chew."

The words weren't simply bravado. Maybe the Wilcoxes were a kinder, gentler clan with Connor in charge, but they still weren't soft by any stretch of the imagination. There was plenty of open land around town, land where a person could disappear and never be found again. Jake knew this for a fact because it was common knowledge that their ancestors had disposed of more than a few enemies in that very same way. Something to be proud of? Probably not; there had been times when he'd winced inwardly at his clan's black reputation with the other witch families. But even though they'd cleaned up their act in recent years, that didn't mean they didn't know how to make sure troublemakers quietly vanished.

Even knowing that the Wilcoxes could handle pretty much anything thrown at them didn't allay all of Jake's fears, however. Making an ordinary person disappear was one thing. But if Agent Lenz vanished in his pursuit of Addie Grant, well, there would probably be a lot of interested parties determined to discover what had happened to him. They might shine a spotlight on Flagstaff, which was the last thing the Wilcoxes—or any of the Arizona witch clans, for that matter—wanted to happen.

Well, no point in borrowing trouble. Either Agent Lenz would never make the connection between Adara Grant and Flagstaff, Arizona...or he would. And if he did, the Wilcoxes would be waiting for him.

Agent Lenz didn't know what he disliked the most about Las Vegas—the insufferable heat, the unending traffic, the throngs of tourists that crowded every place he went, or the neon lights that flashed day and night, searing his corneas.

Actually, it was probably a combination of all

those factors, plus a couple more he hadn't yet thought of.

He sat in his hotel room at the Mandalay Bay, scowling at the club sandwich room service had brought up for him and wondering if he should have ordered something a little more substantial. It was now after nine o'clock at night, and he'd finally given up after visiting ten casinos and a few more of the smaller hotels in the southern part of the Strip. No one had seen Adara Grant or her companion, and the traffic cam footage that hadn't been corrupted hadn't shown a single black Jeep Gladiator.

Which made all this feel like an exercise in futility.

The only bright spot was the report Agent Dawson had sent over before going home for the evening. It was a list of all the Jeep Gladiators sold to men named Jake or Jacob in the United States since the beginning of the year. Since the vehicle was new and hadn't yet begun to roll out in huge numbers, the list wasn't very long, just forty-seven individuals in all.

For the time being, Lenz figured it was safe to focus on those individuals in the western half of the United States. He supposed it was possible that Jake had traveled from the East Coast to "rescue" Adara Grant, but he thought it far more likely that he hadn't driven nearly so far, had come from California or Arizona or possibly Utah itself. How he'd known to show up on her doorstep was an entirely different conundrum, but Lenz decided to leave that question aside for the moment. Where Jake had come from was far more important than why he'd done what he'd done.

He picked up his club sandwich and took a bite as he perused the list. As he did so, he waited for the prickle of intuition that would tell him if any of these felt like a likely candidate.

Jacob Andrews, Elko, Nevada.

Jake Ortega, Mesa, Arizona.

Jake Reynolds, Rancho Cucamonga, California.

Jake Wilcox, Flagstaff, Arizona.

Jacob Day, Fresno, California.

Jake Giles, San Diego, California.

Jacob Delray, Anaheim, California.

The names started to glaze in front of his eyes, and Lenz set down the phone and rubbed his forehead for a moment. None of them seemed any likelier than the others, and he scowled. So much for his intuition.

Well, the next thing to do would be to have Agent Dawson scour the records of the dealerships where the vehicles in question had been purchased and pull up the relevant paperwork. Those files would include scans of the driver's licenses of the men who'd bought those Jeep Gladiators, and that way, he should be able to make a positive visual I.D. of the particular Jake he was looking for. He probably should have asked for that information from the outset, except he'd known it would be more time-consuming, and he'd hoped he'd be able to locate his quarry with some good old-fashioned legwork.

That didn't seem to be the case here, though. As he'd worried previously, there was always the chance that Adara and Jake hadn't come through Las Vegas at all, or, if they had, only stopped there for food and gas before continuing to... wherever it was they were headed.

He glanced at the time on his phone. Almost ten o'clock, meaning it was nearly 1 a.m. in D.C. Agent Dawson would be long gone. Of course, the agency had people working around the clock, but Agent LaRue, the man who worked as Dawson's replacement during the overnight hours, was neither as meticulous nor as quick.

Still, he could at least get started. With any luck, he would have the records in question collated and ready for perusal by the time Lenz was up and ready to go the next morning. Much as he hated to admit it, he knew the couple he sought were probably already long gone. Might as well keep working steadily in the hope that he'd catch up to them when the time was right.

Because, as his father had often told him, slow and steady won the race.

13

EVEN A GOOD THREE HOURS OF SHOPPING DIDN'T make a huge dent in the wad of cash the Wilcox clan had given me, mostly because I'd spent my whole life shopping the sale racks and didn't see any need to change that behavior just because my fortunes had shifted. Still, after hitting the Dillard's and the JC Penney at the mall, and the Kohl's on the opposite side of town closer to the college, I had enough new clothes to see me through a week, along with shoes and sandals and a purse to store the wallet and iPhone Laurel had provided. By the time we were done, I was starving, and all too glad to stop at the Greek restaurant in Woodland Village by the Kohl's and load up on Mediterranean takeout.

Laurel drove me to a neighborhood about five

minutes away from the restaurant, closer to Flagstaff's downtown. There, she pulled up in front of a cute two-story clapboard house that fronted on a park. I spotted Jake's big Jeep Gladiator in the driveway and said, "Trident Enterprises?"

"You got it," Laurel replied. "Let's just leave your stuff in the trunk—you can transfer it to Jake's truck whenever you guys are done here."

"Okay," I said, and unbuckled my seatbelt. I was a little unnerved by the way she just seemed to assume I would be doing everything with Jake, but then again, he was sort of my guide and mentor. Who else was going to chauffeur me around until I was able to get my own car?

And actually, the thought of buying a car made me feel almost cheerful. I'd never had a car of my own—we just couldn't afford it. My mother and I had shared, and most of the time the arrangement worked out okay. Still, even though I wished I could change what had happened, could go back and prevent Agent Lenz from firing that fateful bullet, I couldn't help but be just the teeniest bit excited at the prospect of having my very own car.

I followed Laurel down the front walk and in through the door of Trident Enterprises, each of us carrying bags of takeout. As soon as we were inside, she called out, "Beware of geeks bearing gifts!"

Jake's head appeared in the entrance to the room beyond the front office. His expression was a little pained at his cousin's pun, but he smiled as soon as he caught sight of me. "Go ahead and take it back into the kitchen. We'll be there in a sec."

"Got it."

We went down a short hall into the kitchen, which had been nicely updated with white cabinets and quartz countertops, although I saw no sign of anyone ever preparing anything more elaborate in there than a cup of coffee. The space was big enough that there was a square table with four chairs off to one side; Laurel deposited the bags of food on the table, then went to the cupboard and got out some melamine plates.

"Grab some napkins from the holder over on the counter there, would you?" she asked, and I hurried over to the little antique bronze napkin holder and extracted four.

By the time we had the place settings out and the various food containers extracted from the bag, Jake and his brother Jeremy walked into the kitchen. At least, I assumed the guy with Jake was his younger brother—he looked to be around my age, and, like his brother, he had dark hair and eyes and was very good-looking, although his features were a little rounder, not quite as chiseled.

"Addie, this is Jeremy," Jake said, and Jeremy raised a hand in greeting but immediately took a seat at the table and reached for one of the bags.

"Nice manners, Jeremy," Laurel remarked, and he flashed her a white-toothed grin.

"I'm hungry. All this braining uses up a lot of calories."

"Sure," she shot back, but she didn't bother to chide him further, only sat down as well in the chair opposite his.

Which left Jake and me to take the two seats remaining. I settled in the chair across from him, and tried not to blush as his gaze met mine. The three of them were easy and relaxed around each other the way only people who'd known one another all their lives could be, and I felt more than ever like an outsider. Yes, I supposedly shared their blood, but would I ever feel as though I fit in here?

Honestly, I wasn't sure I'd ever fit in anywhere.

Either ignoring my awkwardness—or maybe not noticing it in the first place—Laurel popped open the containers of food, revealing plates of souvlaki, gyros, special french fries with feta and some sort of yummy mayo-based sauce, along with salad and a stack of pitas. We all fell to, silence reigning for a few minutes as we sated our hunger. Eventually, though, we slowed down enough to pick up the conversation.

"Looks like Agent Lenz is still stuck in Vegas," Jake remarked, and I paused with a forkful of salad halfway to my mouth.

"That's good, right?" I asked.

"For now," Jeremy said, ignoring the withering glance his brother sent him. "We can't really expect him to stay there for too long. If the guy was able to figure out that you went to Las Vegas, then sooner or later, he's probably going to follow the trail all the way here to Flagstaff."

The food I'd eaten suddenly felt like a big lump of glue in my stomach. "If that happens... what then?"

Jake smiled, looking as if he thought being tracked down by a murderous federal agent was no big deal. "We'll handle it."

"Handle it how?"

Laurel's eyes narrowed, but before she could say anything, Jake replied, "It'll be taken care of."

"What my brother is trying to so obliquely say," Jeremy remarked as he slid some souvlaki off a skewer, "is that Agent Lenz is going to find himself disappeared if he sets foot in Wilcox territory."

"'Disappeared'?" I echoed, pretty sure I could guess what he meant, even if I didn't want to believe such a thing. "You mean...?"

"Don't mind him," Laurel interposed. A small frown was pulling at her well-arched brows, although I couldn't tell whether she was troubled because she couldn't believe Jeremy had stated the situation so baldly...or because she knew that was exactly what would happen if Agent Lenz somehow showed up in town. "Nobody's getting disappeared."

"They're not?" I asked. I wanted to believe her, but even though I definitely didn't know much Wilcox family history, I already had the impression that some of my distant ancestors hadn't exactly been angels.

"No," she said firmly. Before either Jake or Jeremy could comment, she went on, "I'm not saying we won't take care of him. But that just means we'll scoop him up, mess with his memories a little, and then dump him someplace a hundred miles from here, like maybe back in Kanab."

That sounded like a much better solution to the problem. I let out a little breath of relief...

although that relief was short-lived, because, undeterred, Jeremy spoke up.

"That's only a temporary solution to the problem. You think a guy like that doesn't check in with his superiors and let them know where he's going and what he's doing?"

"Well, then," Laurel said sweetly, "I guess that's where you, Mr. Computer Hacker, have to step in and make sure any records of those notes and conversations are destroyed."

His mouth lifted at one corner as he gave her a skeptical glance, but I noticed he also looked almost pleased, as if he was glad that she apparently had enough trust in his abilities to believe he could pull off such a feat. I had to say, from what I'd heard, it didn't sound as though her confidence was misplaced. Any guy who could hack traffic cameras and scramble satellite surveillance footage obviously knew what he was doing.

"If it even comes to that," Jake said, his voice smooth and reassuring enough for a radio announcer. I got the impression that, as the oldest in this particular group, he tended to be the one who acted as peacemaker. "So far, there's no evidence to suggest he'll even make it to Flagstaff. For now, we have other things to focus on." His gaze met mine, and I found myself glancing back down at my plate, pretending to be fascinated by the bits of gyro and salad that rested there. "When we're done eating, Addie, you need to go meet Joanna."

"The weather-worker, right?" I asked, trying to sound casual. While I knew I needed to see Joanna and have her show me how to control my unwieldy "gift," somewhere inside me anxiety awoke, roiling up fears that she wouldn't be able to help me, either, that I'd lay waste to a large swath of Flagstaff before I fled the scene entirely.

"Right," he said with a smile. "She's very good at what she does, and I think she'll really be able to help you."

"I hope so," I replied.

"Me, too," Jeremy put in. "Because I'd hate to have a tornado rip up downtown just because you were having a bad day."

Jake's brown eyes might as well have been daggers, but his younger brother seemed completely unconcerned by the death glare that had just been shot in his direction. "Jeremy—"

"It's okay," I said. "I don't want to rip up downtown, either—the little bit I've seen of it is really cute. And I have to be really upset for that sort of thing to happen, so...." I let the words trail off, hoping Jeremy would get the hint.

Apparently, he did, because he leaned against

the back of his chair, mouth twitching. "Oh, don't worry. We're all going to be super-nice to you, aren't we, Laurel?"

She tilted an eyebrow at him. "Yeah, some of us don't have to work at it, dork."

Unperturbed, he dropped another mound of fries on his plate, picked one up, and took a bite. "I am the soul of charm, dear cousin."

That comment elicited a very unladylike snort. The sound was so incongruous coming from someone so pretty that I let out a snicker, and a moment later, we were all laughing. Maybe it was silly, but it also felt awfully good.

Just the day before, I hadn't been sure whether I'd ever laugh again.

Once lunch was over, Jake showed me the rest of "Trident Enterprises." I was definitely impressed by the operation they'd set up in that innocuous-looking house, and had to wonder how much money had been spent on all those fancy new computers—and the house itself, which still smelled of fresh paint. Clearly, they'd put a lot into modernizing the place and making sure it would be both a comfortable environment in which to work, not to mention adequate to their tech needs.

"But enough of that," Jake said after he brought me back downstairs—the upstairs bedrooms were being used for server space, storage, and a sort of flop area with a couple of twin beds, just in case someone wanted to crash there rather than go home for the night. "I need to get you over to Joanna's house."

"She lives here in Flagstaff, too, right?" I asked.

"Yes, but way on the east side, out past the mall. It's going to take about twenty minutes to get over there."

So I followed him out to his Jeep truck—we'd already transferred all my parcels from Laurel's little SUV—and we drove back along Route 66, past the old downtown section. It definitely looked fun, from the bit I could see, and I found myself wishing that was our destination.

Jake must have followed my gaze, because he said, "You want to go tonight?"

"Go where?"

"Downtown. There're some good restaurants, and places where there's live music."

I smiled despite myself. "For our not-date?"

"Exactly."

I thought I could deal with weather-working

lessons if I knew I was going to have a chance to explore Flagstaff's downtown with Jake Wilcox at my side. "Sure," I said, trying to sound casual.

"Great. I'll figure out what we're going to do while you're working with Joanna."

That comment made me look at him with some alarm. "You're not going to leave me there alone with her, are you?"

"No," he said, then grinned as he added, "It's too far for me to want to go back and forth. But I'll probably hang out in the house while you two work out back. Joanna's house is on a lot of land."

I had a hard time visualizing that sort of setup, mostly because what I'd seen of Flagstaff so far made me think it was pretty settled, with lots about the same size as most of the neighborhoods in the various towns where I'd lived. However, once we were out past the mall and heading north, the road sloped down a little, and I noticed that the neighborhoods were farther flung, with places that looked like mini-ranches sitting on at least a couple of acres.

It was by one of these that Jake turned off on a side road where the asphalt quickly turned to dirt, and the properties were separated by tidy, white-painted split-rail fences. Even though the road was unpaved, it looked fairly well-maintained, and so we didn't bounce around too much. It would have taken a much rougher trail than that one to put Jake's Jeep truck through its paces.

When we got to the end of the street, it dead-ended at a property where you couldn't even see the house, thanks to all the ponderosa pines and sycamores and elms that grew out front. There was a solar-powered gate that opened automatically as we approached; no magic, just a motion sensor. We drove down a gravel-paved driveway, and then Jake turned to the left and the house finally came into view.

It was tall, with a steeply pitched roof obviously meant to easily shed snow. Newish, as far as I could tell, the façade set off by river rock accents and a rock chimney. What caught my eye, though, was the large backyard with a smooth green lawn populated by...?

I glanced over at Jake, startled by the long-necked animals I'd just spied. "Are those llamas?"

"Alpacas, actually," he said. I thought I caught a glint of amusement in his eyes, and had a feeling he'd purposely not mentioned the alpacas because he wanted to see how I would react to their presence. "Joanna has an online business selling yarn and loose wool."

"Is there any money in that?"

His shoulders lifted, and he looked toward the house. "What do you think?"

Well, I thought it looked as though Joanna was doing pretty well for herself. Then again, it was probably a lot easier to slide over into the "comfortable" zone when you were guaranteed an extra sixty grand every year.

"Come on," he said then. "She's waiting for us."

With nervous fingers, I tucked a lock of hair behind my ear and then got out of the truck. I'd gotten a stick of gum and applied some fresh lip gloss after lunch, but I found myself wishing we'd had time to stop at Jake's house on the way over so I could have brushed my teeth. Lunch had been tasty but a little garlicky.

But there wasn't anything I could do about that now. About all I could do was hope I wouldn't be too stinky...and also hope that at some point I wouldn't feel so nervous about meeting yet another member of my extended family.

The front door opened as we approached, and a woman wearing jeans and a sleeveless chambray shirt stepped out onto the porch. I stared at her in surprise, then wondered why I should have been so startled by her appearance. After all, Jake hadn't said much of anything about Joanna except that she was the clan's weather-worker, and a very powerful witch. For some reason, that description had made me think she must be an older woman, experienced. But while Joanna was most likely several years older than Jake, I doubted she was even thirty yet. Her long dark hair hung in a thick braid down her back, and, like the other Wilcoxes I'd met so far, she was very attractive, with a smooth oval face, regular features, and gorgeously tanned skin.

"Joanna, this is Addie," Jake said, and Joanna stepped forward, hand extended.

"Nice to meet you, Addie," she said. Her voice was lower than I'd expected, almost husky. As soon as I'd approached her, I'd felt the odd little tingle that supposedly indicated I was around another witch, and I assumed she'd experienced the same thing when she met me. "Jake tells me you were raised in the civilian world and don't know much about controlling your gift."

Although her tone sounded matter-of-fact enough, I thought I glimpsed concern and even a little sympathy in her tip-tilted dark eyes. "Yes," I replied as relief swept over me, even though I couldn't exactly have explained why. "I was hoping you could help with that."

"Oh, I know I can," she told me, looking

undaunted by the task that lay ahead of her. She glanced over at Jake. "You can hang out in the house while we work. There's a pitcher of iced tea in the fridge, and some fresh-baked cookies on the counter in the kitchen."

"Thanks," he responded. I noticed how he hadn't declined the cookies, even though we'd just eaten a big lunch.

"We'll head out back," she went on. "If you do well, you can have some cookies afterward."

I couldn't help smiling a little at that remark. Offering me treats as a reward? Well, I figured I wouldn't be averse to a cookie or two if I somehow managed to avoid summoning a tornado or scaring off all the alpacas with a misplaced bolt of lightning.

Speaking of which....

"Are the alpacas going to be okay with me messing around with the weather?"

"Oh, sure," Joanna replied. "They're pretty placid. Besides, we're going to head out to the back forty, and I made sure it was clear. They won't even notice what we're doing. Come on."

With a wave, she gestured for me to come with her. I sent a questioning glance at Jake, and he gave me an encouraging nod before disappearing inside the house.

Well, it seemed I didn't have much choice. I

quickened my pace so I caught up with Joanna, then followed her as she led me off the porch and across a narrow strip of lawn, and over a tiny footbridge that crossed a cheerful little stream as it wound its way through the property. From there, we made our way along a path that separated two of the alpaca pastures. Eventually, we came to another pasture separate from the other two, one that was, as she'd promised, empty.

"Here we go," she said, lifting the latch on the gate to open it. "All the open space we could need. You can go ahead and set that down," she added, and pointed to the purse that was slung over my shoulder.

Feeling a little awkward, I removed the purse and set it down next to a fence post, figuring that might give it a little extra protection in case things got crazy. Straightening up, I turned back toward Joanna.

"Okay," I said. I almost tacked on, *I'm ready,* but I honestly didn't know for sure how ready I actually was. Well, I supposed I'd find out soon enough.

She put her hands on her hips and regarded me for a moment. Turquoise gleamed from several fingers, and I found myself wondering if she was part Navajo. Yes, all the Wilcoxes were dark, but there was something slightly exotic about her eyes and her features, very different from Laurel's girl-next-door looks.

"Has Jake said much to you about how our powers work?"

"A little," I replied. "I mean, he hasn't gone into a lot of detail. We've had other things on our minds."

Joanna's expression softened then, and I guessed she was reminding herself of exactly why we'd been so preoccupied. Again, the image of my mother lying on the floor of our living room, blood spreading out from beneath her lifeless body, invaded my mind, and I pushed the horrible memory away with what felt like a physical effort. Dwelling on that scene wouldn't change anything. What was important now was learning to control my stupid gift so it couldn't cause any more trouble.

"Well," she said, "it's really not that difficult. These talents are born within us, so it's just a matter of understanding what they are and making them work for us, rather than vice versa. Weather magic is a little different from some talents in that it involves working with an outside force that sometimes has a mind of its own."

"Do you do much to change the weather?" I asked, genuinely curious. It seemed to me that the temptation to make every day a perfect, sunny seventy-five degrees had to be kind of overwhelming.

Her mouth curved in a smile, even as she gave me a single shake of her head. "I try not to. Weather has patterns of its own, and interfering with them too much can cause a lot of problems. I won't say I haven't nudged a monsoon storm out of the way so it wouldn't ruin someone's wedding, or maybe coaxed a bit more snow from the clouds when it looked like the Snowbowl was going to have a bad ski season. Overall, though, it's more about paying attention so I can let key people in the clan know if something bad is coming our way."

"Like a meteorologist," I said.

"Something like that. But because you didn't have anyone around to recognize what your power was when it first awakened, it kept feeding on itself, getting stronger at the same time it got more out of control. Jake says that you bring storms when you're upset about something?"

I nodded, feeling ashamed that I could screw up something I'd supposedly been born with. However, Joanna, apparently guessing that would be my reaction, only shook her head again.

"Don't beat yourself up about it. Like I said, I think you got caught in kind of a feedback loop.

You just need to break the chain so your emotions don't control your gift." A pause as she looked up at the sky, which was a bright, clear blue, with only a small puff of a cloud here and there to break up its vast sapphire-hued expanse. "I want you to take a breath and then focus on the wind. Breathe it in...feel it. Feel where it's coming from, where it's going. Reach out and sense its energy."

For a second or two, I only stared back at her, wondering how in the hell she expected me to do that. After all, wind was wind. How was I supposed to feel this so-called "energy"?

But if I made such a protest, I knew I would be admitting defeat before I even got started. I was here to learn, after all. It was pretty clear that I needed to learn to play by an entirely different set of rules. I wasn't some kind of a freak—I was a Wilcox witch, and I had to learn how to behave like one.

So I closed my eyes and thought about what Joanna had just said.

Feel the wind. Breathe it in.

Become one with it.

I stretched out my arms and let the breeze wash over me, cool despite the warmth of the sun overhead. The wind was blowing from the west, had once been born somewhere far out over the

Pacific Ocean, had traveled across cities and deserts and stretches of deep, cool forest before it arrived in Flagstaff. But no, I couldn't say it had really arrived...it was only passing through, constantly moving, constantly alive. My fingers spread, and I could feel its touch all along my skin, picking up speed, catching my hair to blow it around my face. Almost playful, that wind, although I knew it could turn cruel if it wanted to, strong and rough enough to knock down trees or tear off roofs. It was all about the potential energy buried in those currents, all about what that energy wanted to do.

In that moment, it almost seemed alive to me, a new kind of being, true, not human, but still with a will of its own. And I somehow knew, without knowing how I knew, that it had reacted to the magic in me all those times by translating my own worry and fear into its energies, making them tangible, an active force in the world. All I had to do was understand that, although I should never deny my emotions, I had to realize that they interacted with my magic in a very powerful way.

And with that understanding came control.

I opened my eyes and saw Joanna smiling at me.

"You see?" she said. "It's really very simple."

"How could you tell I figured it out?"

"Look."

My gaze moved upward, and I saw a single small cloud floating in the air directly above the spot where I stood. Although the breeze was brisk and the cloud should have moved out of position almost as soon as I noticed it, the little puff of water vapor didn't seem inclined to do much of anything except remain where it was.

"I did that?" I asked.

"Yes. Now, let it go."

I looked up again. Not even a conscious thought, but more an understanding reached that the little cloud had done its work and was free to move on. And just a second later, it began to drift lazily eastward, riding the wind, letting the air currents do their work.

"It's really that simple?"

Her dark eyes danced in the sunlight. However, I didn't get the impression that she was amused by me, but instead pleased I'd learned the lesson so easily.

"It can be, if you let it." She came over to me, and I realized for the first time that she wasn't wearing sandals or flip-flops, the way the warm weather might have dictated, but a scuffed and very well-worn pair of brown cowboy boots. "You have to remember, Addie, that this isn't like learning a magic trick. It's not something you have to really work at. The power is within you. Just let it be what it is—and give it a nudge from time to time if necessary—and you'll be fine. If you'd had someone to tell you this when you were a child, you would never have had any trouble."

Jake had said much the same thing to me, but in that moment, I truly understood what he'd meant. My weather magic wasn't good or bad...it just was. And now that I knew how to let it flow through me, rather than tense up and try to create barriers which shouldn't be there in the first place, I wouldn't have to worry about causing havoc wherever I went.

Or at least, that was the theory. I supposed I'd find out for sure whether I was right the first time I encountered a situation that triggered any negative emotions.

"Does that mean I get a cookie?" I asked, and Joanna grinned, the corners of her dark eyes crinkling a bit.

"I'd say you've earned it. You're probably hungry after all that work."

I lifted an eyebrow. "It didn't seem that hard. We were only out here for about ten minutes or so."

"Were we?" she returned, still wearing that

amused expression. "You might want to check the time."

Mystified, I went over to the spot where I'd set my purse down on the ground and pulled out my phone. The display said it was a little after three. But...that was impossible. We'd been running a bit late, and so had arrived at Joanna's house closer to two-fifteen than the two o'clock we'd agreed on, but still, there was no way I'd been standing out in that pasture with her for almost forty-five minutes.

"Time can get a little weird when you're doing that kind of focus," she said. "But that's okay. Actually, it's good, because I knew when you went that deeply into it, you were making some real progress. Anyway, let's get back to the house."

Still feeling flummoxed, I put the phone back in my purse and followed Joanna to the house. Inside, we found Jake sitting on a recliner in the living room, feet up as he did something with his iPhone.

"Make yourself at home, Jake," Joanna drawled.

He didn't look at all discomfited, but only grinned at her. "Well, you were out there so long, I figured it couldn't hurt to put my feet up for a bit. How'd it go?"

"Great," she said.

"I'm cool, calm, and in control now," I added, hoping that I was telling nothing more than the truth. "And now I get a cookie."

That comment made him shake his head, although his smile remained in place.

"Kitchen's through there," Joanna said, pointing toward the dining room and the opening I was just barely able to glimpse on the left side.

Sure enough, there was the kitchen, big enough to rustle up grub for a whole team of hired hands, complete with an enormous professional six-burner stove and a refrigerator that looked as though it could have held a couple of sides of beef. Had this place been a working ranch before Joanna started raising alpacas here? No, that didn't seem feasible; I guessed she probably had about five or six acres, but that wasn't enough room for herds of cattle or anything. The house definitely felt ranch-like, though, with its wood-paneled walls and tongue-and-groove ceilings, and the enormous stone fireplace I'd passed on my way to the kitchen.

As promised, there was a plate of chocolate chip cookies covered in plastic wrap sitting on the granite countertop. I slid off the plastic and extracted one, then sealed it up before heading back out to the living room. By that point, Jake had gotten out of the recliner and was talking quietly to his cousin. I caught Connor's name but didn't hear anything else, because they both paused and glanced over at me.

"Got it," I said, and took a bite of cookie. It was amazingly good, rich and filled with actual chunks of chocolate instead of just chips. Had Joanna made the cookies because she knew we were coming over, or did she just have them lying around for whenever? If that was the case, she must have had a killer metabolism, because she was slim and fit and didn't look as though she'd ever eaten a carb in her life.

"Jeremy just texted me," Jake said, lifting his phone. "He wants us to come back to HQ."

It sounded kind of funny for him to refer to the renovated house they were using as their offices as "headquarters," but maybe that was just their little joke. And since we were done at Joanna's place, I supposed there wasn't much reason to keep hanging around. She didn't seem like the sort of person who wanted to waste time with idle chitchat when there were chores to be done.

However, something in Jake's expression had shifted, and I had a feeling Jeremy hadn't made the request because he simply wanted someone to hang out with while he jammed traffic cams or whatever else it was he did on all those computers. A little thrill of cold went through me, but I told myself it was nothing.

"Sure," I said, and consumed the last few bites of cookie, then brushed the crumbs off on my jeans. I looked over at Joanna and added, "Thank you so much. It's such a weight off, knowing that I'm not going to summon a thunderstorm the next time someone cuts me off in traffic."

"You'll be fine," she assured me. "And it's my pleasure. It's not every day I get to meet a long-lost cousin."

I smiled at her, not sure of the best way to respond. Jake came to my rescue, though, thanking Joanna as well, and then guiding me back outside as we made our final goodbyes. A minute later, we were back in his truck and headed down the long gravel driveway to the road.

"So, what's up with Jeremy?" I asked as we bounced along. "Did he find something else?"

"Yes," Jake replied. His mouth was set, but I didn't think his suddenly grim expression had anything to do with the unpaved road beneath our tires. "Your mother's funeral."

And I stared back at him, not sure what to say.

14

JEREMY SEEMED SUBDUED WHEN JAKE LED ADDIE into the front room where all the Mac Pros were housed. He was sitting in front of one of them, watching video of a small white church surrounded by cottonwood trees.

"That's the United Church in Kanab," Addie said, moving closer to the screen. One hand went to her mouth as she observed the scene—about twenty or thirty people, mostly women, leaving the church, a few of them weeping. "And that's Tammy Miller—she worked with us at the diner."

Addie pointed to a woman with brassily blonde hair in a tight black skirt and blue blouse, handkerchief held to her eyes as she blotted away tears. Her own eyes looked suspiciously bright, and she blinked, hard, before looking away from the screen.

"I found this when I went to check back on Kanab, see if anything else was going on," Jeremy explained. Judging by the way his gaze had immediately shifted back to the video, he didn't quite know what to do about the obvious grief on Addie's face.

Jake really didn't know, either. Well, he knew what he wanted to do was take her in his arms and hold her, offer what comfort he could, but he wasn't quite sure whether that was the wisest thing to do with his brother sitting a few feet away.

"Of course, they'd have to do it at a nonde-nominational church," Addie said, her tone almost a murmur, and Jake sent her an inquiring look. "Because she wasn't Mormon...or anything else, really. I guess my grandparents were Baptist, but my mom and I never went to church."

Right. He supposed he should have thought of that—probably should have been glad there was a church in Kanab that would be suitable for Lyssa Grant's funeral—but he was still too focused on how much he wished he could be alone with Addie so he could offer her the comfort she so clearly needed.

"I guess they took up a collection," Jeremy said then. He paused the video, which clearly had been shot earlier that afternoon. "The whole town, that is. They collected enough money to take care of the funeral and to have her buried in the city cemetery."

The tears that had glistened in her eyes now rolled down Addie's cheeks. She reached up to wipe them away. "Sorry," she said, her voice muffled, thick with emotion.

Oh, the hell with it. Jake went over and took her hand, pulled her close. She put her arms around him and leaned her head against his shoulder. No sobs, only those quiet tears flowing down her face, dampening the T-shirt he wore. For a second, Jeremy's eyes met his, and then he gave a single nod, as if absorbing the apparent change in his brother's relationship with the woman he'd found.

"It's okay," Jake murmured, and passed a hand over her hair. "Don't ever feel as if you have to apologize for being sad."

She nodded, then sniffed. "It's just—we lived there for a year and a half, and while people were friendly, we really didn't make any *friends,* you know. And for them to have gotten together and raised the money to give her a real funeral and a spot in the cemetery...I guess it just means maybe we weren't as alone there as we thought."

"People don't always show what they really think until some crisis comes along," he said quietly. "But I'm glad your neighbors and the people you worked with could come together on this."

No immediate reply, only her head moving against his shoulder in what Jake thought was another nod. "I want to visit her grave," Addie said, voice barely more than a pleading whisper.

Sitting in his office chair, Jeremy sent his brother a look of alarm, even as he shook his head. Jake raised a hand, letting him know he'd take care of this.

"And you should," he said, then continued before she could speak. "When it's safe. We don't know whether Lenz still has any fellow agents in the area. He might have her gravesite surveilled to see if you come back."

"Exactly," Jeremy agreed. "Also, everyone in Kanab thinks you're dead, too. They put your name on the headstone and everything. If you show up there, it could cause a little bit of a problem, you know?"

Addie reached up to blot her eyes, then pulled away from Jake's arms. Although he didn't want to, he knew he had to let her go, had to make himself stand still as she passed a hand through her hair and stared at the still image on Jeremy's Mac, her eyes reddened but still beautiful.

"I know," she said, in a small voice that didn't sound very much like hers. "I'm not saying I want to go tearing back there right away. But someday...." The words faded away, and she pulled in a breath, one that had a little hitch in the middle. When she spoke again, though, her tone was much firmer. "Can we go back to your place, Jake? I think I want to lie down for a while."

"Sure," he replied immediately. It was sort of awful that her victory over at Joanna's house should be followed so quickly by such a vivid reminder of her recent loss. No wonder she wanted to check out for a bit. A nap wasn't a cure-all, but in this particular situation, he thought it could only help. "We can go right now."

A dreary little smile touched her lips. "Thanks, Jake." Her gaze moved to Jeremy, and she added, "And thanks for letting me know, Jeremy. It actually does help."

"I'm glad," he said, and wisely left it at that.

Jake guided Addie back out to his truck, and

waited until she had climbed into the passenger seat and buckled her seatbelt before he went around the other side and got behind the wheel. Since the drive was short, he decided it was probably better not to say anything until they were back inside his house.

"Do you want something to drink?" he asked as they entered the kitchen and she set her new purse down on the countertop. "Water? Iced tea? I think there might be a couple of Cokes in the fridge, too, but—"

"Jake." Her tone was quiet but firm, and he made himself stop and look at her. Although her eyes were still a little red, the tears appeared to be gone. "I'm okay. In a way, what I just saw...that helped."

He watched her, studying her face, and he realized she was only telling him the truth. There was a calm in her expression that surprised him, a certain strength in the set of her delicate jaw. "It did?"

"Yes." She tucked a lock of hair behind her ear, and he realized she was wearing a pair of silver hoop earrings. Had she worn them this whole time, and he just hadn't noticed until now? "It gave me some closure. I kept seeing her —seeing her on the floor with blood everywhere. But now I know someone came along and took care of her body. They gave her a funeral service and said goodbye to her, and they gave her flowers and a headstone and treated her like she was part of their family. I couldn't have done any better for her myself. It's...it's good, Jake."

Tears gleamed in her eyes again, and he took a step toward her. She raised a hand, shaking her head.

"It's okay. Really. I just...I just want to go upstairs and lie down for a while. Then I'll be up to going out tonight."

Jake stared at her, wondering if he'd understood her correctly. Would she really be ready to be around people and act as though she was having a good time after witnessing her mother's funeral? "You still want to go out after all this?"

She smiled then, a little sadly, as if she somehow knew that what she'd just said wasn't making any sense to him. "I do. Because I can't honor my mother by hiding and pretending that none of this happened. I knew her, Jake—she was full of life, always looking for the fun in everything. She wouldn't want me to hide in the house and torture myself by trying to think of the ways I could have made all this turn out differently. No, she would have told me to get out there and live my life. So...that's what I'm going to do. I just need a little time for myself, and then I'll be okay."

As he watched, she turned away from him and left the kitchen. A moment later, he heard her footsteps on the stairs, followed by the door of the guest room closing. Curled up on the floor by the stove, Taffy stared at him and gave an inquiring head tilt. The dog had stayed quiet during the entire conversation, as if she'd known they were discussing people topics that didn't involve her, but now she was alone with Jake, he could tell she needed a little reassurance of her own.

Don't we all, he thought as he went over to his dog and knelt down next to her so he could ruffle her lopsided ears and run his hand along the soft fur on her back. Taffy leaned into him, her small weight a welcome pressure, grounding him somehow, reminding him that there were always small pleasures to be had, no matter how difficult the situation.

And in that moment, he resolved to make sure that Addie had the best evening out he could manage. He might not be able to make her forget what had happened to her mother, but at the very least, he wanted to give her a few hours of happiness, something to ease the weight of the world from her shoulders.

Anything less wouldn't be worthy of her.

The hotel clerk squinted at the black and white photo Agent Lenz pushed across the counter toward her and uttered the words he'd been waiting to hear.

"Oh, yeah, I remember them."

A surge of excitement went through him, but he kept his tone flat, almost disinterested. "When?"

The clerk tilted her head to one side. She was a pretty woman, with bright red hair pulled back in a sleek twist and improbably long eyelashes. The glance she gave him wasn't entirely professional, but he did his best to gaze back at her coolly. He wasn't here for dalliances, only to do what he could to track down Adara Grant and the man who had stolen her away from him.

"Day before yesterday," the woman said. "Let me look it up." Her fingers—tipped with long, bright red nails—tapped on the keyboard in front of her. "That's it—Jake Anders, Rancho Cucamonga, California."

"I'll need the address he gave you."

She hesitated at that request, then gave a very small lift of her shoulders. He'd showed her his

I.D. earlier, and so she knew that although technically she could request he provide a warrant, it probably wasn't a very good idea to question the motives of someone working for Homeland Security.

Instead, she picked up a pen and jotted down the information on a pad of paper printed with the logo of the hotel, then tore the top sheet off the pad and handed it to him. "Are they in some kind of trouble?" she asked, looking worried. "They seemed like a nice, quiet couple."

"I'm afraid I'm not at liberty to say," Lenz replied crisply. "But thank you for your cooperation, ma'am."

Her russet brows drew together at the "ma'am"—he had a feeling she didn't think she was old enough to have earned that particular designation—but she only nodded. "Not a problem, Agent Lenz. We're here to help."

"And you have."

He folded the piece of paper and slipped it into his breast pocket, then stepped away from the counter so the next person in line could get their particular business handled. Even the din of the slot machines in the background and the piped-in music blasting through the speakers wasn't enough to dull the excitement surging through his veins.

I've got you...Mr. Anders.

Down to the parking garage, where he got into his car and drove away, getting comped at the gate when he showed his Homeland Security I.D. He'd need to head back to Mandalay Bay and check out, since he hadn't canceled his room there, not knowing when he'd finally track down his quarry.

Now he had a name and an address. When he got to his hotel room, he pulled out his phone and entered the address in the map program, figuring he might as well get the lay of the land before he started his journey to Southern California. When he entered "6351 Haven Avenue" into the phone, though, he found himself frowning immediately.

What the hell kind of joke was this?

Oh, the address was located in Rancho Cucamonga. However, it wasn't in any quiet residential neighborhood, but on a major street, and it sure as hell wasn't a house.

No, apparently that address belonged to a Vons supermarket.

"Son of a bitch," Lenz said aloud, scowling down at his phone. He supposed he should have guessed that Jake might have given a fake address, but he was forced to admit to himself that he hadn't thought his quarry would be quite that clever.

As he sat there, wondering what the hell to do next, his phone rang. Dawson's number.

"Lenz."

"Hello, sir. I have the dealership records you requested. Shall I send them over?"

"Yes," he said, not bothering with a "please." Maybe he could salvage the situation after all. It was one thing to lie to a hotel clerk, and quite another to falsify the information given to a dealership during a vehicle purchase. Not with the DMV and the individual's insurance company involved.

"Sending now." A slight pause, and Dawson asked, "Any leads?"

"They were here," he replied, his tone curt. "They provided a false address, though, so I'll have to hope that one of the records you sent has the correct information."

"I hope so, too, sir. Anything else?"

"Not at the moment. I'll get back to you after I've looked over the information you sent."

"Understood."

He ended the call and pulled his laptop out of its bag, then set it down on the table by the window. Jaw clenched slightly, he attached the phone to the laptop, then entered his authentication and looked for the packet Dawson had just sent.

As she'd warned, the file was large, but nothing his computer couldn't handle. He began to scroll through the data, moving quickly because he was only looking at the driver's license images and not much else.

And there he was.

Jake Reynolds, Rancho Cucamonga, California. So the bastard did live in Southern California, had given the address of a place he knew. Lenz did a quick search of the address provided and confirmed that this one was an actual home and not the local Trader Joe's or whatever. But it was real, in a tract of vaguely Mediterranean-style houses—and only a few blocks away from the Vons whose address he'd given to the front desk clerk at Treasure Island.

"Got you," Lenz said softly.

It was a little more than a three-hour drive from Las Vegas to Rancho Cucamonga, putting him at his destination around six in the evening. That should do fine. This time of year, the sun wouldn't have even set by then.

He sent a message to Dawson, telling her to get a backup team in place for an extraction at eighteen hundred hours. Then it was time to pack up his things and get on the road.

This time, he'd catch up with Jake Reynolds and Adara Grant on Jake's home territory...and the man would find it a lot harder to get away this time.

In just a few hours, Lenz would finally have Adara right where he wanted her.

15

I SURVEYED MYSELF IN THE MIRROR AND THOUGHT I might be halfway presentable. When we were out shopping, Laurel had encouraged me to buy some makeup—*real* makeup, not just lip gloss and mascara—at the Sephora located inside the JC Penney at the Flagstaff Mall, and so I was a lot more "done" than I usually would be, with some eye shadow and liner and actual lipstick instead of gloss. I'd used the concealer I bought to hide any lingering redness around my eyes, and hoped no one would be able to tell that I'd allowed myself a good cry earlier in the day.

What I'd told Jake hadn't been a lie. It really had helped to see my mother given a resting place in Kanab's city cemetery, where lush green trees shaded the gravesites and looming red rock formations provided a starkly beautiful back-drop. Oh, I wouldn't lie to myself and pretend it didn't still hurt, and yet I thought the raw wound within me had begun to enter its first stages of healing. That was the most important thing, to recognize that healing was possible, and neces-sary. If I was going to start over here in Flagstaff, I needed to let that part of me go.

Now, as I scrutinized my reflection, hoping that the silky top and dark jeans and lightweight cardigan were okay for a night out in Flagstaff, I thought I hardly looked like myself. The old Adara Grant wouldn't have bothered with this much makeup, and would have told Laurel that the silky green top wasn't practical. But I wasn't going to be scraping my way through college or waiting tables anymore. Now I thought I almost looked like I could be the daughter of someone like Jackson Wilcox.

Not that I even knew what my father had looked like. I realized Connor hadn't shown me any pictures of him. Maybe he didn't have any at the house in Jerome; I could tell that he hadn't cared much for his father, and probably didn't see the need to have any mementos to remind him of a man who'd been dead for more than twenty years.

Well, someone in the clan must have pictures,

and once I'd been introduced to everyone as Jackson's daughter, I could probably ask to see the photos. In the meantime, though, I had Jake waiting for me downstairs, and a whole evening in Flagstaff to look forward to.

I descended the steps and found Jake in the front room, bending down from the armchair where he sat to scratch Taffy's belly. The little dog lay on her back in front of him, eyes closed in doggy bliss, clearly ready to have her master keep rubbing her tummy for as long as she could keep him occupied.

"Hey," I said softly, and Jake looked up from the dog, eyes widening slightly.

"You look great," he said, in such a sincere tone that I could tell he wasn't trying to butter me up with false compliments.

Still, I brushed a hand against the hem of my silky top and said, "It's not too much?"

"No. It's perfect."

I realized then that he'd changed his shirt, was wearing an untucked button-down in a dark brick color instead of the T-shirt he'd had on earlier in the day. "Well, I'm ready when you are —assuming the dog lets you go."

A quick flash of a grin, and he gave Taffy's tummy one final pat before he got up from the chair. At once, the dog rolled over on her stomach, looking indignant, but then she let out a little huff of a breath, as if realizing she was going to get abandoned for the evening.

"She'll live," Jake said. "She got an extra treat after her dinner, so I think she'll forgive me...as long as we're not out all night."

"*Can* you stay out all night in Flagstaff?" I asked, genuinely curious. After all, even though it was a college town, what I'd seen so far didn't seem that wild. It wasn't New York or Los Angeles or someplace like that.

"Well, the bars close at two, but there are usually a couple of Wilcoxes hosting after-parties at their places every weekend night," he replied, mouth still lifted in amusement. "Not that I would know from personal experience—I'm not exactly a party animal."

That comment wasn't at all disappointing— exactly the opposite, actually. I'd never been what you could call a partier, either. Frankly, the thought of hanging out in bars until 2 a.m. and then going in search of a party after that just made me feel tired.

Some twenty-four-year-old I was.

"I think it's okay if we skip the after-parties," I told him, and his dark eyes crinkled a bit.

"Thank God. I thought we'd just try to wander a little, have some dinner, stop in at a place where I know there'll be some live music."

"Sounds good."

He patted Taffy on the head and told her to be a good girl, then gestured toward the front door. I went outside and waited as he touched the latch to lock it, but was surprised to see him stride down toward the sidewalk rather than head over to the garage where his truck was parked.

"We're walking?" I asked as I hastened my pace to keep up with him.

"It's only a few blocks," he replied. "Parking can be tight downtown on weekend nights, especially during the summer, and since we're going to be drinking, I figured walking was wiser anyway." His glance moved toward my feet; I'd put on my favorite black flats since it seemed safer to wear something broken in rather than one of the new pairs of shoes I'd bought earlier that day. "You can walk in those, right?"

I chuckled. "Jake, I can walk, run, climb a fence if need be. So, no worries about that."

"Good."

We fell into a comfortable silence as he led me down the street where his house was located, then jogged onto a different road, a little busier one. A couple of blocks more, and then we were downtown, walking along a street called Aspen Avenue.

"I figured we'd go to Blendz first, have a drink," he said as we waited for the light so we could cross the street. "Or actually, several."

"You trying to get me drunk, Jake?" I asked, wondering what I'd gotten myself into.

His dark eyes glinted down at me. "Not really. Blendz is a place where you can blend your own wine. They have a ton of varietals to choose from, and you get little test tubes to mix and match. By the time you're done, you've had about the equivalent of a glass of wine, but it feels like more because you've gotten to taste so many different things."

Even though I didn't know much about wine, I had to admit that sounded like a lot of fun. "What happens if you get a blend you really like?"

"You write down the formulas as you go," he explained. "If one turns out really well, you give the formula to the person working there, and they'll make you your own bottle of wine."

"Okay, I'm sold," I said, and he smiled.

"I thought you might be."

The wine bar in question was located near the intersection of Aspen and San Francisco Streets, in an old brick building that looked as though it dated back to Flagstaff's early settler days. Since it was only a little past six, the real bar crawlers weren't out in force yet, and there were only two other couples inside, and a larger group out on the pretty little brick-enclosed patio that opened off the rear of the place.

We sat down at the bar. The guy tending it, who looked like he might be Navajo and around Jake's age, shot Jake a grin. "Hey, Jake. Haven't seen you in a while."

I was a little surprised by the friendly greeting, but then I realized that Jake had lived in Flagstaff all his life and probably knew a lot of the waiters and bartenders...and store clerks and a bunch of other people we might run across. Very different from my own experience, where I'd usually just begun to get acquainted with people before it was time for my mother and me to move on to the next place.

"I've been busy, Nick. This is Addie."

"Hi, Addie," Nick said. For just a second or two, his gaze rested on me, almost speculative. Was I the first girl Jake had brought in here since Sarah had died? I didn't know the whole story; I supposed it was possible that he'd started dating again at some point, but that wasn't the impression I'd gotten.

"Hi, Nick," I said, doing my best to offer him a smile that wasn't at all uncomfortable.

"Well," he went on, "since Jake is an old pro at this, I don't have to give you my spiel about how the whole mixing thing works. Just take a look at the sheet with all the available wines and decide which ones you want to play with."

He slid a couple of pieces of paper and some pencils across the bar. When I looked down, I saw that the sheet had a list of all the varietals offered, as well as places to write in formulas as you worked your way through your particular choices.

"It looks complicated," I said in a murmur.

"I suppose it can seem that way," Jake replied. "But it really isn't. And since we'll be sharing a flight, we only need one sheet. We'll keep a spare just in case we screw up something."

"I thought you said it wasn't complicated."

His mouth twitched. "Okay...not *too* complicated."

About all I could do was shake my head. After that, we got busy choosing the varietals we wanted to play with, and Jake handed off our worksheet to Nick so he could fill up the six test tubes with the wines in question. Once the wines were ready, Jake and I started mixing and match-ing, playing with proportions and combinations.

It really was a lot of fun playing mad scientist with wine. Some of the combos were pretty good, a couple just so-so, but we came up with a classic G-S-M blend—grenache, syrah, and mourvedre —that was really good.

"Then we should get a bottle," Jake suggested. "Something to remember our evening by."

"Oh, we don't have to—" I demurred, thinking of the price, but he only shot me some serious side-eye at my protest.

"I want to," he said. "It's not a big deal."

No, I supposed it wasn't, not when he was living in a house worth more than I wanted to contemplate and drove a brand-new vehicle that had to have cost a pretty big chunk of change. And it probably wouldn't have been a big deal to buy a whole case of our particular blend, even if lugging that much wine around was kind of out of the question.

So we ordered a bottle, and Nick made a custom label for us using a photo from Jake's phone, a shot he'd taken sometime during the winter, with the mountains above town capped with snow against an impossibly blue sky. We decided to call the wine "Peaks Punch" in honor of those mountains, and when we were done, we emerged with the bottle wrapped in a brown paper bag and a nice wine buzz going.

"Hungry yet?" Jake asked.

By that point, I was. The wine tasting had taken us more than an hour, and the sun was almost down. Even though lunch had been fairly late—and big—I could tell that the wine had woken up my stomach and that it was ready for something a little more substantial than the chocolate-chunk cookie I'd eaten at Joanna's house.

"Definitely," I said.

He pointed across the street. "Let's go to Criollo. It's one of my favorite places in town."

I looked at the restaurant in question. It seemed small, housed in another old brick building next to a bookstore. "Do we need a reservation or anything?"

"Not if you're a Wilcox."

Before I could reply, the light turned green, and we needed to hurry across San Francisco Street. We passed by an Earthbound Trading Company and a shop that seemed to specialize in Native American jewelry—plus a gorgeous gallery called West of the Moon that I vowed to go back and visit sometime—and then arrived at the restaurant. The place looked packed, and there were people waiting around outside, but all Jake had to do was go up to the hostess, greet her by name, and ask if there were any tables available. She informed him that one had just opened up, and a minute later, we had a cozy spot at a table near the back.

"Those people waiting to get seated must hate us," I said in an undertone as I picked up a menu.

"Probably," Jake replied, looking completely unrepentant. "And honestly, I try not to abuse the privilege too much. But I told you I was going to show you a good time tonight, and a good time doesn't include waiting half an hour for a table."

I had to admit to myself that he had a point, although I still felt a little guilty about jumping the line, so to speak.

"Do you want to get a bottle?" he asked, and I looked up from the menu.

"Oh, probably just a glass for me," I replied, since I already felt a little tipsy from all the wine we'd sampled at Blendz.

He looked a bit disappointed but, to my relief, didn't press the point. When the waitress came by, we both got glasses of malbec, and then I had to return to my perusal of the menu. The food was an interesting blend, with a lot of Latin influences without being straight-out Mexican. Since everything except the burger looked unfamiliar, I had to guess at what to order—I'd been brought up on good old American diner food, and I was forced to admit that I probably didn't have a very sophisticated palate.

Not that I would confess this particular short-coming to Jake, who was clearly at home in the place and hadn't even stopped to think whether I might be put off a little by the offerings on the menu. Then again, they did have tacos. It was kind of hard to go wrong with a taco, even though I didn't quite know what "al pastor" meant. Still, it was probably time for me to branch out.

"So," Jake said, after the waitress had brought our glasses of wine and taken our orders, "what do you think of Flagstaff so far?"

"It's beautiful," I said honestly. Because it was, with those heavily forested mountains rising above the town, the quaint buildings of the old downtown section, the stunningly deep blue skies overhead. "It definitely has a lot more going on than Kanab."

His dark eyes laughed into mine as he raised his glass of wine and took a sip. "Well, that doesn't sound too hard."

"No, but still. I guess I wasn't expecting Flagstaff to be as big as it is. I mean, you have a Kohl's and everything. We used to have to drive to St. George to shop at one."

I didn't bother to mention that those shopping trips were a special treat, something my mother and I did maybe every six months or so. Even Kohl's prices were out of range for us unless we saved up and shopped the sales carefully.

A pause as he sipped some more wine. I could tell from the way his brows drew together slightly that he had something on his mind, a thought he wasn't sure he should voice aloud.

"What is it?" I asked.

He set down his wine glass and leaned forward slightly. His hands were resting on the tabletop, and I found myself wanting to reach across the table and twine his fingers with mine. There was something almost overwhelming about sitting at that small table with him, even though we'd been closer before then...even though he'd held me as I wept. But this...this felt formal.

This was a date.

When he spoke, his voice was low enough that I had to strain to hear him over the background music and the chatter of the other patrons in the restaurant. "So...do you think you'll be able to live here?"

I gave him a wry smile. "It's not like I have much of a choice, do I?"

His lips pressed together. Still holding my gaze, he said, "That's not what I asked."

No, it wasn't. Did I really want to think about this so soon? I knew it wasn't as though he was asking me to move in with him or anything; of course not. But what he was asking was whether I thought I could be happy in this town that still felt strange to me, even though apparently I had family who'd lived there for more than a hundred years. Whether I could turn this place into home, could finally stop running.

Thanks to Joanna and the insights she'd provided into my gift, I no longer had a reason to run.

"I think so," I said, my voice also quiet. "I mean...this is all really new to me, and I'm still trying to absorb everything. But it's beautiful, and my family is here, and...." The words faded away as I wrestled with a notion that was new to me and therefore alien, not something I'd ever really allowed myself to consider, thanks to more than a decade of moving from place to place and never feeling settled. "And I think I'd like to put down roots here."

His hand moved, touched mine. A little thrill went through me at the brush of his fingers, and I had to wonder at myself for reacting like that to such a small gesture. Then again, I didn't think he'd touched me casually, judging by the intensity in those dark eyes.

"I'm glad to hear that," he said.

Such heat coiling in my belly, awakened by just a whispered touch. Was this normal for witches and warlocks? Yes, I couldn't deny that I was attracted to him, but there were other men I'd been attracted to in the past, and I sure as hell had never reacted like this.

Then again, none of those men had been Jake Wilcox. Guys in high school I'd thought were cute, Tom McKenzie at the community college in Durango—he was the only one I'd actually gone out with, had kissed. He had been fun and attractive, and upset at the way my mother and I had bailed so precipitously, but even though at the time I'd thought he was a good kisser, I'd never had my body run hot and cold and flare out into sudden need simply because his fingers had brushed against mine.

"But I'm mostly just taking it one day at a time," I said, doing my best to act casual as I withdrew my hand and reached for my glass of wine.

Disappointment flickered in Jake's expression, but he didn't protest, only picked up the water glass at his place setting and took a swallow. "Well, no one can fault you for that. And we'll do what we can to see you get settled." A wicked little glint entered his eyes as he added,

"And now that you're street-legal, why don't we go car shopping tomorrow?"

The sip of wine I'd just allowed myself seemed to get caught in my throat. "C-car shopping? I don't even have a bank account yet."

"Well, we can do that first. But you can borrow the money from me and pay me back after Connor transfers the money to your new account."

I stared at Jake, wondering if he was pulling my leg. But no, he looked perfectly serious, head tilted slightly to one side, gaze fixed on my face. "I can't borrow that kind of money from you."

"Sure you can." He winked at me—an honest-to-God wink. "I know you're good for it. Or at least, you will be."

How was I supposed to respond to that remark? Because he was right—Connor himself had said that as soon as I had an account set up, he'd start transferring my inheritance. Probably not all at once, because even a broke-ass college student like me knew that funds in a checking or savings account would only be insured up to two hundred thousand dollars, but what a single account could hold would definitely pay for a car. Several cars, and a down payment on a house, and....

"Okay," I said, figuring there wasn't much

point in arguing about it. After all, I knew I wanted a car, didn't want to have Jake or Laurel or whomever driving me around whenever I wanted to go somewhere. But maybe Flagstaff had Uber? I'd never used the service, partly because most of the places we'd lived didn't have those sorts of modern conveniences, and partly because it was an expensive luxury we couldn't afford even if it was available. Anyway, money wasn't really an issue anymore, so I supposed I could have just called an Uber to get around.

I didn't want that, though. I wanted a car, wanted the sense of freedom one would give me.

"Great," Jake replied. "There are a bunch of car dealerships on the eastern edge of town, out past the mall. We'll go shopping in the morning."

"Any of those dealerships owned by Wilcox-es?" I inquired.

"A couple," he allowed, and I had to chuckle.

"Figures."

Our food arrived after that, and for a few minutes, we were quiet as we tucked into our food. Even though the combinations of flavors were unfamiliar to me, I had to admit to myself that my tacos al pastor were very good, and it looked as though the roasted chicken Jake had ordered was equally tasty.

But once we'd gotten some food in our stomachs to soak up the wine, I asked a question that had been occupying my thoughts ever since I'd met Jake's brother Jeremy. "You haven't said much about your parents," I said. "Are they...?" And I let the words trail off, wondering if I'd made a mistake by bringing up what could have been a delicate topic.

However, Jake allayed those fears with a simple shake of his head and a quick smile. "Oh, no. They're both around. They live in University Heights, which is sort of in the southwest part of town. My dad's an electrical engineer, and my mom works in the registrar's office at Northern Pines University."

"Wow," I said. "That sounds so...normal."

He picked up his fork and ate a mouthful of chicken, then responded, "We're all about normal. Or looking normal, anyway. And it's helpful to have someone working for the registrar, considering that most Wilcoxes go to school there. She can help smooth out any irregularities, if you know what I mean."

Not completely, but I guessed that in a family of witches and warlocks, there had to be the occasional complication that needed to go away. It did sound as though the Wilcoxes had woven themselves pretty thoroughly into the fabric of the town, which made sense. They'd been living there for a very long time.

"And my grandparents are all retired and still here as well, although their houses are more out toward the area where Joanna lives. They don't come down here all that much—they think there's too much traffic."

Well, I had to admit that Flagstaff's streets had seemed busier than I'd expected. But the weather that weekend had been perfect and there were probably a lot of tourists in town in addition to the regular residents, so I supposed that wasn't so strange.

"Their loss," I said lightly, and Jake gave a rueful tilt of his head.

"I suppose so."

We went back to our food after that, and when we were done, we emerged from the restaurant into a cool twilight, a brisk breeze blowing down from the darkening mountains above us. I hadn't been expecting the air to cool down so quickly, and I shivered a little despite the lightweight cardigan I'd put on over my new silky top.

"Cold?" Jake asked. He was still only wearing the short-sleeved shirt he'd changed into for our evening out, but apparently the cold air wasn't affecting him the way it was affecting me.

"A little, but I'm okay," I replied. "I should be fine once we start walking."

For a second, he hesitated, as if he maybe wanted to move closer to me, drop an arm around my shoulders. But it seemed he wasn't quite ready to make so public a display of affection, because then he said, "Sure. The bar where we're headed is two streets over, so maybe the walk will help."

I nodded, and he led me to the corner, where we waited for the light until we could cross San Francisco Street and head back west in the general direction of the neighborhood where Jake's house was located. However, we turned down another street long before we got anywhere close to his house, and then down an alley, where he led me down a steep flight of cement steps to a subterranean door.

"What is this, some kind of speakeasy?" I asked, shooting a dubious glance at our surroundings. Not that I thought Jake would ever take me someplace that wasn't totally safe, but it definitely felt a little dive-y.

His teeth flashed in the tepid light from the bare bulb mounted next to the door. "Actually, that's exactly what it was back in the day. Now it's a club."

He reached for the handle and opened the

door, letting out a blast of industrial music. I couldn't help wincing.

"It'll be better when the band starts," he said, looking almost apologetic.

"Okay," I replied.

Another grin, and then he put his hand on my elbow and led me inside. The place was really dark, so I couldn't make out much except the bar on the opposite wall, mostly because it was outlined by some sloppily hung rope lights. As my eyes adjusted, however, I saw that the walls were cement, patched in multiple places—well, in the spots where they weren't covered by vintage concert posters. There were about ten small round tables placed around the space, and then an open area in front of the raised platform where the band would play. In fact, there were a couple of guys hooking up amps and moving around equipment, so I assumed live music would be forthcoming soon enough.

"I'll get you a drink," Jake said, his voice raised loudly enough to penetrate the music booming out of the speakers mounted in all four corners. "I assume more wine is okay? They only have a wine and beer license here."

Rather than try to shout back at him, I gave him a thumbs-up, indicating that wine would be fine. Actually, even though I'd never been much of a drinker, even I knew better than to start mixing. Once I'd decided on a drink for the evening, I stuck with it.

Jake wandered over to the bar while I took another look around. More people were starting to filter in, telling me that we were probably getting close to the time when the band was scheduled to start. Although it was hard to tell for sure because the lighting in there was so bad, I guessed that almost everyone there was in their twenties. No one had asked us for I.D., but I didn't know if that was because they didn't bother until people actually started ordering drinks, or because it was just sort of generally known around town that this was a twenty-one and over kind of place.

Soon enough, Jake was back with our glasses of wine. He set one down in front of me. "Here you go."

"Thanks."

I picked up the plastic cup and took a sip, and was pleasantly surprised. Not that I knew much about wine, but I knew what the cheap stuff tended to taste like, and this didn't seem like the kind of inexpensive booze that got poured at college parties—if you were even lucky enough to get wine at all.

"That's good," I said, and he nodded.

"Part of the reason they stick with just a wine and beer license here—besides it being a lot cheaper—is that they only serve local Arizona stuff. What we're drinking now is a red from Provisioner."

Before that night, I'd barely even realized Arizona had a wine industry. Playing with all those varietals at Blendz had taught me differently, although a few of their offerings had come from California. "Is wine a big deal here in Arizona?"

He chuckled. "Oh, you sheltered child."

Since I knew he was teasing, I only raised an eyebrow at him. "Well, you did just rescue me from Utah."

"True." A pause as he sipped from his cup. "It's getting to be a big deal. And remember, Connor owns a vineyard down in the Verde Valley."

Right. I'd almost forgotten about that in the blur of other activities. "So, he makes wine?"

"Well, it's Anthony—the husband of Angela's friend Sydney—who handles most of the wine-making side of things, but Connor's sort of the silent partner, the financial backer. I think he used most of the money he made from his art to buy the vineyard. They don't have a tasting room or anything yet, though—they're focused on creating wines right now."

"What do they do with the wines if they don't have a tasting room?" I asked, thinking that this newfound half-brother of mine was turning out to be quite the renaissance man. Artist...father... vintner...head of a whole clan of witches and warlocks.

I realized then that the amazing art I'd seen on the walls of Connor's house in Jerome must have been his.

Jake swallowed some more wine, then said, "They sell their wine through a co-op in Jerome. It's a place where winemakers who don't have their own tasting rooms can offer their stuff. We should go next time we're down there—it's a fun way to try some of the less mainstream Arizona wines."

As opposed to the "mainstream" ones, which I hadn't even known was a thing until this evening. For some silly reason, I found myself strangely happy at the casual way Jake had mentioned a return trip to Jerome, as if it was just a given that we'd continue to see each other and do things together.

I wanted to do things with him...or, more to the point, *to* him. The table where we sat was pretty small, and when he shifted, his knee brushed against mine. I could tell it wasn't anything he'd done on purpose, but even so, that accidental touch was enough to get my blood racing again.

Crazy.

All of the band members showed up on stage then, announced themselves as "Deep Six," and launched into the first song of their set. Not sure what to expect, I was surprised at how good they were—straight-up rock with maybe just the slightest country edge.

There wasn't much chance to talk after that, but it was okay—the music was good, and midway through the first set, a couple of people who turned out to be more Wilcox cousins came by to say hello. Jake introduced them as Tyler and Rashelle, and they hung out for a while before moving on to see some more of their friends. Again, everything was casual and relaxed, as if it was no big deal that some witches and warlocks had decided to hang out with civilians on this particular Sunday night.

And I supposed it wasn't a big deal. This was just part of being a Wilcox; you might keep that part of your life hidden, but you still had to interact with the regular world, had to be a member of society. None of them seemed to have too much trouble balancing the two sides of their existence, and I hoped I could be that effortless about the whole thing one day.

Around midnight, we wandered out of the club, Jake giving me a guiding hand as we went up the stairs, since by then I'd had another glass of wine and that, on top of what I'd already drunk earlier in the evening, was enough to make me pretty unsteady on my feet. Once we were on level ground, I felt a little better, but I was still happy to have him take my hand as we walked back to his house.

After we'd gone inside and he'd closed the door—and Taffy had come running up to us, dancing around, tail wagging, and we'd both bent to pet her—we straightened and looked at each other. I knew I was definitely on the far side of tipsy, and while he was in better shape than I, Jake wasn't exactly stone cold sober, either.

For a long moment, neither of us said anything. He touched my hand, but briefly. What he meant by that touch, I wasn't sure. To see how I would respond? To let me know that he wanted something a little more?

Apparently, neither of those things. He glanced away from me, then said, his tone diffident, "Do you need help getting up the stairs?"

I wasn't firing on all cylinders, but even I could guess the question meant he didn't plan to kiss me. Not that I'd really been expecting him to, and yet...

...and yet, I'd really hoped he would.

"I'm all right," I said, doing my best to sound unconcerned rather than bitterly disappointed. "I've got a banister to hang on to here. See?"

My fingers wrapped around the piece of carved oak in question, and I began to haul myself up the steps. Thank God I was wearing flats and not heels, or I had a feeling I probably would have tripped over myself.

A creak told me he was coming up as well, although he maintained a safe distance behind me, probably so I wouldn't feel as if I was getting crowded. When we got to the upstairs landing, he hesitated, then said, "Good night, Addie."

"Good night, Jake," I replied. "I had a really good time."

A certain tension in his jaw seemed to ease, and he smiled. "Me, too. Car shopping tomorrow, remember."

I gave him a thumbs-up. "Wouldn't miss it."

Then I went inside the guest room and shut the door, and went over to the bed so I could sit down.

Damn. I really wished he'd kissed me.

16

Just as the Google search had indicated, Jake Reynolds lived in a quiet suburban neighborhood in Rancho Cucamonga. By the time Agent Lenz parked his Ford Taurus at the curb, it was nearly seven; a bad crash involving a semi on I-15 had delayed him by nearly an hour. Still, daylight lingered on this quiet June evening, the sun just beginning to touch the horizon. The skies were clear, seeming to indicate that whatever Adara Grant was up to in the house on Valinda Avenue, she wasn't unduly upset by it.

Lenz was also happy to see a black Jeep Gladiator parked in the driveway. Garage too full to accommodate the vehicle, or did Mr. Reynolds prefer to leave it outside so he could flaunt his recent acquisition to his neighbors?

Not that it mattered, except the flashy truck served as a clear sign that Lenz had definitely come to the right place.

His gun was a familiar weight in its shoulder holster. After what had happened in Kanab, he sincerely hoped he wouldn't have to use it. Regret flared in him once again at the accident that had taken Lyssa Grant's life, although he pushed it away as best he could. If Jake Reynolds hadn't interfered, then Adara's mother would still be alive today. Accidents happened.

That was the party line, at any rate.

He pulled in a breath, steadying himself for the confrontation to come. Then he opened the car door and got out.

The air was dry and warm, and smelled of fresh-cut grass. Over on the next block, he thought he heard kids laughing and splashing; playing in someone's backyard pool, most likely. All in all, it was an idyllic suburban scene, one he hoped he wouldn't have to disturb too much.

Twenty steps up the walk to the front door. Because he'd always been in the habit of noticing things, he took note of the carefully spaced day lilies that filled the flowerbeds to either side of the stamped-concrete walkway, the flowerpots of brightly painted Mexican pottery that sat in wrought-iron stands on either side of the home's double doors. Wreaths of woven grapevine and dried grasses decorated those doors, effectively obscuring the peepholes.

Good.

He rang the doorbell. A brief wait, and then he heard footsteps approaching the door. It opened, and a man in his late fifties, trim with closely cut salt-and-pepper hair, stared out at him.

Agent Lenz had never seen the man before. Trying to keep a frown from his brow, he flashed his identification and said, "Agent Lenz, Homeland Security. I need to talk to Jake Reynolds."

The man's brows—still dark, unlike his hair—drew together. "I'm Jake Reynolds. What's this about?"

For a second, Lenz could only stare at him. How could he be Jake Reynolds when it was the Jake with Adara Grant whose image had appeared on the driver's license in question?

Recovering himself, he said, "Is that your Jeep Gladiator parked in the driveway?"

"Yes," Reynolds replied, expression mystified.

Well, the man standing in front of Randall Lenz wasn't the only one confounded by this particular turn of events. What the hell was going on? Lenz would have liked to blame Agent Dawson for making some sort of stupid mistake, but she didn't make mistakes. Besides, the paper-work had been clear enough—the much younger man he was pursuing was supposed to live at this address, not the person who stood before him now.

Thinking quickly, Lenz said, "Have you traveled recently to Las Vegas?"

"No," the man responded, looking more confused than ever. "Haven't been there since my wife and I visited Vegas about five years ago." He paused, a note of worry entering his voice when he spoke again. "Am I in some sort of trouble?"

"I'm afraid there's been something of a mix-up," Lenz said. "Your address was provided by a fugitive at a hotel there. But you don't match the description." Well, aside from being the same gender and approximate height, although this man was old enough to be the other Jake's father.

If the bastard's name was Jake at all. He might have handed Adara a false name. Right then, Lenz wouldn't put much of anything past the man.

"A fugitive? What—?"

"I'm afraid I can't tell you more than that," Lenz cut in, his tone curt. Anger boiled through him—rage at being tricked into making a two-hundred-mile drive for nothing, for letting that other Jake get the best of him. However, angry as he was, he knew the man who stood before him had nothing to do with any of it, was only a convenient scapegoat. "I'm sorry for disturbing you. Have a good evening."

He turned on his heel and strode back to his car, leaving Jake Reynolds to stare after him in shock. In fact, the man was so flummoxed that he stood there in the doorway for a moment longer, and watched Lenz put the Taurus in gear and drive off.

Stupid, stupid, stupid, he growled at himself, although he didn't honestly know whether he should be beating himself up quite so harshly. Whoever this Jake person was, he apparently had someone on his side who was a good enough hacker that he—or she—had been able to get into those dealership records and alter the photo on the driver's license in question. For all Lenz knew, Jake had planted that fake Rancho Cucamonga Vons grocery store address specifically to ensure that his pursuer would follow that one false lead, rather than focusing on his actual quarry.

Well, whatever had happened, he was back to square one. About all he could do now was stay the night here in Southern California and do his best to regroup, try to figure out who the real Jake was out of all the records Dawson had sent him.

If the Gladiator was even his. He could have stolen it. Doubtful, though; Agent Dawson would have run a routine check on stolen vehicles matching the Gladiator's description, and would have notified her boss immediately if she'd gotten a ping.

There was a Best Western hotel almost across the street from the Vons whose address Jake had borrowed. Lenz pulled into the parking lot and went inside, doing his best not to scowl. No point in attracting any more attention to himself than necessary.

At least his miserable luck hadn't extended to encountering a fully booked hotel; there were several rooms available, and a short time later, he was checked in and unpacking his laptop.

No matter what it took, he was going to figure out which Jake was behind all this. And even though he knew he wasn't supposed to make these missions personal, he couldn't help but experience a flicker of satisfaction at the mental image of finally taking the bastard into custody.

Who could blame him, really? The mysterious Jake had brought whatever misfortune awaited on himself.

～

After telling himself to sleep on it, Jake awoke the next morning with pretty much the same condemnation rolling around in his head, the one that had echoed in his brain even as he'd passed out face down on his pillow the night before.

You're an idiot.

He'd been so close. He'd looked down at Addie, her face flushed and beautiful from the walk back to the house, and he'd almost bent down to kiss her...the operative word being "almost."

Why he'd stopped himself before the fateful moment, he really wasn't sure. At the time, he'd thought he didn't want to take advantage of her—after all, even if she hadn't been outright drunk, she was still pretty tipsy, and he didn't want to do anything quite so momentous when she was in an impaired state. True, her gorgeous gray-green eyes had been glowing, and she'd stood there with her lips slightly parted, looking as though she was practically begging for a kiss, but he still couldn't bring himself to do it. He'd wanted to. God, had he wanted to. In the end, though, he'd realized he wanted his first kiss with her to be something she approached with a clear head, not because she was halfway to wasted and not thinking straight.

Maybe it hadn't been such a good idea to spend all night drinking. Okay, probably a bit of an overstatement, since they'd basically had a drink an hour, but still, by the end of the evening, that still equaled a decent amount of booze. At the time, he'd just wanted to keep her entertained and give her a night out she'd remember. Unfortunately, he'd realized partway through their bender that she hadn't spent her college years drinking and building up a tolerance the way he had...just like a lot of his Wilcox cousins, come to think of it.

Well, today was a new day, and he'd just have to see what happened. Lying here in bed and beating himself up wasn't going to do him any good.

He got up and showered and put on clean clothes, deciding that yesterday's jeans needed to be relegated to the hamper. After he was ready, he emerged in the hall and paused for a moment. The door to the guest room was open, and he heard water running in the hallway bath. That meant Addie was ambulatory enough to be up and about. With any luck, she wouldn't be too hungover. That was no state to be in when car shopping.

If it turned out she was feeling a little under the weather, he resolved to take her to breakfast first, although he'd never been that into eating a heavy meal in the morning. However, even he knew that sometimes you just needed to get some hash browns and eggs inside you.

For the moment, though, he figured it was a good idea to get a big pot of coffee brewing. He was just pouring himself a cup when Addie paused at the entrance to the kitchen.

Actually, for someone who'd been up past midnight drinking wine, she looked remarkably well rested. Her hair was still damp, but she'd put on some makeup—not as much as she'd been wearing the night before, but enough to make her look as though she hadn't rolled out the wrong side of the bed. Jeans and a pretty blue top with some embroidery around the low scoop neckline, something she must have picked up during her shopping expedition with Laurel the day before.

"I thought I smelled coffee," she said as she stepped into the room.

Her tone was light, almost casual, but Jake couldn't miss the way her eyes wouldn't quite meet his. Awkward because he hadn't kissed her and she'd wanted him to? Or...awkward because she'd guessed he'd wanted to and she didn't?

Hard to say. He needed some caffeine in his

system before he attacked a thorny problem like that.

"Perfect timing," he replied, then lifted the pot and poured some coffee into the mugs he'd already set out on the counter. Because he figured he might as well plow in right away, he added, "How're you feeling today?"

"All right," she said.

She came over and took one of the mugs. As she did so, Jake was able to catch the faint floral scent of her shampoo from her damp hair, and his groin tightened.

So much for acting casual.

"Did you want to go out to breakfast?" he asked. "I thought you might want some fortification before we go and look at cars."

"No, I'm good, as long as you still have some of those bagels."

Since there was still half a bag left, bagels weren't a problem. Not sure whether he should be relieved that she'd declined the breakfast invitation, or worried that she didn't seem too interested in food, Jake made himself go to the freezer and get out the bag, then put two bagels on a plate so he could defrost them in the microwave. While he was busy with that task, Addie spoke again.

"I had fun last night. Thanks for that."

Surprised, he turned back toward her. She wasn't looking at him, seemed to be staring out the window at the backyard, and he got the feeling she was doing that on purpose so their eyes wouldn't meet.

"My pleasure," he said. "I was hoping you'd have fun...that it might take your mind off things for a little while."

"It did." A shift in position, and now she was facing him, hands stuck in the pockets of her jeans as though she wasn't quite sure what else to do with them. "Maybe too well."

He raised an eyebrow, not sure what she meant by that comment.

Without saying anything, she went over and picked up one of the mugs of coffee, then spent a little more time adding milk and sugar. When she was done, she leaned up against the counter opposite him, her hands cradling the big hand-painted mug, something he'd bought a while back at one of the art fairs held at Wheeler Park.

"I know this probably sounds awful," she said then. "But for a few hours there, I almost forgot. I almost forgot what happened in Kanab...what happened to my mother." Her voice trembled slightly on that last word, but Jake saw how her chest rose and fell as she forced herself to take a strengthening breath. "I shouldn't be forgetting. It's not right."

God, he wished he could go to her and take her in his arms. But Jake somehow knew she needed this space between them for now so she could assess her emotions and try to get a hold of herself. "No one's asking you to forget," he said quietly. "Maybe more like...heal."

"I'm trying to," she said. "I really am. And I think I will. If for no other reason than because that's what she would have wanted." Addie looked up from her untouched mug of coffee, her gaze meeting his directly for the first time that morning. "It's just...I'll be going along, thinking that it's going to be okay, and then I get broadsided by it all over again."

"Do you want to talk to someone?" Jake asked. "I mean, a professional. We don't have any Wilcox therapists here in Flagstaff, but I think there might be someone down in the Phoenix area—"

At once, she shook her head. "No, I don't want to talk to a shrink. I like this better." Those big eyes of hers were fixed on him, steady, with no sign of tears. "I like talking to you, Jake. You listen. So many people don't."

Warmth filled him at her comment, even as he experienced a small twinge of...guilt? Sarah had said almost the same thing to him, once upon a time, and yet he hadn't listened when she'd let him know she was going on that camping and kayaking trip with their cousins. He'd told her that he didn't think any of them were experienced enough to be attempting that sort of expedition on their own, and they'd quarreled over it. Of course, he hadn't tried to stop her from going, and yet afterward, he kept wondering if he'd just sat down and talked over the plan rather than condemning it from the start, things might have gone differently.

Maybe he wouldn't have lost her.

"I try to," he said, then went and got his own neglected mug of coffee. "I always want you to feel like you can talk to me."

A nod, and Addie lifted her mug and took a sip. She was quiet for a moment and he waited, getting the impression that she had more she wanted to say.

When she spoke, her words startled him.

"Why didn't you kiss me last night?"

Jesus. He could tell she wasn't the sort of person to keep secrets—except the biggest secret of all, the secret of her weather-working gift, which she'd had to hide from the world—but he hadn't really expected her to be quite that direct about the situation.

But if she was going to be forthright, then he damn well better respond in kind. Anything less than utter honesty wouldn't score him any points.

"I wanted to," he said bluntly. "But I thought you'd had a little too much to drink, and I didn't want to do anything in the heat of the moment that you might regret later."

Not a blink as she absorbed that response. Then she gave a very small nod, as though his words had confirmed something for her. "I thought maybe that was it. For the record, I wanted you to. It wasn't something I would have regretted...even if I'd had too much wine to be thinking clearly."

Damn. Jake forced himself to swallow some coffee, then said, "Well, maybe we can revisit that idea when we're both sober."

"We're sober now," she said, but a glint had entered her eyes, and he got the impression she was teasing him a little. "But we're drinking coffee, and I know I haven't brushed my teeth yet, so maybe it's better to wait."

"Maybe," he responded, knowing he sounded a little strangled. Coffee breath or no, he definitely wanted to kiss her now, take her in his arms and taste her sweet mouth and breathe in the fresh-washed dampness of her hair.

However, he sensed this was the wrong time. They wouldn't wait much longer—he could tell that much—and so he told himself to be patient.

Whenever they kissed, he knew it would be worth the wait.

17

HAD I REALLY SAID THOSE THINGS TO JAKE? I mentally replayed the scene in the kitchen and confirmed that yep, I'd come out and told him I'd wanted him to kiss me.

Very smooth, Addie.

But he hadn't been put off by that revelation —at least, I didn't think he had. In fact, his gaze had lingered on my mouth for a few seconds, as if he'd wanted to kiss me then and there, and only held off because he could tell I wanted something a little more moonlight and roses for our first kiss.

All right, maybe not anything that overtly romantic, but a kitchen in bright daylight with his dog watching us to see if we dropped a crumb probably wasn't the ideal location for that sort of intimate exchange.

We'd both put the moment aside, and eaten our bagels and finished our coffee as though something hadn't just fundamentally changed in our relationship. No, we hadn't kissed, but we'd both acknowledged it was something that was probably going to happen in the very near future.

Which was why it was sort of a relief to leave the house and go out in public, where those sorts of displays were much less likely. Although the main focus of the morning would be car shopping, we first stopped at a Chase branch near downtown where a Wilcox cousin named Amber worked—that way, she could sort of overlook my current lack of a permanent address or any of the usual roadblocks to establishing a bank account, and managed to get a savings and a checking account set up for me in less than twenty minutes.

"You'll still have the usual wait for your debit card, though," Amber said, looking apologetic. She was probably around my age, a little fairer than the Wilcoxes I'd met so far, with honey-brown hair rather than the usual near-black and big hazel eyes. "I can't really control that part, since those come from corporate. But you can come into any branch with your account number and access your funds that way."

Since I honestly hadn't even been sure whether I'd be able to get any kind of a bank account with nothing but a bogus Arizona driver's license to prove my identity, I was more than grateful for the help she'd provided. When we left the bank, Jake suggested that I text my account info to Connor so he could go ahead and start transferring funds.

"Not that we're going to wait on getting you a car or anything else you need," he added. "But you might as well get the ball rolling."

The concept of having that much money still didn't feel quite real to me, but I dutifully texted the information to the number Jake gave me. Only a minute or so later, Connor replied.

Thanks—I'll get this started today. We've decided to head up to Flagstaff early & plan to make an announcement to everyone tomorrow or the day after. I'll keep you posted.

I supposed I should have been glad that Connor was being so proactive. At the same time, though, I experienced another of those nervous little flutters of worry. Yes, everyone I'd met so far had been nothing but friendly, had welcomed me to the clan with pretty much open arms. Even so,

I wasn't sure how I felt about the whole Wilcox family knowing my father was their former *primus*. Maybe my parentage wouldn't actually end up giving me any kind of special status...but I worried that it just might.

Still, there wasn't anything I could do to stop my brother from making the announcement; it wasn't as if I could request to have my identity kept secret. That wasn't fair to my mother, and it really wasn't fair to Jackson Wilcox, either. He'd never had a chance to meet me, so it seemed selfish to ask that Connor not tell anyone who I really was.

Thanks, I replied. *Looking forward to it.*

That response ended our convo, and I slipped the phone back into my purse. By that time, we were passing the mall, and then drove past another shopping center with a Tuesday Morning and a Petco and a Home Depot. On our left were Subaru, Nissan, and Toyota dealerships, while off to the right was a Mercedes-Benz outlet.

"Pick your poison," Jake said cheerfully. "Do you want a Mercedes? Your father always drove one."

Right—I remembered how my mother had specifically said Jackson Wilcox drove a Mercedes, as if she was proud of herself for hooking up with a man who had expensive taste and a bank account to support those tastes. However, I couldn't see myself behind the wheel of a car that fancy, even if I could afford one. I'd be scared to drive the damn thing, petrified to leave it anywhere as prosaic as a grocery store parking lot.

"No," I replied, my tone serious. "I'm okay with something a little simpler."

"Subaru?"

At once, I shook my head. "No, thanks. My mom and I owned a fifteen-year-old Forester, and I'm okay if I never drive another Subaru."

"Got it." A lift of his shoulders, and he added, "Well, I'll take you down to the Jeep dealership. They sell trucks and cars, too. And I'm kind of partial to Jeeps anyway."

"Hadn't noticed," I remarked with a curl of my lip, and Jake's eyes crinkled at the corners in a way I'd already come to appreciate, since I knew it meant he was amused by something I'd said or done.

However, he didn't reply, only pointed the Gladiator straight ahead, where the street we were driving on sort of dead-ended at another street that fronted the dealership in question. We parked in one of the visitor spaces and started to roam the lot. I'd sort of expected a salesperson to descend as soon as we appeared, but we seemed to have been left alone...at least for the time being.

Jake apparently caught the way I glanced toward the glass-fronted office building, wondering where all the sales staff were hiding, because he said, "I might have called ahead to let Jordan know we wanted to browse in peace. Even when I know I want to buy something, I hate all the high-powered sales stuff."

I supposed I could see his point. While I knew you had to deal with salespeople as a necessary evil in these sorts of transactions, I didn't have any personal experience at that sort of thing. My mother had always bought her cars used, either off Craigslist or via friend-of-an-acquaintance types of arrangements.

"Thanks," I replied, then added, "Who's Jordan? Another cousin?"

"Of course."

Of course. There did seem to be an awful lot of Wilcox cousins scattered all over Flagstaff, but I probably shouldn't be surprised by that, considering there were so many people in the clan.

Jake paused by a big Dodge truck and glanced over at me. "What do you think?"

The thing was huge...and intimidating. "I think I'd need a step stool to get up into it."

Once again, his eyes crinkled in amusement, but he didn't argue. Not that I was overly short—I stood just a hair under five foot seven—but the truck in question definitely had some sort of lifted off-road package and would have been uncomfortable for me to drive.

"Then just wander," he suggested. "Stop and look at anything that seems interesting, and when we have your top two or three, we'll go find Jordan."

Jake's suggestion sounded like a good idea. I went up and down the rows, looking at all the cars and trucks and SUVs on display. Once or twice over the years, I'd thought I might want a Jeep Wrangler, but truthfully, I'd never been off-roading in my life and wasn't sure whether I needed anything quite that sturdy. Besides, those things were expensive—I looked at the stickers on a couple of them and wanted to go into shock. All right, I knew that pretty much any new car these days was going to cost upwards of twenty-five grand by the time you walked out the door, but those fully loaded Wranglers were nearly $50K. No, thanks. The Renegades were cute and more affordable, and yet I still wasn't sure whether I could see myself driving one, although

I'd liked what I saw of Laurel's car when she'd driven me around to go shopping.

Then I stopped next to a vehicle I couldn't quite classify. I supposed it was a small SUV, but much cuter than your normal soccer-mom car, with curved lines and cool dark-alloy wheels and, best of all, a gorgeous deep metallic-green finish.

"I like this one," I said.

"A Fiat?" Jake responded, sounding skeptical. "That might not be the best thing for the snowy winters we get up here."

"It has all-wheel drive," I pointed out as I perused the window sticker. "That's what we had in our Subaru, and it did just fine in Utah winters."

"Flagstaff is a lot colder than Kanab."

I had a feeling he would bring that up. Luckily, I was already armed with a rebuttal. "Colder than Durango? Or Cheyenne?"

His hand ran over the scruff on his chin, letting me know that I'd just scored a point. "Oh, right. I forgot you lived in those places, too."

"I've lived in a lot of places. And a lot of them were cold and snowy. I like this one." I paused before adding, "Maybe this sounds silly, but it feels like...well, it feels like me."

"It's not silly," he said. Now he was smiling a little, although I didn't think that was because I amused him. No, I had a feeling he was just glad I'd found something that made me happy. "Should we go rustle up Jordan?"

For a second, I hesitated. After all, buying a car was a big decision, and if I was trying to be practical, I should have found something else to test-drive as well, just to make sure the little green Fiat was really the vehicle for me. However, I knew in my gut that it was the car I wanted.

"Sure," I said. "Let's go find him."

We went into the sales center, and almost at once, a guy around my age walked over to us. Like Jake, he was tall and dark-haired, although since he was working, he wore a white dress shirt and a tie.

"Addie?" he asked, and I nodded.

"I'm Jordan Garnett. Your cousin...but I suppose you already knew that."

I grinned. "I'm starting to think I'm related to half of Flagstaff."

He flashed me a smile in response. Not as good-looking as Jake, but still, probably the sort of guy I would have craned my head to take a look at if I'd seen him in passing on campus or something. This extended family of mine definitely seemed full of handsome people. "Did you find something?"

"The green Fiat...." My words trailed off then as I realized I hadn't even looked at the actual model name of the car—I supposed I'd been too distracted by that pretty metallic green paint. "Sorry, I can't remember exactly what it was."

"It's okay," he assured me. "We only have one green Fiat on the lot right now. The 550X. Let me just go get the key."

I thanked him, and he disappeared into one of the offices, presumably in search of the key in question. As I waited, I did my best not to look as nervous as I felt. Maybe I was letting myself get distracted by something I thought was cute rather than a vehicle that would be truly practical. But then, wasn't an economical little car with some extra cargo space and all-wheel drive practical? It wasn't as though I was across the street at the Mercedes dealership buying a seventy-thousand-dollar luxury sedan.

Jordan reemerged, and we headed over to the Fiat. After he handed me the key fob, I got behind the wheel, adjusted everything—well, once he showed me how it all worked, since the old Subaru I'd been driving had manual controls—and then waited as he scrunched himself into the back seat and Jake took the passenger seat next to me. I had to acknowledge that the back seat wasn't huge, but it wasn't like I planned to haul around a basketball team or something.

The test drive, which involved taking a back road from the dealership down to a freeway on-ramp about a mile away, then driving on I-40 to get back to where we started, went well. Even though I knew the engine couldn't be all that big, it felt peppy and loads more powerful than anything I'd experienced before. And it felt like I'd need an advanced degree in computer science —or maybe Jeremy's help—to get the stereo and navigation systems figured out, but even that wasn't too big a deal.

"Well?" Jordan asked as I maneuvered the car back onto the lot.

I supposed I should have played it cool, but I'd never been very good at acting blasé. "I love it," I said simply.

"Should I get the paperwork started, then?"

Hesitating, I looked over at Jake. "You love it," he said. "I don't think there's anything more we need to discuss, is there?"

"Not really."

"Well, then."

We all got out of the car and went inside. While I knew that buying a vehicle involved a lot of paperwork, I thought the transaction should be simpler in this case just because there wouldn't be any financing involved. However, there was still a lot of back and forth, signing this and signing that, a break for a hurried call to a Wilcox cousin who was an insurance agent and who got me set up on the spot, so more than two hours elapsed from the time I'd agreed to buy the car to the time when Jordan put the key fob in my hand and said simply, "It's yours. I'll bring it around front for you."

Feeling a little dazed, I went out front with Jake to wait for my new car. He looked down at me. "Happy?"

"I think so," I replied cautiously. "Honestly, I'm feeling a little shell-shocked."

"It is kind of an ordeal," he agreed. "But I hope you're not too tired—I want to make another stop before we head back to the house."

Right then, I just wanted to follow Jake back to his place and then order takeout for lunch or something. "We're not buying anything else, are we?"

His brown eyes twinkled. "Just one more thing."

I got the feeling that any protests would fall on deaf ears. "Okay...as long as we're not chasing all over town."

"Nope," he said cheerfully. "We just need to

go to the Best Buy we passed on our way over here. No chasing involved."

Best Buy? Was he going to buy me a washing machine or something?

However, after I'd gotten behind the wheel of the Fiat and followed Jake's Gladiator to the store in question, I thought I understood what he'd been talking about, since he took me over to the Apple kiosk toward the back of the store and paused by the laptops.

"You really need a computer."

Well, probably I did, but I wasn't sure a Mac was necessary. I could get by with some sort of inexpensive PC, and told him as much.

"Maybe," he allowed. "But you need to stop selling yourself short, Addie. That is," he went on after a hard look at my face, "if you're more of a PC kind of girl, then sure, I can understand why you wouldn't want a Mac. If it's all about the cost, though...." He let the words sort of evaporate after that, as though trying to remind me that Jackson Wilcox's only daughter shouldn't be wasting her time with penny pinching.

And that's what it was, really. In high school and college, I'd eyed my fellow students' shiny MacBook Pros and MacBook Airs with envy, wishing I could have afforded one. I'd used Macs in the computer labs at school and really liked them, found them easier to work with than a PC. But there was no way in the world I could ever have justified the cost, and so I'd done my best to tell myself that a Mac certainly wasn't a requirement for doing well in school.

With Jake still staring at me with that one lifted eyebrow, as if he knew all too well the thoughts that were passing through my head, I guessed it would be stupid to lie.

"Okay," I said at last. "Yes, I want one. But a MacBook Air—I want something light and easy to carry around."

"Not a problem," he replied. "It's your computer, after all."

So we chose the one with the maxed-out memory and processor, along with a nice padded laptop bag, and Jake put the whole thing on his credit card. That made it probably around thirty-five grand I owed him after that day's little shopping expedition, and I vowed to myself that I'd go to Chase the next day and get a cashier's check for the entire amount. I hated the thought of owing anyone money—especially that much money—even though I knew he honestly didn't care how slow I was about paying him back.

Afterward, I followed him back to the house, parking my new car in the driveway while he put the big Gladiator in the garage.

"Hungry?" he asked.

"Yes," I said, adding quickly, "but can we get takeout or something? That kind of wore me out."

"You like Indian food?"

I had absolutely no idea, since I'd never had any. When I confessed that lack to Jake, he shook his head.

"Well, then, I'll order some and you can tell me what you think. Time to broaden your horizons a little."

Looking at him, I thought I'd like my horizons broadened...and soon. In the meantime, though, it sounded like fun to try some Indian food.

"Sure," I said. "Only nothing too spicy. I'm kind of a wimp about that kind of thing."

One eyebrow lifted, but he only said, "No problem," and pulled out his phone and called in an order of things I'd never even heard of before —samosas and naan and chicken tikka masala.

While we were waiting for the food to arrive, I got out my new laptop and started setting it up. Jake gave me the info for his wifi network, and in less than fifteen minutes, I was up and running. I was even able to get my Gmail account conncected to the mail program on the MacBook, although there really wasn't much to see, except a couple of reminder emails from the college about signing up for the fall semester. Obviously, the admissions department and the financial aid department weren't very good about keeping tabs on one another.

Seeing those emails sent a pang through me. I wouldn't be going back to U of U. Everything I'd left behind was pretty much gone, and I still wasn't quite sure how I felt about the situation. Sad...but with a certain guilty excitement under-lying the sorrow. I probably shouldn't have enjoyed my morning as much as I had, and yet I was thrilled with my new car and my shiny new laptop, eager to see what would happen next.

"Everything okay?" Jake asked as he glanced up from his phone. He'd probably been checking emails or texts, but must have spotted the trou-bled expression on my face.

"Fine," I told him. "Just looking at some emails."

His dark gaze was searching, but he didn't probe, only said, "Okay."

At that moment, my phone pinged from inside my purse. Since I wasn't used to the iPhone's alert sounds, I didn't quite know what that meant. However, I still leaned over and dug out the phone from my purse, then checked the screen.

A couple of new texts from Connor.

I realized you probably would want to see our father, he wrote. *I don't keep old family photos around, but then I remembered I had a few on my phone. Our cousin Marie digitized a bunch of Wilcox pictures and put them in a database Jeremy set up—he can give you a username and password so you can access them whenever. But here are a couple to get you started.*

Attached to the message was a photo. I clicked on it, and found myself having to swallow hard against the sudden lump in my throat.

The picture was of a man in probably his late thirties or so, which meant it must have been taken long before he'd ever met my mother. He stood in front of a tall Christmas tree and had two boys with him, one on either side. The younger child had dark hair and gray-green eyes, and I realized I was looking at Connor himself. He'd been maybe five or six, while the other boy was much older, high school age, tall and handsome already, with black hair rippling back from his brow and eyes so dark, they looked black as well.

Damon, I thought. The brother I'd never met, would never be able to meet, because he'd died more than five years earlier. Maybe someday, someone would tell me exactly what had happened to him. Probably not Connor, though; I already got the feeling he really didn't want to talk about it.

However, my real focus was on the man in the middle. There was a strong resemblance between him and Damon, more so than Connor. Maybe Connor took more after his mother. However, I could still see certain echoes in Connor's features as well—the strong black brows, the well-defined chin. He'd been handsome, that unknown father of mine, with the kind of looks I guessed had aged pretty well. No wonder my mother had been attracted to Jackson Wilcox, even though he must have been old enough to be her father.

I didn't think I looked all that much like him, even though Connor and I shared some similarities in appearance. For all I knew, that was simply because we resembled our mothers in a lot of ways, and that softening of Jackson's somewhat harsh features had somehow worked its same magic on both of us. Even so, I knew at once that he was my father. There were just enough echoes of his appearance in my face for me to realize I couldn't deny he was the one my mother had been with all those years ago.

Not that I'd planned on making those denials, when I had the whole Wilcox clan apparently ready to embrace me as their own.

Still, it felt more than strange to finally put a face to the man who'd changed my mother's life forever.

The other photo was of Jackson alone. He was older in that shot, probably closer to the age he'd been when he encountered my mother in that Flagstaff bar twenty-five years ago. And yes, I'd been right about one thing—age had only tempered his looks, made his features more chiseled and that much more striking. I didn't know who'd taken the picture, but they'd managed to catch him in what I guessed was a rare unguarded moment. He sat behind a desk, but his attention didn't seem to be focused on any of the paperwork I saw spread out before him. No, he stared off somewhere in the distance, expression brooding and almost sad. Had he felt his mortality creeping up on him, guessed that he might not have too much longer on this earth?

Impossible for me to say, but in that moment, I felt an irrational stir of anger toward my mother. She'd always been emphatic about not telling my father I existed, had said that it was her decision to keep me and she wasn't about to go begging him for money. When I was younger, I'd been proud of her for standing on her own, even if I'd secretly wished I could have met the man who contributed half my genetic makeup...

and possibly somewhat resentful that maybe our lives wouldn't have been so hard if she'd only swallowed her pride and reached out to him for some support.

Sitting there in Jake's living room, though, I could only wonder if Jackson Wilcox might have looked a little happier if he'd known he had a daughter, someone who apparently had managed to escape the Wilcox curse.

I knew that was pure conjecture on my part, and yet...

...and yet, he looked so sad. Too bad my talent wasn't time travel. Then I could go back to him and tell him who I was, that the curse didn't have quite as much of a stranglehold on his existence as he thought it did.

"What're you looking at?" Jake's voice. "Is everything okay?"

I started, then gave myself a mental shake as I tried to bring myself back to the here and now. Jake stood near the end of the sofa, watching me with concern in his eyes.

"Fine," I said. "Connor sent me a couple of pictures of my father." I tilted the phone toward him so he could see the screen, and he frowned slightly.

"Wow. I don't think I ever saw Jackson look like that around other people."

Not surprising. Everyone had done their best to dance around the issue, but even so, I got the impression that my biological father hadn't been the nicest person in the world.

"Do you know who took this photo?"

Jake shook his head. "Not really. Maybe Marie—she's the only person I can think of that Jackson might have let his guard down around."

Marie again. "She's kind of an important person in the clan, isn't she?"

"Yeah, I suppose so. She's a seer. In most witch clans, the seer—or seers—consult with the *primus* or *prima* a lot."

I stared at him blankly. "Seer...as in see the future?"

"Basically. Their visions aren't always perfect, though, or require some interpretation. But still... seeing the future is sort of a big deal."

There was an understatement. Yet another talent that sounded infinitely preferable to mine. Then again, I didn't know for sure if I'd really want to know what was about to happen. Life was difficult enough without always trying to maneuver to avoid a frightening future.

The doorbell rang then, and Jake went to answer it. A minute later, he came back carrying two large bags of takeout.

"You planning on feeding an army?" I

inquired, eyeing the bags with some alarm. Yes, I was hungry, but still....

"Indian food makes great leftovers," he said with apparent unconcern. "Let's eat—I set the table while you were looking at your phone."

Speaking of which.... I took one last glance at my father's handsome, sorrowful face, and locked the screen on the iPhone and put it back in my purse before following Jake into the dining room. As he'd said, he'd set the table already, using some placemats that looked handwoven from cotton rags, the sort of thing you might buy at an art fair or something, and heavy stoneware plates fired in comforting shades of soft blue and brown and tan. Folded-up paper towels instead of real napkins, but since my mother and I did the same thing most of the time, I wasn't too concerned by the lack of ceremony.

The food was good. Spicier than I'd expected —but not so spicy that I couldn't manage—and in an almost dizzying variety of flavors and colors and textures. I tried one dish after another, focusing on the unfamiliar seasonings and combinations, on how it was all so different from anything I'd ever had before.

"Good?" Jake asked when I slowed down to take a sip of water.

"It's great," I replied. "Thanks for suggesting

Indian food. Now I know what I've been missing all my life."

"We have some pretty good restaurants in Flag," he said. "I mean, it's not like the variety you'd get down in Phoenix, but still, we do okay."

From what I'd had so far—the takeout this afternoon and dinner the night before at Criollo and the Greek takeout we'd shared with Laurel and Jeremy at "HQ"—I thought Flagstaff was doing more than okay. And in that moment, I realized I was doing okay, too. The pain still lay deep inside, coiled within me, but I could manage it. With any luck, each day would get a little better.

I hoped.

"I like Flagstaff," I said. Maybe a juvenile remark, but it was the truth. I liked this town, liked the variety of experiences it offered and the beautiful mountains that soared above it and the deep quiet of the ponderosa forests that spread out for miles on all sides. It was the sort of place that wanted to be home.

I wanted it to be my home.

Jake's eyes caught mine. He set down the half-eaten piece of naan he'd been holding and said quietly, "I'm glad. I wanted you to like it here."

Just like that, heat flooded through me. I could have lied and said it was only the spiciness of the tikka masala I was sensing, but I knew better. No, the warmth pooling in my stomach and rippling out to my fingertips had very little to do with the meal and everything to do with the answering warmth I saw in his eyes.

Since I hadn't responded, he added, in an even lower tone, "And I like you."

A whisper, a breath. "I like you, too, Jake."

His hand reached across the table, and I extended my own hand so my fingers could twine with his, feeling again the strength in them, the welcome heat of his tanned skin. My heart seemed to skip a beat, and I had to force myself to stay there, to allow this moment to happen. It was frightening, the way I reacted to him, when all he'd done was touch my hand. What would happen if we went any further than that?

I realized I was about to find out, because he pushed his chair back and stood, making me rise with him, since our fingers were still entwined. A breath, and another, and then he pulled me close and placed his lips against mine. Gently, as though he knew he needed to make it easy for me to pull away if I wanted to.

No chance of that. As soon as our mouths touched, the heat flared in me again, hotter and stronger and brighter than anything I'd ever experienced before. I'd never realized that a kiss could feel like this, could make me run hot and cold at the same time, make me feel as though I would tremble to pieces at his touch...but also seem as if I was suddenly strong enough to leap over the tallest of the San Francisco Peaks.

He tasted of spices, savory and exotic at the same time. Then his arms were around me, holding me close, the muscles of his chest hard against my breasts. In that moment, I wanted to tear our clothes off, remove the annoying pieces of fabric that prevented me from feeling his bare skin against mine.

Somehow, though, I managed to hold it together. And sometime later—an eternity or so—he ended the kiss, lifting his mouth from mine so he could gaze at me intently.

"Wow," he said.

"I second that motion," I joked weakly, and then we both laughed, more to break the tension than because my remark was really all that funny. A pause, and then I said, "Is this—?"

"What?"

"Is this normal?" I placed a hand against his chest and could feel his heart beating beneath my palm, strong but fast. Clearly, he was just as stimulated as I.

He ran a hand through his hair, making adorable little pieces stick up from the rest. Right then, I got an idea of what he might look like when he woke up in the morning...which was probably not the sort of thing I should have been thinking about in that particular moment, not with his bedroom right upstairs. Way too dangerous.

"Define 'normal,'" he said with a twitch of his lip.

"Normal for witches and warlocks," I said. "I mean—that wasn't my first kiss. But it might as well have been."

Jake laced his fingers through mine, and led me out of the dining room and back over to the sofa. It was probably also dangerous to sit close to him, but I found I couldn't force any distance between us, had to sit so our legs were touching. He noticed, I could tell, but he didn't comment on my closeness, only frowned a little as he appeared to consider my comment.

"It's maybe a little different for us than it is for regular people," he told me, his tone quite different now, serious, almost earnest. "We tend to recognize the person who's our match—our soul mate, for lack of a better term—when we're pretty young. Divorce rates among witch-kind are very low. I don't know if that's an echo of the consort relationship, or—"

"'Consort'?" I echoed, interrupting him. "What's that?"

His fingers tightened on mine; we'd remained holding hands that whole time. "In most clans, it's a woman who runs things. And that woman—the *prima*—has to meet her consort sometime during her twenty-first year and bind herself to him, for lack of a better term. It's a very intense relationship, from what I've been able to tell. Anyway, some people think that the way most witches and warlocks also find their soul mate early on is sort of a reflection of the *prima*/consort relationship. So...." Jake released a breath and shifted on the sofa so he was looking directly at me. "So I guess you could say that the way we reacted to each other is normal, for a witch and a warlock. I just...."

The words sort of drifted away, and his gaze moved from me as well, apparently fixed on a painting that hung on the opposite wall, what looked like an original oil of Flagstaff's San Francisco Peaks with a field of sunflowers in the foreground.

"You just what?" I prompted, wondering why he seemed so hesitant.

Still looking away from me, he responded, "I just never thought I'd feel anything like that again."

"Because you felt it with Sarah?" Even though I knew it was probably foolish to feel that way, I couldn't quite repress a stir of jealousy at his obvious devotion to his former fiancée. *Good one, Addie,* I chided myself. *Getting jealous of a dead girl.*

"I did," he said simply. "We were crazy about each other. And when she was gone, I thought that was it for me. People just aren't lucky enough to find two soul mates in a lifetime."

What could I say to that statement, uttered in such a matter-of-fact tone? Did his comment mean he thought I might be his soul mate as well? Asking the question outright felt horribly presumptuous, so I only sat there in silence, hoping that my need and my worry weren't too obvious in my expression.

But obviously Jake saw something, because he said, "And yet...I think I might be that lucky. Maybe it's crazy to be thinking that kind of thing when we've only known each other for a couple of days, but on the other hand, that's sort of how it works with witches and warlocks. If we're right for each other, we know it early on."

Those words awoke a cautious joy in my heart. I wanted to be right for him. He was the first person who'd ever made me feel like this, as though I could do anything, accomplish anything, as long as I knew I had him by my side.

"I think I know it," I whispered, and he took my hand and pulled me to him so he could kiss me again, the touch of his mouth enough to make me tremble with need.

"I know it, too," he replied. "So now...now we just need to figure out what to do next."

18

RANDALL LENZ WAS STARING AT THE SIGN ON THE back of his hotel room door, the one that stated checkout was at 11 a.m., and wondering whether to stay another night or get the hell out of California, when his phone rang. He'd left it sitting on the nightstand, and so he had to hurry over to pick it up before it went to voicemail.

Agent Dawson.

"I think I might have something, sir," she said.

"What is it?" he asked, his ennui of a moment before disappearing as if it had never existed in the first place.

"Well, as you requested, I had the name 'Adara' flagged because it's unusual. There are fewer than fifteen hundred women in the U.S. with that given name."

"Yes, I know that," he said, not bothering to keep the testiness out of his tone. He didn't need a lecture on "Adara" and its statistical popularity —he needed to find out where the hell one particular Adara had gone.

Without missing a beat, Dawson said, "Yes, sir. This morning, I had two flags pop up—one was a set of checking and savings accounts registered to an Adara Wilcox at Chase Bank, and then a vehicle purchase by an Adara Wilcox."

Wilcox. Why did that name sound vaguely familiar to him, as if he'd run across it in the not-too-distant past? "Where?"

"Flagstaff, Arizona."

The location also felt as though it should be tripping some mental circuits. Wait a minute—

He hurried over to his laptop, which he'd left sitting on the table by the window. It wasn't currently connected to his phone, and therefore didn't have any internet, but that didn't matter. The file in question was still sitting open on the screen.

Lenz's gaze scanned down the list of names and came to a halt at one of them.

Jake Wilcox, Flagstaff, Arizona.

Coincidence?

His time working for Homeland Security had taught him there was no such thing as a coincidence.

"Dawson, do a scan for a Jake Wilcox in Flagstaff, Arizona. Transmit any information you find directly to my phone."

"Working."

A pause while she got to work, her fingers making faint clicking sounds on the keyboard as she performed the requested search. A moment later, she said, "Sending the files now."

"Thank you, Dawson. Hold for a moment."

He put her on hold, then went to his email and found the information she'd just sent. As an image of Jake Wilcox's Arizona driver's license appeared on the screen, Lenz felt a slow smile spread across his lips.

There was his man. Definitely the same person who had come to Adara Grant's doorstep in Kanab, Utah, the same man caught on surveillance video in that St. George convenience store.

And there was his address: 52 West Birch Avenue. He should be easy to find—and Lenz had no doubt that wherever he found Jake Wilcox, he'd find Adara Grant as well, no matter which last name she was currently using. Had she taken Jake's last name in an attempt to make herself more difficult to find? Most likely; he doubted that the couple had gotten married in a quickie ceremony while hiding in Las Vegas, although after the week he'd had, he supposed anything was possible.

It wasn't her surname that had given her away, though, but the unusual first name her mother had bestowed upon her at birth. Adara was going to regret that oversight. If she was going to change her name at all, then she should have changed the whole damn thing.

A quick calculation on his phone told him the journey to Flagstaff would take around six and a half hours. If he left now, he could be there by five o'clock.

He took Dawson off hold and said, "Leaving now. Flagstaff ETA is approximately seventeen hundred hours."

"Should I assemble a team?"

It was standard procedure. However, having a team at his disposal hadn't helped much in Kanab. Something told Lenz that this time around, he would do better on his own. Jake Wilcox, although fit enough, certainly wasn't a match for a trained agent. And since his house appeared to be located in a quiet neighborhood of historic homes, the sort of place where people tended to know one another, having a large law enforcement presence would only attract the kind of attention Lenz had been doing his best to avoid.

"No," he said after a pause. "I'll handle this on my own. However, have an extraction team waiting at Flagstaff Pulliam Airport. Once I have Adara Grant in custody, I'll want to fly her out of there."

"Understood. Anything else?"

There was probably a good deal else, but right then, the most important thing to focus on was removing Adara from Jake Wilcox's clutches and getting her into custody. Agent Lenz still couldn't quite figure out what connected the two of them—he knew that Wilcox had never crossed Adara's path before their fateful meeting a few days earlier—although he supposed he would get those answers out of her once he had her someplace safe for questioning.

"Nothing else," he told Dawson. "I'm going to leave the hotel as soon as I end this call. If you have any new information, contact me on the road."

"Yes, sir."

He touched his finger to the screen and returned the phone to his pocket, then quickly and methodically went about packing up his few personal items. No need to go to the lobby to check out; he followed the instructions on the TV screen and left the plastic key card for the room sitting on the dresser. In less than five minutes, he was back in his car and pointing it east so he could pick up Interstate 15 northbound.

As he went, he smiled. Yes, he'd suffered a few setbacks, but he felt it in his bones that he was on the right track here. By the end of the day, he would have Adara Grant in custody...

...and then he'd finally get some much-needed answers about who Jake Wilcox was, and why he'd taken such an interest in her.

Jake had a feeling that sitting around the house after he'd shared that spectacular kiss with Addie would be problematic, to say the least, and so he suggested they spend the afternoon at Lowell Observatory, located less than a mile from his house. She'd looked a little startled by his proposal, but then she shrugged and said sure, that sounded like fun.

And so there they were.

He'd been coming to the Observatory since he was a little kid. Back in those more innocent times, he'd thought it might be kind of cool to be an astronomer, although even then he'd known that astronomers often had to go where the jobs were, which meant traveling. And that was one thing no witch or warlock could safely agree to, not when they were supposed to stay in their home territory and not venture out very much.

Besides, by the time he'd struggled through calculus in high school and realized his brain just wasn't suited for that sort of thing, he'd admitted to himself that he wasn't the kind of math genius who could be a successful astronomer.

Still, he'd been a member at Lowell for the past five years or so, figuring he might as well put some of that Wilcox cash to good use by supporting a worthy institution like the Observatory. One of the benefits was that he could pop in with a guest whenever he liked. He thought that Addie would probably like the place, if for no other reason than the standard tour offered there also provided a lot of local Flagstaff history, and it would be a good way for her to learn more about the place where her father's family had lived for generations.

And it got them out of the house for a while. His body told him how ready he was for her, but Jake knew that falling into bed would be rushing things...to say the least. She'd lost her mother just a few days earlier, and now was not the time to take a huge step like that, no matter how combustible their chemistry might be.

To his relief, she seemed intrigued by the Observatory, and was game for taking every tour on offer that afternoon, including the one that covered the discovery of Pluto and Lowell's role in that major step in humankind's knowledge of the solar system. Afterward, they hung out in the gift shop and bought some T-shirts, acting like a couple of tourists. Actually, he'd been meaning to come by and pick up a few anyway, since he'd messed up one of his favorites by getting paint on it while helping his cousin Aidan paint the new addition to his house.

Eventually, though, they'd pretty much exhausted Lowell's offerings, and so it was back down the hill in search of entertainment. Addie drove because she wanted to play with her new toy, but when they came to the intersection where they needed to turn left to go back to the house, Jake was seized by inspiration.

"Head to the freeway, then go west," he told her, and she lifted an eyebrow, even as she turned the car so they'd go back out to Milton Road and from there to the freeway.

"Kidnapping me?" she asked with an amused lift at the corner of her mouth.

"It's kind of hard to kidnap someone when they're doing the driving," he pointed out, and her smile widened.

"Okay, carjacking," she allowed, then added, still smiling, "But where are we going?"

"Williams."

"What's in Williams?"

He shrugged. "Just someplace new to see. I figured it couldn't hurt for you to get more of the lay of the land up here."

"Is it still Wilcox territory?"

"Definitely. All of northern Arizona is, starting about ten miles or so below I-40 and then stretching all the way up to the Utah border."

A very small frown tugged at her brows. "Isn't part of that Navajo land?"

"Yes, but we've been cooperating with the Navajo for generations." Since Addie didn't look very convinced by that comment, Jake added, "Really. The Wilcoxes have a lot of Navajo blood in them."

"Like Joanna?" she asked. "I thought she looked like she could be part Native American."

"Right—her mother is Navajo. Anyway, it's not like we tried to settle on Navajo land or anything...it's more like everyone knows that the Wilcoxes control this part of the state and that it's better to stay out." Almost at once, he realized what that remark must have sounded like, so he hastily added, "I mean, that's the way it used to be. Once Connor took over, a lot of things changed. Even now, though, it's considered good etiquette to ask permission to travel through another witch clan's territory."

"I'll keep that in mind." Addie sent him a quick sideways glance, a look that had a certain warmth to it he liked very much. "Not that I'm planning on going anywhere anytime soon."

"Good." Yes, he definitely wanted her to remain close—as close as possible. Maybe it was a little weird that she was staying at his house, considering the way their relationship status had shifted that day, but then again, having her right across the upstairs hall might be just what the doctor ordered.

They drove in silence for a little while after that, ponderosa forest passing by on either side of the highway. There was a good bit of traffic, but everything flowed, and he could tell she enjoyed driving the car and putting it through its paces. Eventually, they came upon the first exit for Williams, and he directed her off I-40 and into the town's historic district.

"What now?" she asked after she parked the car in one of the town's pay lots.

"Wander around, I guess. There's a wine tasting room just down the street."

Her gray-green eyes sparkled. "Now you're speaking my language."

The wine tasting room in question was fairly busy on that Monday afternoon, since they were now into June and people everywhere were on vacation, but they were still able to snag a couple of stools at the bar. They split a tasting, since they had to drive back to Flagstaff after that, and decided to buy some of the winery's fun wine in a can. After a detour to put their purchase in the car, they began to roam again, with Addie pausing here and there to look in a shop window.

"You should've gone in," he told her after she began to walk away from a store that specialized in Native American jewelry and had some pretty spectacular pieces on display.

She shrugged. "I don't need any jewelry right now."

"Forget about 'need,'" he said. "What about 'want'?"

That question made her stop and look up at him, her full, pretty mouth pursed slightly in amusement. "I think I've probably spent enough money today. You know, with the car and the laptop and all that."

All right, she had a point there. Even so, he

hoped she wouldn't spend the rest of her life in some kind of scarcity mentality just because that was how she'd been raised. "It's okay to buy nice things for yourself."

"And it's okay not to."

It wasn't the first time he'd glimpsed her stubborn streak. Not that Jake minded; he appreciated the way she stuck up for herself and wasn't afraid to make her opinion known. Still.... "What if other people buy things for you?"

For a second, she stared at him, and then comprehension dawned in her eyes. "Don't you dare get me anything, Jake Wilcox."

"Or what?"

"Or—or—" She flailed for a moment, obviously trying to think of a punishment that fit the crime of daring to buy her a piece of jewelry. "Or I'll *leave* you here."

That was actually a valid threat. Or at least, it would have been, if he didn't have at least twenty Wilcox cousins who lived in town and who could come to his rescue if necessary.

"That's a risk I'm willing to take."

Jake turned and went back to the store, then headed inside, leaving a startled Addie standing on the sidewalk, staring after him. There was an almost dizzying assortment of jewelry on display, everything from earrings to huge squash blossom necklaces to fancy concho belts. He doubted she would want anything too splashy—and he'd seen the turquoise ring that never seemed to leave her finger, and so knew she probably wouldn't want another one—but he spied a pretty pair of earrings in the lightly veined greenish blue from the Kingman mines, simple drops with rope bezels and sturdy ear wires, and thought the color should match her ring pretty well.

"Could I have those, please?" he asked, pointing.

The saleswoman got them out for him. "Those are some very nice pieces of turquoise. The designer is Andrew Yazzie—he's Navajo."

"They're perfect," Jake told her. "I'll take them."

She smiled and put them in a box, and he handed over his credit card. All told, the entire transaction had probably taken less than three minutes. When he came back outside, Addie was still standing there, pretending to be absorbed in reading something on her phone.

"All done?" she asked tartly as she looked up at him.

"Yes," he replied with a grin, then gave her the box. "Here you go."

"Jake—" she began in warning tones.

"Just open it. And don't worry—I didn't buy you the crown jewels or anything."

With an exaggerated sigh, she slipped the phone into her purse, then used her newly free hand to lift the lid off the box she held. Almost at once, her eyes widened in surprise...and delight.

"They're beautiful!"

"I thought they went with your ring."

"They do. It's a perfect match." She tipped the earrings into her palm and put the empty box in her purse. A moment later, the plain silver hoops she'd been wearing had been replaced by the turquoise dangles. They showed up clearly against her long, dark hair, and somehow seemed to intensify the green hues in her eyes. "Thank you, Jake."

"You're welcome." He wanted to bend down and kiss her, but they were standing on a sidewalk on Route 66, and he'd never been one for public displays of affection. Well, she could properly thank him once they got back to Flagstaff.

One hand went up to touch the smooth turquoise drop hanging from her right ear, but she only said, "Now what?"

He'd been saving the best for last. "Are you afraid of heights?"

That question elicited a puzzled glance. "No...why?"

"Come on—I'll show you."

Still looking mystified, she gamely followed him to the next street over and to the platform where the Route 66 Zipline was located. As they approached and she appeared to realize it was their destination, she glanced up at him again. "A zipline?"

"It's not your standard zipline," he said. "You sit in tandem seats, and it sends you riding through the air above the street. It's a lot of fun."

"Sounds okay," she said, even though her tone was still dubious. Then she added, her expression brightening, "Actually, it sounds like a lot of fun. Who knew Williams was hiding something like this?"

Well, he did, because he'd done the zipline with Sarah about five years earlier. However, Jake figured it was probably better not to mention that particular fact. He didn't want Addie to think he was trying to duplicate experiences with her that he'd shared with Sarah. It was more that he knew the zipline existed and so wanted Addie to see how much fun it was. No more, no less.

They bought their tickets and had to wait about ten minutes for their turn. Then they fastened their seatbelts, hung on, and were sent soaring out over historic Route 66.

Addie let out a delighted sound that was half

laugh, half squeak of excitement, her hand finding his and holding on to it tightly. The air rushed past, cool at this altitude, but the sun shone warmly as it made its way westward, and so conditions were just about perfect. Down below, Jake watched cars and tourists and shops and restaurants rush past, all a happy blur. He looked over at Addie, saw her lovely face shining with sheer delight as the wind lifted her hair and tumbled it into ribbons of dark silk.

It almost hurt to see how beautiful she was— and in that moment, how free of worry and sorrow and doubt. No room for that as they soared over the town at nearly thirty miles an hour, free of all the cares they'd left behind them in Flagstaff.

In that moment, Jake vowed to do whatever he could to make sure she always looked like that —happy and free, the creature of pure spirit she was meant to be.

Eventually, the ride ended, and they had to get out of their chairs and return to solid ground. However, he couldn't miss the delighted flush in Addie's cheeks, or the way she continued to smile as she held his hand and talked excitedly about the experience they'd just shared.

"You're going to spoil me, Jake," she said on their way back to the parking lot. "You're going to make me think that life as a Wilcox is continuous dinners out and wine tasting and underground clubs and ziplines. We have to come back to earth sometime, don't we?"

He couldn't help smiling. "Well, okay—most of us aren't quite this free to roam around. It's just that I'm working on the project right now, and since you're part of that project, it's important to keep an eye on you and show you a good time."

That comment made her pause, hands on her hips. "So, that's all this is? Keeping an eye on me?"

To hell with his plan to avoid public displays of affection. Jake bent and kissed her full on the lips, then said, "You know it's a lot more than that."

Obviously, she'd been teasing him, because her mouth curved in a smile. "All right. Yes, I suppose I do."

He kissed her again, this time on the cheek, and then they continued to the car. Once they were on I-40 headed east, however, some of the amusement faded from her face.

"I've been thinking," she said, and Jake shifted in the passenger seat, trying to get a better read on her expression. When a person prefaced a comment with that phrase, it rarely meant anything good.

"About?" he asked, trying to sound casual.

"About me staying at your house," she replied. "I mean, I think it was important last night, to help me sort of get acclimated, for lack of a better word. But now...."

Although he had a suspicion as to where this was going, he did his best to seem neutral as he asked, "Now?"

Her fingers tapped on the steering wheel. "I don't really know what we're doing. Are we dating?"

"I'm not sure we have to be that formal about it."

"Well, whatever it is, it feels weird for me to be staying at your place. I think it might be better if I went back to the cottage."

A stab of disappointment went through him, even though he actually understood why she would feel that way. It was one thing to have her sleeping across the hall when there was nothing going on between the two of them. But now that a relationship had clearly begun to develop between them, it maybe wasn't the best idea to have a setup that looked as though they were cohabiting or something.

And, he did his best to tell himself, it wasn't as though she'd just proposed moving clear to the other side of Flagstaff, or down south to Kachina Village or something. The cottage was right on his same street, only two houses down. No biggie.

"Okay," he said.

"You're mad."

"No, I'm not." He reached over and touched her knee, just a quick gesture of reassurance. "Really. In a way, I think that's smart. You can have your space, but we'll still be close enough to have coffee in the morning or whatever you want to do."

Her shoulders relaxed slightly, and she gave him the briefest glance, not much more than a quick flicker of her eyes in his direction before she returned her attention to the road. "Thanks, Jake. This isn't—this isn't me rejecting you or anything. And I suppose there really isn't anything 'normal' about my situation, but I suppose it's me trying to make it *feel* normal."

Which he completely understood. Her life had been upheaved in ways he could hardly imagine, and he knew he needed to support her in her quest to try to restore some sort of balance. If that meant staying in the cottage until she could get more permanent housing set up, then fine.

Even if he found himself hoping that she'd

want to come back to his place after a few weeks or a month in the cottage.

"Then let's be normal," he said. "We'll get back, and I'll help you move your stuff over to the cottage, and then maybe we can go have dinner somewhere and see a movie."

"That sounds totally normal," she responded, looking even more relieved that he seemed willing to go along with her plan. "What's playing?"

"I have no idea," he confessed, and for some reason, they both started to laugh.

It was fine. It was all going to be fine.

Agent Lenz sat in his car, which he'd parked across the street and partway down the block from Jake Wilcox's big Victorian house. How a kid who wasn't even twenty-seven could afford such a place, Lenz had no idea, but that wasn't his present concern. If he'd really cared, he could have asked Dawson to dig up Wilcox's bank records and tax returns. However, at the moment, he didn't much care. Jake Wilcox's finances were no concern of his.

The house was empty. Lenz knew that because he'd been sitting in the same spot for more than an hour, watching the place, and there hadn't been a single sign of life. Just his luck that his quarry was off somewhere else.

But Jake would have to come home sometime.

Sure enough, about ten minutes later, a small green Fiat station wagon/SUV crossover slowed as it approached the house, then pulled into the driveway. Watching it, Lenz frowned. Definitely not the Jeep Gladiator he'd been expecting. Had he gotten the address wrong somehow?

His fears were allayed as the Fiat's doors opened, and Adara Grant and Jake Wilcox emerged. She'd been driving, and he guessed the car was the new acquisition that had caught Agent Dawson's attention. It had paper dealer plates, so that theory seemed to check out.

Jake came around to the driver's side and took Adara by the hand, and led her up the porch steps. They seemed to have some sort of laughing exchange at the front door, and then Jake bent down to kiss her. No peck on the cheek, either, but a full-mouthed kiss that lasted for quite some time.

Interesting.

Eventually, though, they went into the house. Lenz waited in his car, wondering if he should approach now or wait until evening fell. Sometimes it was better to have the cover of darkness.

The couple weren't inside for much longer than ten minutes before they emerged again, this time carrying a haphazard collection of shopping bags. They walked down the porch steps and followed the sidewalk to another, much smaller house, two doors away. Once there, they headed indoors and disappeared for some time.

Even more interesting.

He noted the address of the cottage and texted it to Agent Dawson, telling her to send him any information she could locate on the property. As he waited for her reply, he kept watching the small house with its cheerful dark red shutters and trim, but he couldn't see any further signs of activity, although eventually one of the lights in the front room was turned on.

Agent Dawson's text came back. *Property is owned by something called the Wheeler Park Trust. I'll have to do more digging to see who's behind the trust.*

Keep on it, he responded, even though he wasn't sure if the actual ownership of the property was really that important. Possibly, it was an Airbnb or some other type of short-term rental.

About ten minutes later, Jake Wilcox emerged from the cottage and walked back to his house.

He had his hands in his pockets and sauntered along in a casual way, smiling to himself. Whatever had occurred during those ten minutes, it didn't appear to have been an argument.

But again, the reason why he'd left and gone back to his house by himself wasn't the issue here. No, far more vital was the simple fact that his departure meant Adara Grant was now alone. This chance might not come again.

Time to move.

19

I TOLD JAKE TO GIVE ME A FEW MINUTES TO GET myself put together for that night's date. After our outing in Williams, I knew I was windblown and a little disheveled, and I didn't see the point in making him sit there and cool his heels while I fussed with my hair and put on another coat of makeup. Also, I wanted to change my top, and although I knew it would be fine for him to sit on the couch in the living room and wait while I changed behind a closed bedroom door, the thought still made me a little uncomfortable.

And while I didn't want to confess such a thing to him, I also knew I needed a little time to myself to gather my thoughts and mentally adjust to this sudden change in our relationship. Deep down, I realized we'd probably been on a collision course toward one another from the very moment we met, but everything had come to a head that afternoon, and I needed to process what all these events actually meant. I'd never felt like this before; to be honest, I'd never really thought I *could* feel like this. In that context, a short space of time to center myself seemed vital before we went any further.

So, I shooed him away and told him I'd be over in about ten or fifteen minutes, and quickly put on one of my new acquisitions, a white peasant-style blouse with aqua embroidery that I knew would go perfectly with the earrings he'd given me. I was just reaching for my mascara when someone knocked at the door.

Feeling halfway amused—what, Jake couldn't even stay away from me for a whole fifteen minutes?—I left the bathroom and went to the front door. It didn't have a peephole, but that didn't bother me too much. After all, no one except Jake and a few members of the Wilcox clan even knew where I was staying, and I sort of doubted any solicitors would be canvassing the neighborhood at seven o'clock on a Monday evening.

I opened the door, and saw Randall Lenz's icy blue eyes staring down into mine. "Hello, Ms. Grant."

Without thinking, I grasped the door and tried to slam it shut, but he was too fast for me, interposing himself between it and the doorframe.

"You're quite a hard woman to find," he went on as he advanced into the living room, casually closing the door behind him with one hand. "You might have been even more successful if you hadn't bought that car or opened that bank account. Those sorts of transactions leave traces, you know."

My mouth was dry, my heart pounding so hard that I wondered if it was going to bruise itself as it rattled against my ribcage. Somehow, though, I heard myself blurt out, "I changed my last name."

"You did," he agreed. "But you have such an unusual first name, Ms. Grant, that you really weren't too difficult to find."

Damn it. Here I'd thought we were being all careful and cagey, and all we'd actually been doing was telegraphing my presence to Randall Grant and his cohorts.

Still, circumstances had changed since the last time he'd tracked me down. There in Kanab, I'd been alone and scared, and had absolutely no idea who I really was or how to control the strange power that lived within me. Only a few days had passed since then, and yet I now felt like a completely different Adara.

"Well, I'll be more careful next time," I replied, and his lips lifted in a thin smile.

"Oh, I don't think there'll be a next time," he said. "No, you'll come with me quietly. After all, I would hate for anything to happen to your new friend."

Of course, he meant Jake. Anger flared in me, even as I thought that Agent Lenz really didn't know what he was dealing with here. I had no idea how he'd managed to get the drop on me when supposedly the Wilcox clan had been told to keep an eye out for him, but all the same, he was now in a place where there were plenty of people with very special powers who'd be more than happy to take care of such an interloper.

And it wasn't as though I was entirely defenseless, either.

"And I'd hate for anything to happen to *you*, Agent Lenz," I shot back. "I assume you're just doing your job, aren't you? At least, that's probably the party line for situations like this. Anyway, I know why you've been tracking me, but it seems you've forgotten why the people you work for think I'm so valuable."

Something in his eyes went still and cold then, although he still wore that half-smile. "No, I haven't forgotten anything, Ms. Grant. However, your power is something of a blunt instrument, isn't it? I'm sure you don't want any harm to come to your neighbors...or to Jake Wilcox."

A little trickle of worry worked its way down my spine, but I tried damn hard to appear unconcerned by Randall Lenz's veiled threat. Again, a few days earlier, I would have been far too afraid to try wielding my power like a weapon, since the collateral damage could be significant. However, now I knew far more about how to control it, thanks to the gentle insights Joanna had provided. It was all about flow, rather than resistance.

"No, I don't," I said calmly. "I don't even want any harm to come to you, despite what you did to my mother."

His jaw tightened. "That was an accident."

His words confirmed what I'd already guessed. Not that it made my mother's loss any easier to bear, but at least I now knew for certain that he hadn't intended to kill her. "Even so, it's the sort of thing that might make a person bear a grudge. I'm not that kind of person, though. I just want you to leave me alone."

Not even a blink. "I'm afraid I can't do that."

All right, so he wasn't going to give me any choice. I'd feared as much, but I knew I couldn't have lived with myself if I hadn't given him that one last chance to walk away.

He was just about to find out what a huge mistake he'd made.

Lightning was a crazy thing. It could strike from a cloudless sky—or at least, a sky without visible clouds, traveling more than twenty miles to hit its target. There were no clouds directly over the neighborhood where we stood, but a few lingered around Mt. Humphreys, the highest of the San Francisco Peaks...and that was all I needed.

The Adara Grant from three days earlier couldn't have done what I was about to attempt. However, I now knew how to reach up to those clouds, to sense the potential energy trapped within them. To cause them to flare, and charge, and send out a single targeted bolt.

It came through the window, shattering the glass and setting the curtains ablaze. For one timeless second, the lightning arced in place, illuminating the room with a white-hot flash, as if a nuclear bomb had been detonated nearby. Randall Lenz's eyes widened, and I saw fear come alive in them as he realized what I had just done.

No time for him to do anything about it, though, as the bolt connected with him and for a moment, his entire body pulsed with that white-hot glare. Soundlessly, he slumped to the floor, his dark suit smoking from the contact, his eyes staring at me without seeing.

Shit. Oh, shit. I'd had to do it, but....

I'd spotted a mini fire extinguisher in the kitchen pantry earlier, and I ran in there and grabbed it, then hurried back to the living room so I could put out the curtains before they caught the whole house on fire. Only once I knew the structure was safe did I set down the fire extinguisher and go to Agent Lenz's prone body. With a shaking hand, I reached down to touch his throat, to see if I was just as much a murderer as he was.

A pulse. Faint and thready, skipping here and there, but alive. How, I didn't know, although I'd read once that more people survived being struck by lightning than not. Still, I doubted there was much time to waste.

I didn't call 911, though. Instead, I ran for my purse and called Connor, since his was the only actual number I had programmed into my new phone.

To my infinite relief, he picked up after the second ring. Maybe, as the head of the Wilcox clan, he was used to getting phone calls at all hours. "Hello?"

"Connor," I gasped. "It's Addie. That agent— Agent Lenz—he showed up at the cottage. I blasted him with lightning, but now he's half dead and I don't know what to do."

"Whoa, whoa," he said. "The government agent you told me about is here in Flagstaff?"

"Yes," I said. "He said he found me because of the bank account I opened and the car I bought. That's not important, though. What should I do?"

"Just hang on," he told me. His tone was calm, not rattled at all, so I assumed this wasn't the first crazy emergency he'd had to deal with in his tenure as *primus*. "I'll call Eleanor, the clan's healer, and send her over there. And Angela and I will be over as well. Good thing we decided to come to Flagstaff early—we're already in town."

That news made me want to sag in relief. I didn't know why the knowledge that Connor and his wife were nearby made me feel so much better, but I'd take it. Right then, I was willing to grasp at just about anything.

"Where's Jake?" Connor asked next.

"At his house. I—I would have called him, but I don't have his number since we've been together pretty much the whole time and I never thought to ask."

"It's okay. I'll call him and send him over. Just hang tight. Is the guy breathing?"

"Yes."

"Pulse?"

"It feels weird, but it's there."

"Okay, then he'll probably be able to hold on until Eleanor shows up. Cover him with a blanket, because he's most likely in shock."

It hit me then that Connor seemed to know an awful lot about treating a victim of a lightning strike. "How do you know about all this?"

"We get a lot of lightning up here in the high country. It's good to know the basics. Anyway, I'll call Eleanor—she only lives about five minutes from you, so she should get there pretty quickly. Hang tight."

He ended the call, and I set the phone on the coffee table and hurried down the hallway, where I thought I'd spied a linen closet. Sure enough, right before the bathroom was a cupboard filled with extra sheets, towels, and blankets. I grabbed one of the blankets and hurried back out to the living room, then spread it over Agent Lenz's body. He didn't move, and once again I knelt next to him so I could feel for a pulse. Still there, but even harder to locate. Would Eleanor get to the cottage in time?

Tears sprang to my eyes, and I blinked them back. This was no time to lose it. If I really had been that worried about Randall Lenz's well-being, then I wouldn't have attacked him in the first place. I'd had no choice, though—letting him take me back to wherever he intended to hide me really wasn't an option.

"Addie!"

Jake, bursting through the door and looking down at me with wild eyes. At once, he came and knelt next to me and took me in his arms, holding me tight.

"Are you okay?"

"I'm all right," I said, once again blinking furiously to keep those damn tears from flooding down my face. Somehow, I knew if I lost it with Jake, I'd be a useless sobbing mess, and none of us had time for that at the moment. "I—I didn't want to hurt him, Jake. I just didn't know what else to do."

"It's okay," he soothed me, one hand stroking my hair. "Connor told me Eleanor is on the way. She'll take care of it."

I had to hope Connor was right. I'd never met Eleanor, of course, but I guessed that anyone who'd been healer to the Wilcoxes for any appreciable amount of time probably knew what they were doing.

The healer must have beaten a land-speed record getting over to the cottage, because she showed up just a minute later. Like Jake, she didn't bother to knock, but came right in and headed straight for Agent Lenz without saying anything to either Jake or me. She laid a hand on the agent's head, then ran her hands lightly over his body, as though using her powers to locate everywhere he'd been injured and to use those same powers to heal the damage the lightning bolt had caused.

Whatever she was doing, it appeared to be working. While he didn't regain consciousness... although I thought I saw his eyelids flutter once or twice...his cheeks seemed to regain some color, and his skin didn't look as clammy and pale. At the end, she placed her hands palm down on his chest and left them resting there for a moment while she sat with her eyes closed, her face tight with concentration. Now I was able to get a better look at her, I could see Eleanor was probably in her fifties somewhere, hair still dark except for an attractive streak of gray right in the front, but with friendly lines around her eyes and the sort of calming presence people probably appreciated in a healer.

"Is he...okay?" I asked, the words not coming out in much more than a whisper.

"He'll live," she replied. She straightened the blanket, which had become somewhat askew during her ministrations, then got to her feet. "If the circumstances were different, I'd say he still needed to be moved to a hospital. But from what Connor told me, that really isn't an option, is it?"

I shook my head, and she let out a little sigh, looking resigned.

"Well, we should at least move him to the couch until Connor and Angela get here."

Thank God that Connor and Angela were coming to the cottage. In my panic, I'd almost forgotten he'd told me they would be over, but it made sense. After all, they were the ones in charge, so I supposed it was their job to clean up any messes their clan members might have created. I just wished I hadn't made quite such a huge mess so soon after arriving in Flagstaff.

"You should sit down, Addie," Eleanor said then, her tone turning brisk. "You've suffered a shock as well. Jake, help me move this man to the couch, and then you can make her a cup of tea."

Obviously, Wilcoxes were used to doing what their healer said, because he didn't argue, only took Agent Lenz by the shoulders while Eleanor lifted him by the feet. Together, they managed to haul him over to the couch, where the healer once again made sure he was covered by the blanket. Afterward, Jake went into the kitchen, and Eleanor looked over at me.

"Go ahead and sit down," she said. Even

though she still spoke in that same no-nonsense tone, I could see the concern in her dark eyes. "It's going to be okay."

"Is it?" I asked, my gaze moving toward the unconscious man on the couch. While he did look improved, he also didn't give any indication that he planned to wake up any time soon, despite the movements of his eyelids I'd noticed a few minutes earlier.

Maybe that was a good thing.

"Yes," Eleanor said. "Connor will know what to do. In the meantime, you need to take care of yourself. Come and sit."

She patted the back of the armchair that stood next to the couch, and I got up from where I'd been kneeling on the rug and went over and sat down. My knees felt surprisingly shaky, so it seemed she knew what she was talking about.

A moment later, Jake came back in with a big mug of yellow-glazed stoneware in his hands, the tag for the teabag still hanging over the side. "Here you go," he said, carefully folding it into my hands, which I wrapped around the mug, taking a faint bit of comfort from its warmth. "Do you need anything else?"

I shook my head. "No, I'm okay."

Hands now free, he reached up to rub the scruff on his chin as he stared down at Agent

Lenz, whose lashes looked surprisingly thick and dark against his pale cheeks, revealing a vulnerability I sure had never seen in his face while he was conscious. "I can't believe he found you."

"We weren't careful enough," I said. "My name gave me away."

"You didn't use your name."

"My *first* name," I pointed out, and Jake frowned.

"Jesus."

About what I had thought, too. I didn't know what else to say, though, so I lifted the mug to my lips and took the tiniest of sips, since the tea was still really too hot to drink. An uncomfortable silence fell, one only broken by a soft knock at the door a few minutes later.

Jake went to answer it, and let Connor and Angela in. They both looked troubled but also calm in a way, as if they'd already come up with a plan and now only had to execute it.

After uttering some quick greetings, Connor asked, "He's stabilized?"

Eleanor nodded. "I can't say that he won't have some lingering problems—headaches, dizziness, that sort of thing—but overall, he's all right. He didn't break any bones or suffer any real burns."

"So, he can be moved?"

That question made all of us send Connor a startled glance. Angela took over then, saying, "We decided that the best thing to do is get him out of Flagstaff as quickly as possible. The plan right now is to take him back to Kanab and dump him there."

"'Dump him'?" I repeated, knowing how aghast I sounded. "The guy just got struck by lightning!"

"We're not planning to leave him on the side of the road or something," Connor said quickly. "We'll put him in a motel room. He'll be okay."

"And then he'll come right back after me," I said, my tone flat. "I don't think even a bolt of lightning is enough to deter this guy."

The *prima* and *primus* exchanged a glance. "He won't know where to come."

That comment didn't seem to make any sense. "What?"

"We're going to erase his memories," Angela said. The statement was made in such a matter-of-fact tone of voice, it took me a minute to properly process what she'd just said.

"You're *what?*"

However, even as I stared at him in shock, I realized that Laurel had mentioned basically the same sort of contingency plan just the day before. Clearly, she knew what her *primus*—and his *prima* wife—were capable of.

Connor sent me a humorless smile. "I know it sounds crazy, but Angela and I working together can do a lot of things that are beyond the scope of a normal witch or warlock. We're going to erase all his memories of you, of being in Flagstaff. He won't remember anything."

On the surface, that sounded like a good plan. However, while Randall Lenz wasn't a warlock, he also wasn't exactly your run-of-the-mill civilian, either. "Even if you do all that, this guy was still working for the government. There have to be other people in his agency who know what he was up to, who have records of his mission here."

"Which is where Jake's brother Jeremy will come in," Connor said, apparently unfazed by all those complications. "I'm going to give him Agent Lenz's phone and his laptop—if he has one with him—and Jeremy is going to make sure every single trace of this trip is erased. It'll be like none of this ever happened."

That sounded better. I wouldn't question Jeremy's ability to go into those devices and remove all the pertinent data; what I'd seen so far had already convinced me there wasn't much he couldn't do when it came to hacking data.

And really, what other choice did we have? Killing Agent Lenz wasn't an option, so about all we could do was make sure there was no way in the world he could ever trace me back to Flagstaff, Arizona. He'd wake up with a couple of missing days in his memory, there would probably be an inquiry, and once it was determined there was nothing to be found, he could go back to his life...and I'd try to rebuild mine here in the town where my father was born.

"Where *is* his laptop, though?" I asked. Randall Lenz hadn't been carrying a briefcase or anything when he showed up.

"He probably has a car parked somewhere nearby," Connor replied. He went over to the unconscious agent and went through his pockets as gently as he could, in the process extracting a cell phone and a key fob. A quick glance at the fob in question, and he added, "Yep, Ford Taurus. I'll go look for it."

He let himself out, while Angela met my gaze and offered a reassuring smile. "It's going to be okay. We've already called Jeremy to let him know what's going on, and he's on his way over now. By tomorrow, this will all seem like a bad dream."

It already seemed like a bad dream, but maybe there really was a way to wake up from it.

"Do we need to stay here?" Jake asked. "Addie's had kind of a shock, and I think it might be better if I took her back to my place."

"Of course," Angela replied. Her gaze strayed to the broken window and its frame of scorched curtains. "No one can stay here until that window gets repaired anyway."

I wanted to protest that I was fine and didn't need any coddling, but I knew that would have been a lie. Instead, I told everyone that I needed to get my things, and so for the second time that day, I went and gathered my various purchases and loaded them back in their bags. By the time I was done, Connor had returned, laptop in hand. He put it down on the coffee table, since the small table over by the window was covered in broken glass.

Just seeing the laptop made me feel a little better. Once Jeremy had worked his magic on it, there wouldn't be any trace left of Agent Lenz's dubious mission.

Right then, I only wanted to get away and try to forget how I'd summoned lightning to strike a defenseless man.

I couldn't say that we exactly relaxed that night,

even though Jake coaxed me into binge-watching *The Good Place* on Netflix, a show I'd never seen before. We ordered pizza, and partway through the evening, Jeremy called to say that Randall Lenz's cell phone and laptop had both been scrubbed, and so that loose end had been tied up.

"And Eleanor's son Travis and our cousin Leland are driving Lenz out to Kanab tonight," Jeremy had added. "So, we're pretty much done here."

Jake relayed this information to me, and I absorbed it without knowing how relieved I should be. On the surface, everything seemed fine. But I couldn't help worrying that there might have been something we overlooked.

I didn't say anything to Jake about my misgivings. No, I watched TV with him until I was too tired to keep my eyes open any longer, and then we both went upstairs. He kissed me before I disappeared into my room to change for bed, but it was a gentle kiss, tender but not too passionate, as if he understood that the evening's events had wiped out any opportunity for romance.

"It's going to be okay," he said quietly.

"I know," I lied.

Afterward, I lay in bed and stared at the ceiling, thoughts racing. I imagined those two

Wilcox cousins making the three-hour trip to Kanab so they could leave Randall Lenz at one of the motels in town. What kind of possible explanation could they give for dumping a comatose man at a motel? Maybe they wouldn't have to offer one at all; for all I knew, one of them had a talent for making other people believe anything he said. Or invisibility—they could conceal Agent Lenz altogether and pretend the room was for them. When warlocks were involved, all sorts of possibilities opened up.

Would all those contingencies be enough, though? I knew how tenacious Randall Lenz was. Even with his memories erased and all evidence of his travels in Utah and Arizona gone, would he still somehow come up with a way to piece together the puzzle and figure out that his quarry was right there in Flagstaff?

I wanted to tell myself that no, of course he couldn't. He might be a very resourceful man, but he didn't possess superpowers. Those memories, once gone, couldn't return.

Or...could they?

I rolled over on my side and reached for my iPhone to check the time. Twelve-fifteen. So much for falling right asleep. I might have been tired earlier, but right then I felt as wired as if I'd just drunk a couple of cups of coffee.

The problem was, Connor and Angela had offered me reassurances, but they didn't know—*couldn't* know—for certain that all the measures they'd taken would be enough. I doubted they'd ever faced this sort of situation before. They'd never had to deal with someone who had the resources of the United States government behind him.

Which meant...what?

That there was always a chance Randall Lenz could remember enough to come after me again. Only this time, he'd probably be pretty pissed off. Did I want to take the chance of having him gunning for Connor...Angela...Jake?

Well, I knew the answer to that question, didn't I?

The real question was, what did I intend to do about it?

As long as I was in Flagstaff, Jake—and my new extended family—was in danger. The only real solution was to leave so I couldn't draw that danger to them. After all, Agent Lenz was hunting me, not the Wilcoxes. He still thought I was only a girl with strange powers, not a witch whose gifts were hereditary. God only knew what he'd do if he ever found out that thousands of people with extraordinary powers were scattered across the country.

Even though the room was warm enough, the bed cozy, I felt cold all over. I knew what I needed to do...and didn't know whether I had the will to do it. How could I leave when I'd only just started to learn what it was like to be a Wilcox?

How could I leave Jake when I'd only just begun to realize how much I cared for him?

But it was precisely because I cared so much that I needed to go. It would break my heart to leave, but better a broken heart than knowing I'd brought ruin on the man I loved, on the people who were my only family in the world.

That argument seemed to settle it.

I got out of bed, moving as quietly as I could. Because I'd been so tired, I really hadn't unpacked anything except my little baggie of toiletries, which was still sitting on the bathroom counter.

A peek into the hallway told me Jake's door was closed. Perfect. Even if he caught me as I was going down to retrieve my things, there was nothing so strange about having to get up and go to the bathroom in the middle of the night.

But his door remained shut, and I was able to pick up the baggie and my toothbrush without being disturbed. Once I was back inside the guest bedroom, I hurriedly got dressed and then used that old trick of shoving the pillows under the bedcovers to make it look as though someone was still sleeping there. A silly subterfuge, maybe, and yet I thought it might gain me a few precious minutes. Then I got my purse and the shopping bags that contained all my worldly possessions, and slowly crept down the stairs.

One thing I hadn't counted on was the dog, but she didn't make any sound as I entered the living room, only came over and pressed her muzzle against my leg. I couldn't really pet her without setting down my bags, so I settled for whispering, "Good dog. Go back to sleep, Taffy," before I went out the front door.

The night air felt biting for early June. The altitude, I supposed. I couldn't stop to worry about it, though, but only hurried over to my car, which was still parked in the driveway where I'd left it. I put the bags in the trunk and got in the driver's seat, praying all the while that Jake wouldn't hear the sound of the engine starting up. Luckily, his room was on the opposite side of the house, and so I thought the likelihood of that happening was pretty low.

I eased the Fiat out onto Birch Street, then slowly turned so I was heading toward Route 66. From there, I could get on I-40 and...what? Where was I even going?

There were three directions I could go, since

due north was sort of out of the question, thanks to the Grand Canyon being in the way. Besides, Randall Lenz was in Kanab, a hundred miles north of where I stood, and I didn't want to go anywhere near there.

All right...west, south, or east. West sounded alluring—I'd always wanted to visit California— but I wouldn't be able to get too far before I reached the Pacific Ocean and didn't have anywhere else to run. South, and I'd hit the Mexico border before too soon. I didn't have a passport, so that didn't sound like a very good idea.

East...well, if I headed east, I'd have most of the United States to lose myself in. Even Randall Lenz might have a hard time finding me in that vast amount of space.

There was my answer. East, toward the rising sun.

There hadn't been paper or a pen in my borrowed room, which I supposed was a good thing. As much as I'd wanted to leave Jake a note, I was worried that anything I wrote might give too much away. And maybe...just maybe...if I made him angry enough, he wouldn't try to look for me.

I got onto the freeway, following the signs directing me toward Albuquerque. At least, I was pretty sure that was what they said. My vision was blurred with tears, and at last I let myself sob for everything and everyone I was leaving behind.

I'm sorry, Jake.

I love you...and I'll never forget you.

~

Jake and Addie's story continues in *Thunder Road* and concludes *in Winds of Change.*

Don't miss out on any of Christine's new releases —sign up for her newsletter today!

To get sneak peaks, cover reveals, insider info about the "Witch" series and much more, join Christine's reader group on Facebook!

(Paranormal Romance)

Sympathy for the Devil

Charmed, I'm Sure

A Wing and a Prayer

THE WITCHES OF CANYON ROAD*

(Paranormal Romance)

Hidden Gifts

Darker Paths

Mysterious Ways

A Canyon Road Christmas

Demon Born

An Ill Wind

Higher Ground

Haunted Hearts

THE WITCHES OF CLEOPATRA HILL*

(Paranormal Romance)

Darkangel

Darknight

Darkmoon

Sympathetic Magic

Protector

Spellbound

A Cleopatra Hill Christmas

Impractical Magic

Strange Magic

The Arrangement

Defender

Bad Blood

Deep Magic

Darktide

THE DJINN WARS*

(Paranormal Romance)

Chosen

Taken

Fallen

Broken

Forsaken

Forbidden

Awoken

Illuminated

Stolen

Forgotten

Driven

Unspoken

THE WATCHERS TRILOGY*

(Paranormal Romance)

Falling Dark

Dead of Night

Rising Dawn

THE SEDONA FILES*

(Paranormal Romance)

Bad Vibrations

Desert Hearts

Angel Fire

Star Crossed

Falling Angels

Enemy Mine

TALES OF THE LATTER KINGDOMS*

(Fantasy Romance)

All Fall Down

Dragon Rose

Binding Spell

Ashes of Roses

One Thousand Nights

Threads of Gold

The Wolf of Harrow Hall

Moon Dance

The Song of the Thrush

THE GAIAN CONSORTIUM SERIES*

(Science Fiction Romance)

Beast (free prequel novella)

Blood Will Tell

Breath of Life

The Gaia Gambit

The Mandala Maneuver

The Titan Trap

The Zhore Deception

The Refugee Ruse

~

STANDALONE TITLES

Hearts on Fire

Taking Dictation

Night Music

Golden Heart

* Indicates a completed series

ABOUT THE AUTHOR

USA Today bestselling author Christine Pope has been writing stories ever since she commandeered her family's Smith-Corona typewriter back in grade school. Her work includes paranormal romance, fantasy romance, and science fiction/space opera romance. She makes her home in Arizona's beautiful Verde Valley.

Don't miss out on any of Christine's new releases —sign up for her newsletter today!

Christine Pope on the Web:
www.christinepope.com

www.ingramcontent.com/pod-product-compliance
Lightning Source LLC
Chambersburg PA
CBHW060217030726
47499CB00004B/1086